BADD BOY

A BADD BROTHERS NOVEL

Jasinda Wilder

BADD BOY: A BADD BROTHERS NOVEL

ISBN: 978-1-948445-06-1

Cover art by Sarah Hansen of Okay Creations.

Formatting: Champagne Book Design

BADD BOY

ONE

Xavier

I AM ABSOLUTELY OUT OF MY ELEMENT.

I'm sitting in the saloon of a stunning 35' yacht in Ketchikan harbor beside a beautiful young woman who might as well be one of Homer's sirens. And, to be fair to myself, I'm pretty sure any guy would be tongue-tied right now. Less than an hour ago I helped this young woman after she twisted her ankle.

The fact that I'm out of my element is no surprise, given the fact that the only time I am ever truly comfortable is when my nose is stuck in a book, and my hands are assembling little robots. The rest of the time, I'm uncomfortable being around people, especially people I have never met. Being around people makes my skin feel too tight, makes my head feel too full of thoughts and sensory stimulation. When there's a lot of chaos in my surroundings, my thoughts tend to run even faster, which makes it feel like I have a fire hose of mental activity on full blast inside my head.

Women, especially, confuse and overwhelm me. Learning to be—or at least *appear* to be—comfortable around my sisters-in-law Dru, and then Mara, and now Eva, Claire, Tate, Aerie, and Joss… has required constant effort on my part. I never know how to act around them. My brothers are all funny, charismatic, interesting, outgoing—with the exception of Lucian, but now that he has Joss, he's learning to open up and loosen up, and in doing so we are finding his true personality is much less reserved than even he once assumed. I share none of those characteristics with my brothers. I don't know how to crack a well-timed joke. Or make some pithy commentary. Or put in some kind of wise, worldly, tidbit. Or turn someone else's statement into a sexual innuendo. All my brothers have a woman in their lives, and they've each become much more physical in their demonstrations of affection—and not just with their significant other, but also with each other and with me.

So, where do I fit in? I don't want to just fade into the background, but what do I say? How do I act?

Especially right now. Women make me edgy, and this girl in particular, sitting next to me—Low, she calls herself—has got the fire hose in my brain turned on full blast.

She's so beautiful it literally makes me question my own eyes, my sanity, my existence. Can she be real? Can a woman this perfect truly exist? Yet here she is, in defiance of all logic. Sitting beside me. Close—very close. Her leg brushes mine, sending an electric shock arcing through me—I do not mean that as hyperbole, either—the touch of her leg against mine was something I feel with acute awareness, a vicious tingle so powerful it is like touching an exposed live wire. I vibrate, all over, from the touch of her leg against mine. It was innocent—I know this. There was no hidden meaning or intent behind this—she was merely sitting on the couch beside me, as one human does with another human. That's all.

Yet…I wonder.

All too often, I find out after the fact that I have missed a social cue, or overlooked a hint, or missed a subtlety in a situation. This is, in many ways, a defining characteristic of mine.

She's talking right now, and I have to remind myself to tune in, to pay attention.

"…I shouldn't have even attempted that variation on the sequence, especially on the deck of a boat. My yoga teacher back home would probably say something like 'your yoga practice is for *you*, for your emotional, physical, and mental well-being, it is *not* a tool with which to impress people.'" Then she laughed, and the sound of her laughter could be recorded and sold as music. "I know better, I really do. That's the kind of thing that keeps you humble, I guess, right?"

Is a response required of me? I honestly don't know. I hesitate, probably for too long. "I would think it rather challenging to do any kind of yoga on the deck of a boat, much less something complicated like the Warrior Three sequence or whatever it was you were attempting."

Another of those musical, bell-like laughs. "Well, it's not like I was trying an inversion. And it wasn't the rolling of the boat that toppled me, it was me being distracted."

"There isn't much roll on this boat, is there?" I asked.

She shook her head. "No, not all. It's very gentle, and it just adds a fun little bit of extra challenge to anything requiring balance." She pulled away the bag of ice from her head, probing the bump with her fingertips. "My head is getting cold, and the ice is melting, and the condensation is getting my hair wet."

I took the bag of ice from her. "Would you like me to refresh the ice for you?"

She shook her head again. "No, that's okay." She stretched her leg out, rolling her ankle. "It's actually my ankle that's bothering me, at the moment."

"Did you twist it?" I asked, after throwing the ice overboard.

Low shrugged. "I think so—it's definitely sore now, but I think hitting my head probably eclipsed anything else that happened."

I knelt on the floor in front of her. "May I examine your ankle?"

She smiled at me, and I had to look away quickly. "Sure. Examine away, Xavier." She lifted her leg, and I cradled her ankle in my hand.

Propping her calf on my knee, I allowed her ankle to dangle freely, and then I gingerly, carefully probed the area, moving it in circles, testing the range of motion while watching her reactions. She winced a little as I rotated her ankle, but nothing more.

I smiled, attempting to look reassuring. "Twisted, but nothing worse. It isn't swollen or tender to the touch from outside, so I think if you restrict the use of it for a day or so, you will be as good as new."

"Are you *sure* you're not a doctor?" she asked, leaving her leg propped up on my knee.

I gently set her foot onto the floor and stood up, wiping my hands on the front of my shorts—an automatic response to touching someone, a habit

I've never been able to break. "I am very certain." I laughed. "I think I would remember eight years of medical school and a residency."

She laughed, and I felt myself wishing I could make her laugh all the time, because the sound was addictive. "I guess you would remember that, wouldn't you?" She patted the couch beside her again, as I hadn't sat back down yet. "I'm feeling better, but you don't have to leave yet."

Once again, I'm left wondering what she means. Does she want me to stay? Does she like talking to me? Is she being polite? Is this one of those situations where she's saying I don't have to leave yet, but she really means the opposite?

I don't want to leave. I like her. I enjoy sitting with her, talking to her.

I looked at her as I sat down, trying to decipher her meaning, her intent. But I got distracted by what she looked like, how otherworldly, ethereally, indelibly lovely she was.

She was tall—I couldn't even begin to guess at her height in feet and inches, but I think she was around the same height as Dru who was, she once mentioned, five-eight. If anything, Low was a little taller. Much of that height seemed to come from her legs, which were long—and being encased in calf-length yoga pants tight enough to be considered a second skin, I could see that those legs were not only elegant and graceful but strong and muscular as well. Her hips pinched inward dramatically to a narrow waist, and her abs had clear, hard definition. The sports bra she wore was pale blue, with a complicated arrangement of thin straps and a diamond-shaped cut-out in the middle showing a hint of the creamy white skin between her breasts.

I had always been under the impression that a sports bra was intended to minimize the size and weight of a woman's breasts during exercise, to reduce the impact of kinetic energy upon the body during movement. The one Low was wearing, however, seemed…rather inadequate to that purpose. Every movement of her body created ripples of kinetic energy, each of which drew my attention—causing my gaze to fix on them for an embarrassingly long moment. She caught me staring—I knew she did, for even I couldn't misunderstand the smirk and the way she glanced at me. She said nothing, however, only allowing the smirk to blossom into a full smile.

Which confused me. I didn't think women appreciated being ogled—and I had been openly and disgustingly ogling her.

I forced my eyes up to hers, which was safer from a manners perspective, but far more dangerous from a hypnotic perspective. Her eyes were…I struggled for an apt descriptor for the shade of blue. Somewhere between cerulean, sapphire, and indigo. If I wasn't physically present, and only seeing a photograph, I would have assumed the brightness and vividness and intensity of the blue of her eyes had been digitally enhanced. Her hair, too, seemed too perfect to be real. A true strawberry blonde, her hair seemed to grow in natural spirals—I found myself lost in those curls, too, following the pattern of the spirals, which were a perfect natural representation of the golden spiral. Her hair wasn't a single shade of strawberry blonde, either, but an iridescent mix of red and gold and copper, the different shades more prominent depending on the angle of the light. I wondered if there was a mathematical expression for the shifting shades of her hair, or if I could capture in code the way her hair changed shades.

"Xavier?" Her voice betrayed confusion.

I blinked rapidly, fisting my hands to keep them from betraying a tic. "Yes?"

"I asked if you were born and raised in Alaska."

I cursed myself mentally, realizing I'd spaced out—or, what others termed spacing out, but which was really just my mind spiraling off into a maze of interconnected thoughts. "Sorry. Ahh—yes. I was born and raised in Ketchikan."

"So you've lived here your whole life?"

"I attended Stanford for a year, but other than that, yes, I have lived here my whole life."

She frowned, a puzzled tilt to her head. "Why'd you drop out?"

"My father passed away. He left a somewhat complicated will, which stipulated that for any of his estate to be released, all of his sons had to live and work here together for a full year. At the time, you see, everyone but our oldest brother had moved away. The will meant none of us got any of the money unless we all came back. So, I dropped out of Stanford and came home."

"Wow. That's—why do you think he did that?"

I shrugged. "I do not know for certain, but I think when we all went our separate ways to pursue our various interests, it upset him. Which is ironic, in a way because he always encouraged us to follow our interests. I think he wanted us back together. He wanted to make sure we stuck together as brothers."

"Why is it ironic?"

I sighed. "Well, that is a complicated question to answer. Our mother passed away when I was seven years old. It sent Dad into a deep depression he never recovered from. I was, for all intents and purposes, raised by my eldest brother, Sebastian. Dad was around, but…not of much use." I fixed my eyes on the wood floor of the yacht's main saloon—the living room of the ship, basically—counting the lines of darker shading in the grains until I felt able to respond; I reached fifty-nine. "The irony is that he was absent from us, mentally and emotionally, so when we left, it didn't seem like it would matter much to him. Clearly, he felt differently."

"That's…that's heavy, Xavier."

"You asked."

"I'm sorry, I didn't mean to bring up anything that would upset you."

"I know you did not intend that."

She eyed me. "So, do you resent having to leave Stanford?"

I resumed counting lines in the grain of the wood, and reached eighty more. "Resent? I do not know if that is the correct word. I enjoyed the educational challenge, and having the resources of a university at my disposal. But my brothers are my family. There is nothing I was being taught at Stanford that I could not find a way of teaching myself. So, I do not resent it, no. I was glad to be able to come home and reunite with my brothers. I am closer to all of them now than I ever was growing up."

"Do you think you'll go back?"

I frowned. "To Stanford?" I counted from eighty to one hundred and nine; usually, my long hesitations between responses bothered people, but Low seemed to not care, or if she was, she was not showing it. "No, I do not believe that would add value to my life in any way."

There was a silence, then. I felt an expectation to fill it, but had no idea what to say. Questions of my own? What should I ask?

Just then a small brown bird landed on the bow of her boat, visible through the open doorway, and I watched as it cheeped and chirruped, its tail flicking, beak parting, its small body swiveling this way and that.

"Where are you from, Low?" I finally asked, after it flew away.

She smiled at my question, and shifted closer to me. "I'm an LA girl, born and raised."

"Have you received upper education?"

She blinked at my question, and then laughed, leaning into me. "You're so weird and funny, you know that? Yes, I went to NYU."

"What did you study?"

"Fine arts." I expected her to elaborate on this, but she didn't.

"And why are you here in Ketchikan?"

Reading facial expressions properly is something I'm terrible at, part of the curse of my social issues, but it seemed to me that her gaze went distant, as if somehow a shutter had gone down behind her eyes.

"I needed to get away from LA." She shrugged a thin shoulder. "It's so hectic down there, you know? I needed to be somewhere quiet and peaceful and beautiful."

"If you want real peace and quiet, take your boat out into some of the smaller channels. You can just drop your anchor and sit and, chances are, you won't see or hear another soul all day long."

"That sounds nice."

"You have a boat, why do you not just…go?"

She shrugged, waving a hand. "Oh, I gave Captain Fisk and the rest of the crew time off. I needed to be alone."

"Do you have a launch?" I asked.

Low frowned. "A what?"

"A smaller boat within this one, usually with an outboard motor and typically only large enough to hold a few people."

She shrugged a shoulder again. "Probably. I wouldn't know where it is, though, or how to launch it or how to drive it, or where to go."

I wasn't sure why I was suggesting this, but the words emerged anyway. "I am a fairly capable person, and I know the area. If you wanted to do a little local sightseeing, I could show you around."

She stared at me for a moment, her eyes boring into mine intently, and I would have given anything to know what she was thinking, for I could not read her expression whatsoever. "I…that…I wouldn't mind seeing some of the other channels in the area."

There was significant hesitation there, but I couldn't parse exactly what, or why.

"We could go up past Beaver Falls, maybe," I suggested. "Toss an anchor over and see if we can catch some fish."

Her frown was disbelieving. "Fishing?"

"Have you never tried it?"

She smirked. "No, as a matter of fact, I have not. It never seemed very interesting, and my life thus far hasn't provided an opportunity."

"Fishing as an activity by itself is the most boring thing on the planet, if you ask me," I said. "But as an excuse to sit out in the beauty of nature for a few hours, it is unparalleled."

This turned her smirk into a hesitant smile. "That sounds nice." She was sitting so close to me now that her thigh and hip were against mine, and her arm nudged mine, and I could feel her hair tickling my cheek. She smelled good—lavender, and something less definable but sweet and heady. "You wouldn't mind showing a city girl how to fish?"

"If you are looking for someone to teach you how to really fish, my brother Brock would be your better bet—he takes tourists out to his favorite spots

Canaan and his wife Aerie are musicians and are on tour pretty much permanently, and Corin and his wife Tate just had a baby—Tate and Aerie are also identical twins. Corin and Canaan have their own production company, which Corin primarily runs by himself while Canaan tours. Luce and his girlfriend just opened a coffee shop and bookstore that they run together. And then there is me."

"So you're the youngest?"

I nodded. "Yes." I shot her a quick look, not letting myself stare too long. "And what about you, Low?"

The shuttering of her expression happened again, and I wondered if she perhaps didn't like talking about herself. "Only child, and my parents live in Carmel-by-the-Sea."

"That is truly the name of the city?" I asked.

She laughed. "It really is. It's actually a pretty magical place."

"Did you grow up there?"

She shook her head. "No. We lived in suburban LA most of my life. My parents retired recently, and that's where they retired to."

"What do you do, Low?" I asked. This question was followed by a long, long pause, which even I could register as a serious reticence to answer the question. I smiled at her, attempting to diffuse the sudden and intense awkwardness. "It is not important. What one does for a living does not compromise the whole of who one is, after all." I chuckled. "At least, for my own sake, I certainly hope not."

She frowned at me, an expression that managed to be adorable and confused and alluring and elegant all at once. "Why do you say that?"

I sighed. "Well, there are many who would say that considering my…intellectual capacity, or what one might term my potential—that I am certainly not living up to or fulfilling what my raw, basic abilities would indicate I am capable of."

Low laughed, and I breathed in deeply, trying to soak up the sound of her laughter into my pores. "Xavier, I hope you won't be offended if I say you sometimes talk like an AI program written to sound like a professor with, like, three PhDs."

I blinked rapidly, processing what she'd said, trying to determine if I was, in fact, offended. "That does not offend me. It would seem rather accurate, I suppose. I do not have even an associate's degree, much less a PhD but, again, I would hope that lack does not equate to lack of ability. I *could* have a PhD, were the circumstances of my life somewhat altered."

"You *could* have a PhD? How old are you?"

"I just turned twenty recently."

"A PhD takes, like, eight years to earn, doesn't it?"

"Not if one is motivated, has the work capacity, and the raw intellectual ability." I shrugged. "If I'd had parents to push me to leap ahead educationally, within the accepted system, I would be in a much different place at this moment, educationally. But my mother died, and my father became a workaholic, and turned to alcohol as a coping mechanism, and my oldest brother had all he could do as little more than a child himself to take care of the rest of us. So, I never skipped grades, despite my intellectual capability."

"What do you mean, intellectual capability? Are you, like, a MENSA genius or something?"

I nodded. "Something like that. I've never taken a test to measure it. I see no point. It would not prove anything, nor gain me anything. I am what some would call a polymath."

She chewed on a lip, frowning, staring up and to the right, a sign that she was accessing her memory. "A polymath—like Da Vinci? Very good at several disciplines?"

"Precisely. I have a naturally perfect memory—an eidetic memory, it's called—which I have honed over the years through practice, and I have a rather prodigious innate facility with mathematics, as well.

Memorizing and understanding literature is as easy for me as mentally performing complicated mathematics. Learning things like robotics and coding are as simple as reciting Shakespeare or Homer."

Low snorted. "Who quotes Homer? I went to NYU for fine arts and I had a hard time with Homer."

"I taught myself classical Greek one summer, because I was bored and it seemed fun. I have read Homer in his original tongue, which makes understanding it in English a much simpler process."

She blinked at me. "Wait, wait, wait—you taught yourself classical Greek…for *fun*? When was this?"

I realized I might perhaps be approaching territory where it would sound like bragging. "I had *The Iliad* memorized in English by eighth grade, and taught myself Greek the summer between ninth and tenth grade, the same year I taught myself Latin."

"Any other ridiculous accomplishments you'd like to casually mention?" she asked, laughing.

I didn't see them as accomplishments, merely things I'd done to try to challenge myself; I didn't say so though—I'd learned that the hard way. People didn't see it the same way, I'd discovered.

"I exchanged emails with a math professor at MIT for many years, beginning in the ninth grade.

"I thought perhaps we could invite all seven of my brothers and their seven significant others. The more the merrier, yes?"

Low's expression morphed immediately, scrutinizing me. "I…um—"

I lifted an eyebrow. "That was an attempt at jocularity, Low."

She breathed out, a huff of either embarrassment or relief, or maybe both. "I knew that."

"Humor is not my forte."

"Nor mine, it would seem." She smiled again, and the sun suddenly seemed to shine brighter. "I'm on vacation, and I'm not really in a mental or emotional place where I want to be around a lot of people."

"You chose Ketchikan for that very reason."

"Yeah."

"It would be just you and me, Low."

She bumped me with her shoulder, and my bare arm tingled where her skin sizzled against mine. "Sounds like a lot of fun."

My phone chirped, then. I glanced at it—I had a text from Bast: ***we just had a bachelorette party walk in. 34 hungry drunk women. Need you back asap.***

I typed a quick response. **I shall return shortly. X**

Bast's response was immediate. ***I know it's you,***

bro. You don't need to sign a text message. Unless your trying to send me a virtual kiss?

You're

Don't correct my grammar, dork knob. Just get your ass back here.

I pocketed the phone and glanced up at Low. "My apologies. I am needed back at the bar."

Low patted my leg, her hand coming to rest on my thigh, just above my knee. "Thank you for rescuing me, Xavier."

"I merely provided a little assistance, that is all."

"Well, thank you, all the same."

"You are welcome." I stood up. "It was a delight and pleasure to meet you, Low."

I wanted to do something to impress her; a gesture of some kind, but the only thing I could think of was to kiss her hand. Which I was afraid would only freak her out, or make her think I was even weirder than she already did.

Yet, when she held out her hand, probably meaning for me to shake it, I found myself bowing over her hand and pressing my lips, ever so lightly, to the back of it. She sucked in a sharp breath when I did so, her eyes fixing on mine. There was another pause, rife with what felt like a million subtleties and subtexts I couldn't fathom or comprehend.

And then, standing, Low made a funny,

faux-prim face. "The pleasure was assuredly all mine, Mr. Badd," she said, affecting a shockingly accurate proper, posh British accent. She dropped the face and the accent, leaning close to me and smiling. "Tomorrow?"

"Tomorrow."

I left then, my heart beating absurdly hard, my lips tingling from the warmth of her skin, a million questions racing through my mind.

TWO

Harlow

I watched Xavier Badd hop from my boat to the dock and then jog back the way he'd come, stuffing his earbuds back in and then increasing his speed until he was pounding down the dock at a punishingly fast pace.

When he was out of sight, I flopped back on the couch, groaning. I really didn't need a complication like Xavier. I'd come to Ketchikan to get away from everyone and everything. I'd intended this to be not just a vacation, but a total hiatus from my entire life—from people and from everything. I just wanted to sit on my boat, alone, read, and watch movies, and do yoga, and drink tea, and maybe work on that script idea I'd had back in college. Boys didn't fit into my plans *AT ALL.*

But…

An insidiously insistent and persuasive part of my mind cropped up with all the reasons why it may not be such a bad idea to let myself have a little fun with Xavier. I mean, how much trouble could I get into? He doesn't know who I am, I don't think, which is kind of nice. Really, *really* nice, if I'm being totally honest with myself. Refreshing. Fascinating. He's hard to read, but it seems like he's interested in me—attracted, if the constant roving of his eyes is any indication—but also interested. Conversation with him is unlike anything I've ever experienced—he challenges me mentally, keeps me guessing. He's a mystery. I mean, I really, truly do not understand him in any way, which I like.

All the other men I've known and dated and slept with were open books—utterly predictable. Which wasn't a bad thing, necessarily. I knew what they wanted, even before I was famous. They wanted to get into my pants, and stay there as long as I'd let them. Harry, my only serious boyfriend, obviously liked me and cared about me for a lot more than that, but even with Harrison, it had started as mostly just sex, and the *more* had grown out of that. Harrison was smart, funny, interesting, sexy—he had ticked all the boxes. He was fun to talk to, great in bed, and seemed to genuinely care about me.

Our breakup had been mutual, an understanding that our lives and passions were leading us in totally different directions—he'd been a finance major with a minor in Mandarin, and upon graduation had accepted a highly coveted internship at a mammoth corporation in Hong Kong, while I was headed for Hollywood and the big screen. The other men I've spent any kind of time with? Sex. Good sex, and sometimes even meaningful sex with something resembling an emotional component, but largely just physical. It was something I was unapologetic about, and refused to qualify to anyone. I kept it intensely private, however, and after my fame had begun to grow, I'd made it a point to be very clear with anyone I spent time with that what we may or may not do together is a private matter—and so far, all the trysts I'd engaged in had remained off the public radar.

God, my mind was wandering. Why was I thinking about this?

Oh yeah—Xavier. He was the opposite of anyone I'd ever dated or slept with or even gone out with. Closed off in some ways, but open in others. Hard to read, with opaque motives and desires. I'd caught him staring at my chest—reassuring me that at the very least he was straight…or straight enough to like looking at my tits. But he hadn't done or said anything that I recognized as flirting, or anything like an obvious overture. He certainly hadn't hit on me.

I was interested in him, in a way I'd never been interested in a man before. Just in terms of sheer intellectuality, he was an enigma and a challenge to me—it was rare that anyone could truly challenge me intellectually, even more so because no one ever tried; they assumed because of my looks that I was a dumb bimbo who probably spent half the morning staring at a carton of orange juice simply because it said "concentrate" on it. Xavier seemed empty of those preconceptions. He spoke to me earnestly, genuinely, and without seeming like he was talking down to me, or trying to impress me. Even when he was talking about knowing classical Greek and Latin, he didn't seem like a braggadocio, it was more a matter of fact, and he almost seemed reluctant to talk about it for fear of seeming that way.

Also, he was sexy.

I wasn't sure he even realized it, which was part of his charm. He obviously worked hard on his body, because I know from personal experience that you don't get as ripped as he is without a lot of brutally hard work, but he never once came across as arrogant or self-important. The men I'd known in Hollywood, even the nice, down-to-earth ones, had an air about them that they knew they were good looking. I mean, duh, right? They're movie stars, of course they know they're hot. But it's just...off-putting.

Do I come across that way? I don't know. Probably.

He tensed every time I touched him. I wonder what that's about? He never moved away or tried to prevent me from touching him, though. And he kissed my hand! Who does that? I've never had my hand kissed, even for a role. My heart may or may not have pitter-pattered. For that matter, there may have been some pitter-patter happening a little further south, if you know what I mean. He did it so intently, so honestly, without pretense or guile. As if kissing my hand like a knight or lord out of something by Sir Walter Scott was an instinctive gesture.

I don't know. Maybe I'm misreading him. Maybe he's a really great actor and all this is just an elaborate ploy to get me to sleep with him.

Question: Is it working?

Answer: So far...yes.

Problem: Assuming he really doesn't know who I am—what if he finds out? If he goes public with whatever may or may not happen between us, my little hiatus away from Hollywood and the paparazzi is ruined, as is the privacy and secrecy regarding my personal sexual life.

Is it worth risking my privacy and solitude to spend time with Xavier?

My gut reaction is that it would be, and that he's genuine—no pretense

, no guile, no subterfuge. He doesn't know who I am, and he seems to like me for more than my body—although he also does seem to like that, too…which I don't mind. After all, I spend a fortune on personal trainers and nutritionists and hours in the gym to look this way, to keep the pounds off my hips, thighs, and ass, to keep my abs visible. The trick is keeping my fat percentage low enough that I have abdominal definition without sacrificing the body fat necessary to actually have boobs—if I dropped too low, those puppies would vanish. It's a delicate balance, and one that's nearly impossible to maintain without the kind of professional assistance I can afford.

Point is, he likes the way I look enough to steal glances, and even to be caught staring, although he was far more careful after that first time. Almost to the point of not looking at me at all.

Come to think of it, he rarely looked me in the eye. Was that on purpose? Embarrassed at having been caught staring at my tits?

I'm so scattered today. Xavier threw me off, that much is obvious.

Now that yoga is out of the question for the day,

if not for the next few days, what am I going to do?

I pressed a button hidden in the arm of the couch, and a panel slid away on the opposite wall, revealing a 75-inch flat screen smart TV. There was also an iPad disguised as a hardcover book, meant to appear as part of the decor; I flipped open the cover and the iPad came to life, which controlled the audio and video. I have a satellite connection onboard available nearly worldwide, feeding me Wi-Fi wherever I go, granting me constant access to my Netflix and Hulu subscriptions. I mean, a girl has to be able to stream her shows, right?

Yes, I'm spoiled.

And, no, I don't care.

What's weird is that I haven't had a blow-out since leaving LA for the *Westworld* shoot in Utah, nor a manicure or a pedicure, or a massage. And you know what? I don't miss it. Well, the massages I miss, but the hair and nails? It's a lot of upkeep. It's part of my lifestyle, having perfect hair and nails all the time, everywhere I go, and it's a lot of upkeep, quite honestly. When you know you're going to be photographed from every angle possible everywhere you go, doing even the most mundane things, it's a fact of life that you never leave the house without looking your best. Going to the gym at four in the morning? Better make sure your ponytail is perfect, with no

hysterical, because Low needs a distraction.

I was woken up at dawn the next day by the obnoxiously chipper chirruping of a bird, which landed on the railing right outside my bedroom window and it decided to tweet and whistle and sing as loudly as possible. At first, I was irritated—I wanted to sleep in, dammit. But then I opened my eyes and saw the little creature, sitting on the railing, joyful as can be, happy to be alive. And I was less irritated. Marginally, at least.

I stretched luxuriously, the absurdly high thread count of the sheets softer than silk against my bare skin; I sleep naked, and have for years—I just sleep better that way. I slid out of bed, testing my ankle. It was a little sore, but not debilitating. I could probably go back to yoga tomorrow if I was careful and not too overzealous. My head was a little sore to the touch where I'd hit it, but other than that, my stupid accident was just a memory.

The other boats near mine left yesterday, so I was all alone in my slip there at the end of the dock—it was early in the morning, before six, the sun just beginning to peek up over the horizon, which meant there shouldn't be anyone about, and certainly not down this far on the docks. Feeling daring, I stepped out onto the small balcony of the main cabin, still naked. The air was cool and crisp, with a gentle breeze blowing, and not a cloud in the sky. I stood and raised my arms over my head, inhaling deeply, and then bent to touch my toes, grabbing my ankles, holding the stretch, and then straightening into a gentle back-bend—the first few movements of the sun salutation. I left it there, not wanting to push my ankle too far, and the balcony wasn't really big enough for the full series anyway. It was nice to just stand and let the sunlight kiss my skin, orange on my closed eyelids, warmth soaking into me.

And then, in the distance, I heard a footstep.

My eyes flicked open, and I saw a thin figure in the distance, way down the dock, approaching at a leisurely walk.

Xavier.

Could he see this far? He was barely a stick figure from this distance, but still.

I darted back inside, started to shut the door, but then stopped myself. So what if he saw me? Unless he had eagle vision, from that distance I could have been wearing a bikini for all he knew. Or if not, he wouldn't have been able to really see anything.

And if he had?

The thought of Xavier having seen me naked,

even from a distance, sent thrills through me. Dark, delicious, and naughty jolts of electricity.

I had a fleeting and ridiculous notion of not putting on anything at all, just to see his reaction when he got here. But I was nowhere near that daring or forward. I liked to take things in logical steps. Even if it was nothing but temporary physical fun, I wasn't the type of girl to just jump right into bed. I didn't do one-night stands, and I certainly didn't answer the door naked for a guy I'd literally just met and spent maybe thirty minutes with. It was a fun idea to think about, though. Would he be scandalized? Would he get an immediate erection? From what I could tell about Xavier, he would probably not know what to say, or where to look.

Maybe I could still play with him a little. Just to see what his reaction would be.

I hunted through my closet until I found what I was looking for: a short silk kimono, purchased on a press trip to Japan for my film with Dawson. It was custom made for me, sewn by hand to my precise measurements. The hem came to mid-thigh, the sleeves draped loose, and the front edges were designed to only sort of overlap when closed, leaving a good bit of cleavage on display. It was unbelievably comfortable, yet sexy as hell—a provocative blurring of the line between lingerie and loungewear. I tied it closed and examined my reflection in the mirror, messing with my hair a little, making sure a strand or two hung loose artfully, making sure nothing was revealed which shouldn't be—yet making sure I was still displayed at my best...in a casual, accidental sort of way.

Satisfied that I looked pretty damn good, but not like I was trying, I headed down to the main level and turned on the automatic espresso machine to brew a latte. By the time the machine was done with the clanking and hissing and steaming and whooshing, Xavier arrived at my slip.

"Low?" he called out, not too loudly—his voice pitched so that if I was awake I'd hear, but if I wasn't I wouldn't be woken up. It was a wonderfully thoughtful thing, which made me smile to myself.

I took my mug with me as I stepped out of the cabin onto the deck, going forward to greet Xavier. He had a large brown paper bag in one hand, and two paper cups of coffee in a cardboard drink holder in the other. He was deliciously gorgeous, wearing tight, dark blue jeans slouched into loosely tied combat boots, with a tight black T-shirt stretched around his lean torso, the symbol for pi printed on the chest.

"Good morning, Xavier." I gave him my brightest, happiest, most welcoming smile—which I didn't have to fake at all; I really was genuinely happy to see

a perfect amount of cream cheese and sautéed spinach. The bacon was crisp but not burnt.

"This looks truly amazing, Xavier. Thank you. It was very thoughtful of you, especially this early in the morning."

He smiled, shrugging. "I am always up early. I was not sure if you would be up this early, but I took a chance you would be. It seems to have paid off."

"Early riser, huh?"

He shrugged, taking a bite. "I require less sleep than the average person."

"I was hoping to sleep in, but a bird woke me up."

We ate in a surprisingly companionable silence. The omelet was even more delicious than it looked. He'd used a generous sprinkling of herbs and spices, so it was intensely flavorful with a hint of spiciness. When we were finished, Xavier finished the last of his cappuccino and shot me a glance.

"Would you like to go on that boat ride this morning?" he asked.

I nodded, smiling. "Absolutely. It sounds like a great way to spend the morning."

His gaze flicked momentarily from my face to my cleavage, and then back. "I will see if I can find your launch and figure out how to get it into the water while you change."

I smirked at him. “You mean I can’t wear my kimono to go fishing?”

He shook his head seriously. “I am afraid not. As ravishing as it looks, and as becoming as you are in it, a kimono is not appropriate attire for a fishing expedition. You would be cold, and there is a chance you may get wet.”

Ravishing? Becoming?

He was serious?

I couldn’t help a snickering laugh. “Xavier, I was being sarcastic.”

He blinked at me owlishly. “Oh. I suppose that would make more sense. You are most likely sensible enough to know better, even for a city girl.”

I frowned at him. “Yes, Xavier, I’m sensible enough to know better than to think something like *this*—” I swept a hand down my body in gesture, “is appropriate attire for a fishing expedition.”

His gaze followed my hand. “That was meant to be sarcastic.”

“Oh,” I laughed. “I’m not quite sure you have the hang of sarcasm, Xavier.”

Another slow blink. “I hope I did not offend you.”

I reached across the table and patted his forearm, and then let my hand rest there, tracing the patterns of his tattoos. “No, you didn’t.”

“That kimono is a very beautiful article of

clothing." His gaze flicked down, and then back up. "Or rather, it looks beautiful upon you." He licked his lips. "Both statements are equally true."

I smiled coyly. "Thank you. It's very comfortable."

"It does not appear to be tied closed properly in the front," he said, and then blushed, ducking his head. "That was not a thought I should have voiced, I do not think."

I glanced down, realizing—or pretending to realize, rather—that the edges of had parted a bit, revealing a considerable expanse of the insides of my breasts, the edges only barely covering my nipples. One wrong jostle, and I'd be exposed; I think he was more than half hoping I'd move wrong, for that precise reason.

"Silly old thing." I said, smirking at him. "It doesn't like to stay closed, does it? It's super comfortable, just not very modest, I guess. I wasn't expecting you this early."

"I hope it was not an inconvenience." His gaze kept flicking up and down, as if the war he was waging with his impulses was losing one.

I almost told him I didn't mind if he looked, but that would ruin the fun of flirting with him. "Not at all," I said. "As long as you don't mind seeing me in this old thing. I know I'm not exactly dressed for company."

He swallowed hard, and his eyes remained steadfastly on my face. "I...certainly do not mind."

I bet not—I didn't say that, though. "I'm going to go get dressed. I think the launch is toward the back somewhere."

"I believe the correct term for the rear of the boat is 'stern' as a matter of fact."

I stood up and traipsed inside, glancing over my shoulder to catch his gaze darting away from my butt. "Yeah, I know. But I just own the thing, I don't sail it or drive it or whatever."

I smiled to myself as I went up to my cabin to change. I dressed in a pair of jeans, a thin cotton V-neck T-shirt, and a thick sweater, with a pair of cute hiking boots I'd purchased several months ago, with the idea that I'd start hiking Runyon Canyon. After working some scented leave-in conditioner into my hair and brushing it backward, I tugged it into a ponytail and then donned a baseball cap and a pair of large-framed, darkly tinted sunglasses. I watched from the window as Xavier fiddled with a set of controls near the rear—the stern, I suppose I should say—of the boat, eventually figuring out how to get the ship's automated system to send out the smaller boat, what Xavier called the launch.

Xavier watched a panel on the side of the yacht open to reveal the smaller boat. I'd have called it a dinghy, or better yet, a baby boat. It was an adorable little thing, finely crafted of blonde wood and polished to a shine. It had a motor built into it, rather than the kind that hung over the back of the boat, and it had an actual steering wheel. Xavier shook his head as if in disbelief. He peered over the railing at the launch, leaning forward on his toes, hands at his sides, rhythmically patting his legs with his palms.

I went down and joined him at the railing. "I see you figured out how to launch the launch." I laughed at my own phrasing. "Launch the launch. That's stupid."

He patted his thighs with his palms a few more times, and then glanced down at his hands with a slight frown, stuffing his fists into his jeans pockets. "Yes, I did. This is a highly automated craft you own, Low." He jutted his chin at the launch. "That is quite a thing, that. Rather more…expensive…than a typical dinghy. It is a work of art in its own right."

I shrugged. "It came with the boat. This is actually the first time I've even seen it. It is pretty nice, isn't it?" I glanced at him. "So…how do we get down there?"

He laughed. "Actually, I was wondering the same thing. There does not appear to be a ladder, or a platform."

"Maybe there's an entrance down in the side of the boat."

"That is a logical suggestion."

I laughed. "Okay, Spock, well, let's go look, shall we?"

Xavier stared at me. "Spock?"

"Yes, from Star Trek?"

"Obviously I am familiar with the character of Spock. But why did you refer to me as him?"

I led him through the boat to the stairs and then to the lower level. "You talk like him—you know, properly, formally, without contractions and with all sorts of fancy words, and saying things like 'that is a logical suggestion.' You just remind me of Spock, that's all."

"I shall choose to take that as a compliment, I believe."

I rubbed his shoulder, noting again the way he tensed at my touch. "It was meant as one."

I found a door I'd never bothered looking behind, which lead down to a small, low-ceilinged platform, just large enough to contain the launch when stowed. It was a mystery to me how the mechanism worked, and I didn't really care. It was cool, and useful. And kind of impressive, honestly.

Xavier made his way across the platform and hopped into the boat, while I made my way with less surety, hesitating at the hop from the platform onto the boat.

Leaning forward, Xavier reached out for me. "May I offer you my assistance?"

I leaned forward, and his hands wrapped around my waist, and he lifted me into the boat. The boat shifted, and I toppled forward against him. His hands, already on my waist, slid farther around to my back, holding me in place against him, his hard, lean body supporting mine for a moment. His startling green eyes met mine. His breath caught, and his fingertips dimpled into my back.

"Hi," I whispered. "You caught me."

His hands slid up my back, hesitating mid-spine, and then he held me by the arms and gently righted me. "Indeed I did. In such close quarters, I could hardly fail to catch you."

He met my gaze for another moment or two, and then looked away, as if unable to hold my gaze. I was somewhat disappointed that he let me go so soon. His hands had felt nice on my back, and his body had felt strong against mine. Hard, firm.

I'd almost thought, for a moment, that he intended to kiss me. But he didn't. With gentlemanly decorum, he had set me upright and backed away, as if to not take advantage of my clumsiness.

A momentary pause, then, as Xavier stared at me with an unreadable expression on his face, his fingertips tapping against his thighs. What went through his mind? What caused him to continually pull away from the obvious openings I was leaving him? He was a mystery. Fascinating, compelling.

"I…if you will take a seat, I will cast us off," he said.

So, I took a seat and Xavier untied the line between the launch and the boat. He cast us off and started the engine, which gurgled to life and then caught with a throaty, powerful rumble. He spent a few moments examining the layout of the controls.

"Can you drive this?" I asked.

He nodded. "It is somewhere between a car and an outboard motor boat. I have not operated one of these particular kinds of boats before, but I think I will be able to manage."

He slowly reversed us away from the larger boat, and then brought us in a wide arc so our bow—or is it prow?—was facing open water. With a gentle nudge of the throttle, the bow lifted and the engine snarled, and an immediate sense of momentum slammed me against my seat, making me cackle in surprised laughter.

Xavier barked a laugh as he backed off the throttle. "This is no ordinary launch."

"It does seem kind of powerful."

"Um, yes, rather. Once we get away from the docks and into more open water, I would like to open it up, if you would be agreeable."

I laughed, leaning back in the seat. "You could just say, 'I want to go fast.'"

"Would you be frightened if I opened the throttle all the way?"

He'd barely touched the throttle and I'd been pushed against my seat; if he opened it up all the way, how fast could we go? The idea sent a thrill of excitement through me. "That sounds like fun. Do it!"

We trundled away from the docks, slowly, so as not to send a wake that would rock the other boats as we made our way away from Ketchikan. A mountain loomed green, with a white crown, behind the little city, which was tucked in against it, nestled in the teeming mass of the forest. Water rippled silver and green and blue, winking diamonds in the sunlight. There was a cruise ship approaching, huge and white. A trio of seagulls wheeled directly above us, cawing and screeching, as if discussing us far below them.

I breathed deeply of the clean, fresh air, soaking up the sunlight on my skin. I let my eyes close for a moment, enjoying the breeze against my face, the sounds of the gulls, the rumble of the engine underneath me…the peacefulness. I didn't even have my phone with me. No assistant, no script to memorize, no upcoming shoots or events, no galas or brunches, no leaks or rumors.

"This is perfect," I murmured.

"Mmm. Yes, I agree." Xavier's voice was low.

I peeked through my eyelashes, and saw that he was watching me as he navigated us away from land and past the approaching cruise ship, which towered dizzyingly above us as we passed it. His expression was obvious, this time: appreciative, raking over me from head to toe, openly, thinking I still had my eyes closed. I liked his gaze on me; I enjoyed wondering what he was thinking, not knowing what he would say or how he would say it, what cute and funny thing he would do next. I enjoyed the anticipation of wondering how this thing would go. There was clearly an attraction between us, but how would it play out?

"Are you ready?" he asked. "I'm going to open the throttle."

I sat up, whipped off my hat and clutched it in my hands, grinning at him. "Go!"

He'd used a contraction, I noted with interest.

He pushed the throttle forward in a smooth arc, and the powerful engine responded beautifully, roaring to life. The bow lifted until I couldn't even see the water ahead of us, and then we leveled off as our speed increased. Our bow sliced the water, sending white spraying off to either side, wind whipping against us. I laughed as he continued to nudge the throttle forward, until it was as far as it could go. The sense of speed was so intense it forced disbelieving laughter out of me. I *owned* this thing? How had I not known? Had I even been told the yacht came with a freaking speedboat?

Xavier angled us toward open water, or what seemed like it. I had only a vague notion of the geography around here, and I felt like we were in a channel of some kind, so we weren't heading for actual open ocean, just a more open section of channel.

"This is fun!" I shouted in his ear, grabbing his arm.

He only smiled at me, glancing down at my hand, wrapped around his bare bicep. His jaw tensed, and his eyes narrowed, and he sucked in a deep breath, held it, and then I watched as the tension bled out of him. He smiled again, relaxing, and turned back to driving the boat. Did he have an issue with being touched, maybe? He didn't seem to mind it, now, so I held on to his arm, letting my fingers press into the smooth skin and hard muscle.

After a few minutes of daring, breathtaking speed, he backed off the throttle until we reached at a nice, leisurely pace, cruising down the channel. Another mile or so, and another channel or something opened up on our left, and he angled toward it. I was enthralled with the lush, green beauty of this place. I'd seen plenty of movies set in Alaska, and they always featured scenes exactly like the one I was in: forested hills to either side, placid, glassy water, clouds wisping across the sun, fish leaping up to splash dramatically, gulls wheeling and cawing. I scanned the sky, half expecting a bald eagle to soar overhead, keening. Really, the movies didn't do it justice. The beauty was almost overwhelming, making something in my chest expand and throb, the sheer, unadulterated, majestic beauty filling some primal void inside me. The natural beauty just…resonated.

"It's really, really amazing here, Xavier," I said, after a while.

He nodded. "I grew up here, and it never gets old."

I spent the next few moments openly examining Xavier's features, the sharp lines of his jaw, the column of his neck, his thick, dark eyelashes. Curly, artfully messy, thick black hair. He really was incredibly beautiful. Hot wasn't a good enough word, not to properly encompass what he truly looked like. Hot guys were a dime a dozen. Truly beautiful men? Not so much. He was masculine, utterly so—in his posture, in the way he carried himself, his stride. Even sitting at the wheel of the boat, he was effortlessly and unconsciously posing in a definitively masculine posture, one arm tossed over the side, the other hand confidently steering the boat. His vivid green eyes were always moving, always darting, and his hands were never still. One would slide around the steering wheel, tracing the leather, the stitching, the seam, and the other would be tapping at his knee, or his thigh, or plucking at his shirt or a thread of his jeans—other than his eyes and his hands, though, he was otherwise utterly motionless, a strange dichotomy of stillness and restlessness.

A thought occurred to me. "We were going fishing, weren't we? I don't think there's any tackle or whatever it's called on this boat."

He gestured ahead, at a large red and white seaplane with two propellers, which was anchored in the distance, off to one side of the channel, engines off. A pair of figures could be seen sitting on the floats, fishing poles angled up and away, lines vanishing into the water. "That is my brother, Brock. He has plenty of extra fishing gear, which he has agreed to loan to me. We were going to be in the same area, so I figured we may as well just meet up with them for a moment."

Meet up with his brother.

Shit.

SHIT.

I froze, tensed.

I had sunglasses on, and a hat. My hair was in a ponytail, pulled through the back of the hat. I was still recognizable, though. Shit. How did I get out of this without getting recognized? I didn't want to have to switch into entertainer mode. I didn't want to have to answer questions or sign autographs or take selfies. I wanted to sit in a boat alone with Xavier and pretend I was just any other girl.

Was that so much to ask?

THREE

Xavier

I GLANCED OVER AT LOW AS WE APPROACHED THE seaplane: she sank lower in the seat, tugged her hat brim down, and settled her bug-eyed sunglasses higher on her nose. Was she shy? She didn't seem shy, but for some reason her body language indicated, as best I could read, that she was uncomfortable in this situation for whatever reason. Was it me? Was she a recluse? She had allowed me aboard, and was willingly spending time with me, so it didn't follow that she was a recluse.

I knew I would not be able to figure it out or understand on my own.

"Are you uncomfortable in some way?" I asked.

She shrugged one shoulder. "You said it would be just you and me. I wasn't expecting to meet anyone else."

"It's just my brother and Claire. We're only staying long enough so that I can borrow Brock's fishing supplies."

She hesitated, and then sighed. "Okay."

I slowed the boat to a stop as we pulled alongside the seaplane; Brock and Claire were sitting on the float, fishing poles in hand. As we stopped, Brock waved, and Claire wiggled her fingers at me.

"Nice boat, Xavier," Brock said by way of greeting.

"It belongs to my friend, Low," I said, gesturing at her. "Low, this is my brother Brock, and this Claire."

"Nice to meet you," Low murmured.

Claire's brows drew down as she glanced at Low, but then Brock hopped up onto the float and reached into the open door of the airplane. He withdrew a tackle box and two fishing poles, with bobbers and lures already set, the hooks latched onto the eyelets near the reel so the lines wouldn't dangle or tangle. He handed these to me and I set them onto the backseat of the boat behind Low and me.

"Didn't know you liked fishing," Brock said, smirking at me.

"I do not enjoy it as a sport or activity by itself,

she's—wow. I mean, *damn*, girl, way to deep-throat, holy shit."

I wasn't watching, as I'd learned very quickly that Claire and Brock had no qualms about their sexual activity, and when Claire wanted Brock, she didn't care who was around. "Just...look away, Low. That's just how Brock and Claire are."

I already had the boat puttering forward and away before Claire warned us, but not before I heard Brock start to curse. Once we were a few feet away, I nudged the throttle forward a bit, still slowly so as not to create a wake.

"That's a big motherfucking fish, Claire!" Brock said, clinging to the strut of the wing with one hand and lifting the fish on the line into the air with the other.

Claire's response was unintelligible, sounding something like "*omph-oh, om-uh-omph*," which could have meant anything.

"Would have been kind of funny if you'd sent a big wake to knock them over," Low said, glancing at me with a smirk.

"I suppose that would have been humorous. I did not think of that."

Low shook her head. "So they're...open."

I shrugged. "Yes, they are rather blasé about conducting sexual encounters regardless of whomever may be watching."

"Is all your family like that?" Low asked.

I shook my head. "No, not at all. There is a lot of sexual innuendo flying around pretty much constantly, but no one is willing to do whatever whenever the way those two are."

"I mean, she just started sucking him off right then and there. You're his kid brother, and they don't even know me!"

"Well, she did warn us."

"Still, that's a little...kooky, if you ask me."

"My family is...far from normal."

"I didn't mean for that to sound so insulting."

I smiled at her, hoping it was a reassuring smile. "I did not take it as an insult. My family, as I said, definitely falls within the definition of kooky. Particularly Claire. She is very...aggressively and openly sexual, I suppose one might say."

"Yeah, that's for sure." She glanced back once more. "Wow, she's still going."

"I have a feeling they will spend more time fornicating than fishing."

She turned to me with an odd look in her eye. "I mean, except for the part about having an audience, I think that actually sounds...fun."

I blinked at her. "I...um..."

How was I supposed to respond? Was that an

innuendo directed at me? A joke? A direct come-on? I had no clue how to interpret her expression nor her words. A roiling in my stomach and a tightening in my jeans and the thunder of my heart made me aware that I was hoping, absurdly, most likely, that she meant it as a direct come-on to me, that she wanted that with me. But how to know? If I acted on that assumption and was wrong, I would be mortified beyond all comprehension.

"We are approaching the spot I have scouted out as the best location for potentially catching fish." I knew my cop-out response was cowardly, and hated myself for it.

My head was buzzing with thoughts, wishes, desires, fears, doubts—a swirling maelstrom of them.

How could she want *me*? That's ridiculous.

But yet…she met me on the boat clad in nothing but a partially tied scrap of silk, so surely that meant she did not—at the very least—mind me seeing her in a state of undress, which would logically lead one to theorize that she also felt a measure of attraction to me. She has put her hands on me, innocently, albeit, several times; does that hint at potential desire?

What about her reticence to meet my brother and Claire, and her obvious discomfort around them?

Her latest comment contained more than one potential meaning and inference, all of which would lead me to theorize she felt some kind of chemical, physical attraction to me. But how could she be attracted to *me*? I'm so awkward, so unsure. I am not at all confident like Bast, or Zane, or Bax. Or any of my brothers, really. Women are attracted to confidence, I have read—so how could she be attracted to me, when I lack that kind of direct, alpha male bravado?

Perhaps I could fake it.

Perhaps if I did, she might be attracted to me.

And if she were to be attracted to me, she might be inclined to pursue a physical relationship with me. Which I want.

But also, I am scared of that.

I doubt very seriously my own ability to carry out such a thing, to go through with it, to allow it. Any kind of physical contact is difficult for me, even my own. Her hand on my arm nearly sent me into a paroxysm of discomfort.

But yet…there was something beneath that discomfort, a sizzle, a tingle, a fleeting, ephemeral sense of…*perhaps*. Of potential pleasure. A lessened discomfort at her hand on my skin.

"Xavier?" Low's voice was confused.

I was jolted back to awareness, and realized I'd stopped the boat and had been staring into nothingness, lost in my thoughts.

"My apologies. Sometimes my own thoughts

"What kind of robots do you build?"

I shrugged. "They don't really do anything useful." I felt myself relaxing into the conversation, evidenced by my use of a contraction. "They are more for fun, for amusement."

"What do you mean? What do they do that's amusing?"

"Have you ever seen a wind-up toy? Like those little swimmer toys that go in the bathtub? Or the monkeys that clap their hands? A range of movement or motion limited to a single repeated behavior? My robots are somewhat like that."

"And what is quantum mechanics? I know quantum means, like, things are relative. The cat in the box that is neither alive nor dead until you look at it."

"The Schrödinger's cat thought experiment, yes. That is part of it, the uncertainty principle." I went on to explain the basics of quantum mechanics, and found myself lost in the fascinating details.

Eventually, Low reached out and put her hand on my shoulder. "I'm afraid you lost me at 'quantization of energy,' Xavier," she said, laughing. "You're making me feel dumb."

I blushed, stumbling to a stop in the middle of explaining the correspondence principle. "Oh. I—I apologize. I myself am somewhat like a wind-up toy, in that respect. Wind me up on certain topics, and away I go." I noticed her hand had slid from my shoulder to my forearm, resting there with familiarity. "I did not mean to make you feel that way. I truly am sorry."

She just laughed. "I don't know how many people could listen to you talk about quantum mechanics and *not* feel at least slightly stupid."

"It is a matter of education, not intelligence. I believe you are a vastly intelligent person. You simply do not have the basis of knowledge in physics to follow what I was lecturing you about." I laughed, shaking my head. "What fun, eh? Sitting in a boat, fishing, and being lectured about quantum mechanics. If anyone should feel dumb, it is me."

She slid across the bench seat closer to me. Her hip bumped mine, her shoulder brushed mine, and her hand, once on my forearm, slid to my knee. "I'm having a good time."

My heart hammered in my chest. Her proximity made my head swim, made my pulse slam out of control, made my whole body feel too tight. The region between my belly and thighs, behind my zipper, was aching in a way that made it difficult to think.

I swallowed hard. "You are?"

She nodded, smiling at me. "I told you, I like hanging out with you."

Say something direct, Xavier, I told myself. *Say*

something bold.

"I...I like you—um, hanging out with you, too...I mean."

Her head tilted to one side. "Why'd you change your answer? I was fine with the first one."

"I...well...both are true. I like you. And I am enjoying our time together this morning." I felt a swell of pride in my chest just from that tiny bit of directness.

Discussing myself, my feelings, what I wanted—these were usually impossible for me. I'd spent my whole life trying to be invisible, to avoid being noticed, to seem normal, to fit in, even slightly.

We sat in easy quiet, listening to the birds sing, watching our bobbers, as the sun moved slowly across the sky.

The silence was broken when Low squeaked as her pole was nearly yanked out of her hand. "Oh! Oh my god! I think I have a fish!"

I was shocked out my thoughts at her sudden outburst of excitement. Her pole was bent nearly to snapping, and she was standing up and being pulled forward in the boat, having a hell of a time merely holding on. Whatever she'd hooked, it was huge.

"Give it line," I said. "Don't reel it in. It's too big—it'll snap the line."

"How do I do that?" She was holding on to the

rod with both hands, panicking, now.

I tossed my own rod to my feet and, without thinking, stood up behind her and reached around her with both arms, taking the rod and pressing the button to release the line. I was effectively hugging Low from behind, her hair tickling my nose, her body framed by mine. Even as I focused on bringing in the fish, I was hyperaware of her—of her proximity, of her scent, of her warmth. Of the fact that, standing like this, her backside was mere millimeters from thc front of my jeans, my zipper, and the aching beast behind it. I had never been so aware of myself in my life as I was in that moment, nor so aware of another person.

Low kept hold of the fishing pole with me, as if she'd forgotten to let go as I fought the fish, reeling it in and then letting it swim away, reeling it in and letting it go, tiring it out. She was leaning backward, now. On purpose? Shifting backward into me. Pressing her back to my chest, clapping as I brought the fish closer to the boat. Her buttocks were pressed flat against my groin, now. Could she feel the evidence of my excitement? I dared not move, for fear of drawing attention to my situation.

She gave no sign of being aware of it, if she was.

"You've almost got it!" Low said, laughing clapping. "It's huge!"

"You do it, now," I encouraged. "Reel it in. It's tired out, so it should come in more easily."

She took over and I let go of the rod, but didn't step away. My head was spinning crazily—I was almost dizzy. Her scent was powerful—jasmine, today, and lavender, and coffee. Her body heat was radiating against me. Her buttocks felt...squishy and yet hard at the same time, pressed against the front of me, against my thighs and pelvis; an intoxicating combination. My hands were shaking, as if merely being this close to Low was causing the adrenaline to rush through me.

She reeled and reeled, and then pressed the button like she'd seen me do, letting the monster fish flip away a few feet, and then reeled it in again. The next time she gave it line, it just floated in place, not trying to swim away, exhausted now.

"Reel it all the way in," I said.

The reel sang, and then the pole was bending over, the tip dripping as she lifted the fish, with no small amount of exertion, out of the water.

"Grab the line and lift it up so we can see it." I dug my phone out of my back pocket and held it up, bringing up the camera as she held the monster fish up beside her. "Smile!"

Low's grin of excitement faltered. "No pictures, please." Her response was immediate and sounded almost automatic, or practiced.

I frowned. "I thought you would want a photograph of yourself with your first fish, which is a rather impressively large specimen."

She stared at me, and then glanced down at the fish. And then a new smile flashed across her face. "Sure. Yeah, you're right." She held up the fish, smiling brightly, pointing at the fish with her other hand. "Cheese!"

I laughed as I snapped a few photos. "I've never heard an adult say cheese for a picture outside the presence of children. That was rather adorable of you, I must say."

"Can I see them?" she asked, sounding anxious.

I handed her the phone and took the rod and the fish. "Is there something wrong?"

She sighed, lowering the phone to smile at me. "No, not at all. I'm just…I'm weird about having my picture taken."

"I do not see why you would be." I reminded myself to be bold, to be direct. "You are a devastatingly beautiful woman, Low. Any camera fortunate enough to capture your image is truly blessed indeed. And I, spending this time with you, am most fortunate of all."

Low's laugh was disbelieving, her smile so excruciatingly lovely I could no more look away than I could swim to Hawaii from here. "You have one hell of a way with words, Xavier."

"It is nothing but the truth."

"Well, thank you." She held up the phone. "I'm going to send this to myself."

"All right." The fish flopped and wriggled on the line. "I'm going to release him, now, all right?"

"You know it's a boy fish? How?"

I unhooked the fish and tossing it into the water, where it sank for a moment and then flicked its fin, darting away.

"Oh, no," I said, laughing. "I don't know its gender. That was merely an expression."

I heard my phone bloop as the photo sent, and she handed the phone back to me. The message she'd typed to accompany the photo:

Xavier, I'm very private, so please do not share my phone number with anyone. But feel free to message me, if you want to.

I clicked the phone to sleep and put it in my pocket, casting a glance at Low, who was sitting down again, arm stretched out across the back of the seat, face tipped toward the sun, smiling happily.

"You seem to have some very specific feelings regarding privacy and solitude," I remarked.

I sat down beside her, not casting the lines again just yet; I sat close to her, but not as close as she'd been a few moments ago, before the fish had bitten her hook.

She spoke without looking at me, face still tipped up to the sun. "Yeah, I guess I just like my solitude, and prefer to stay private."

"I do not know your reasons for those preferences, nor shall I ask," I said, hesitating over my next words. "But…I hope you will believe me when I say I will not ever do anything to violate your privacy. And if my presence ever begins to infringe upon your solitude, I trust you'll make me aware? I would never wish to overstay my welcome in your presence."

This got her to look at me. "Thank you, Xavier. It means more than you know to hear you say that."

"Do you want to keep fishing?"

She shook her head. "No, not particularly. I'd rather just troll around in the boat, if that's all right with you." She grinned at me. "Although, that was pretty exciting."

I put the rods away as Brock had done, and turned over the motor. "My brothers will not believe me when I tell them how large your fish was. They will say it is a fish story."

She eyed me with a pleased grin. "It *was* pretty big, huh?"

I nodded. "Easily a foot long and nearly ten pounds. They will be quite jealous." I watched her expression shift, the grin falling away at my words. "You seem unhappy again. Why?"

"You plan to show them the photo?"

I shook my head. "That would be breaking your trust, as I assumed you would not want me to share that photograph with anyone. So no, I will not."

"What if they ask if you took a picture?"

I grinned. "A tertiary benefit to my unusually formal manner of speech is that others are frequently unable to decipher when I am lying."

"I bet." She poked me in the arm. "I wouldn't have pegged you for someone who told lies, though."

"I am not. I rarely have reason to."

"That's good," Low said, her voice oddly inflected, in a way I couldn't read. "Truth is good."

I took her the rest of the way up the inlet, rounding the two islands and returning south again. We went slowly. We were both inclined to silence, it seemed, and it was not a tense or awkward silence, but rather a companionable one, in which we both enjoyed the beauty of our surroundings.

A shadow slid across the surface of the water and I glanced up; above us was a bald eagle floating lazily. I reached over and tapped Low on the shoulder, and then gestured to the massive, magnificent bird, which was only a hundred or so feet above us and clearly visible.

Low's breath caught, and she clapped her hand over her mouth. "Wow! It's...god, it's huge!" She glanced at me in awe, grinning. She whipped her sunglasses off and shielded her eyes with her palm, watching as the eagle circled. "What do you think it's doing?"

I shrugged. "Just circling, perhaps? I do not know. It may be tracking a fish."

She clapped her hands. "Do you think we might see it catch one?"

"I don't know. I have never seen that happen either. That would be exciting indeed!"

I slowed the boat to a stop and cut the engine, and we both watched the eagle soar. It just circled for a few minutes, and then floated down to settle on the branch of a tree jutting out over the water. We were within two hundred of feet of it, our boat bobbing in the gentle swells. For a long while, we just sat and watched the eagle. I was about to start the engine again when the eagle spread its wings, leaned forward, and with one powerful downstroke, took off, angled low, darting across the water.

"Oh my god! Oh my god!" Low said, in an excited whisper. "It's—look, Xavier! It's gonna catch one!" She reached out and grabbed my hand, her entire being humming with excited energy, a smile so wide and so bright her features were utterly transformed.

The eagle tucked its wings in, stooping down toward the water, and then, at the last moment, its wings slammed forward and its feet extended, wickedly curved talons grazing the surface—and then it struck, water splashing, its wings curving to catch at the air. It happened in a split second, the strike. And then it was beating its wings and streaking skyward, a huge salmon writhing in its talons. It flew across the channel and landed on a branch, its beak slicing into the luckless fish.

Low, laughing, leaned into me, her whole body catching up against mine. "That was amazing! I never thought I'd see something like that actually happen in real life!"

It was difficult to breathe. Her scent choked me, her heat suffused me, overwhelmed me. Her weight against me left my whole body trembling.

She pulled away to look up at me, mere inches away. Her eyes were so large, and so blue, and utterly hypnotic. I could feel her pulse. The softness of her breasts against my chest left me aching.

I was suddenly overwhelmed.

I fought it.

Don't panic.

This is normal.

A part of me was deliriously overjoyed at her closeness, at the mere fact that a woman, any woman, was voluntarily this near to me, touching me. That she seemed to genuinely like me. That she was spending time with me, and didn't seem put off by my quirks and strange speech patterns and formal syntax.

Another part of me was doubtful—what ulterior motive did she have? Surely she had one. Why else would a woman as obviously wealthy and worldly wise and beautiful want to have anything to do with me? Why would someone like Low deign to waste her time with an awkward, nerdy nobody like me?

Memories of a certain experience from high school bubbled up inside me. I pushed them away, but it was futile.

Have you ever been with a girl, Xavier? That sly, lascivious tone of voice, the way Brittany had slunk toward me, stalking, prancing, preening under my naive attention.

Do you like me, Xavier?

Do you think I'm pretty?

You want to touch me, don't you? Go ahead, I don't mind. In fact, I might even like it.

And then, moments after she'd said that, the knife had been inserted, directly into my back and twisted. A metaphorical knife, but no less painful. I clamped down on the memory, involuntarily tensing and shrinking away from Low.

Low frowned up at me. "Is something wrong?"

I breathed deeply in through my nose and out through my mouth, pushing away the panic the memory brought up. "No, it's fine."

Her hand was on my chest, resting directly over my sternum, and then sliding to cover my heart. "Your heart is beating really hard," she murmured, still so close I could smell the coffee on her breath and the scent of her hair and feel her body heat. "Are you okay?

I didn't know what to do with my hands. One hovered near her shoulder, the other rested on the side of the boat—I clenched my jaw and forced my hand to relax, to drift down and to settle on her shoulder. I felt the softness of her sweater, and the firmness of her bone and muscle and flesh beneath the fabric.

"Yes. I am well." I sounded even more robotic and Spock-like than ever, because I wasn't well.

I was in a bewildering daze of panic and sensation, memory and present, desire and fear. Her body was so close, pressed almost intimately against mine, leaning against me, gazing up at me. If this was a movie, the hero would dip down and kiss the lady, and she would lift up and wrap her arms around his neck, and he would do something clever that somehow removed her clothing without breaking the kiss. James Bond, were he in this situation, would lay her flat down on the bench, and her feet would wrap up around his back. She would laugh, lustily, as he kissed her with masterful skill.

I, being me, panicked.

"Low, I—" My breath caught, choking off my words.

She seemed to sense my distress and lifted up, but in so doing, dragged her breasts up my chest—even disguised by the thick sweater, it was clear she was exceedingly well-endowed, and I had a mental image of the way she'd looked earlier, on the yacht, those beautiful breasts only barely covered. That image was burned into my mind.

"Xavier, you have to breathe, you know." She said this with a teasing laugh, her fingers tapping at my chest. "Breathe, Xavier. Take a breath."

I gasped, her words reminding me that I had in fact stopped breathing.

She laughed again, breathily. "You told me you think I'm beautiful, but I didn't think you meant *literally* breathtaking."

My hand had been on her shoulder, resting on the slope of it, and when she had lifted up in concern, my palm had slid downward, so I could feel the strap of her bra underneath the sweater. This only made my distress worse. "No, I—I…yes, I meant it literally. You are so beautiful that you actually, in literal point of fact, make it hard for me to breathe."

"Well, geez, Xavier, don't, like, pass out, okay?"

"If you were somehow to become even the slightest amount more lovely than you are, I would pass out."

She laughed, shaking her head. "Oh, Xavier."

I frowned. "What?"

"The things you say. You're gonna give a girl a complex."

"What does that mean?"

She was so close, her nose was nearly nudging mine, and I felt the breath of her words on my skin, on my lips. "It means when you say things like that, I get…" she trailed off with a breathy giggle.

"What? You get what?"

"All fluttery inside. Nobody has ever said anything to me the way you say things."

"It's just the truth."

"Flatterer," she murmured, smiling.

"It is not flattery if it is truth."

"Yeah, well…flattery can actually get you pretty far. As long as you mean it."

"Where would it get me?"

Her hand drifted up my chest, and then her fingers danced through my hair. "I have a feeling you just may find out."

My heart was crashing, skipping beats, staccato and arrhythmic. My lungs were squeezing, and my veins were on fire.

It seemed impossible to misread the intent behind her words, behind the way she was behaving with me. Dare I take the bait?

What if she was like Brittany, though?

God, the doubt, the fear, the panic—combined with the overwhelming barrage of sensations her physical proximity engendered inside me—it was too much. Too much.

"Low," I muttered, her name falling from my lips. What did I want to say? I had no idea.

A buzzing overhead broke the moment. It was a loud buzz at first, and then a roar—the distinct sound of a double-engine airplane. I looked up to see Brock's seaplane approaching. Low backed away from me, watching Brock's passage overhead—he waggled his wings as he swooped down toward us, getting close enough that Low shrieked in fear, curling in against my chest, huddling into me until the huge red and white aircraft angled upward and away, heading southeast.

"He buzzed us!" Low shouted. "The jerk! That scared me!"

I only laughed. "He used to be, and still is, I suppose, a stunt pilot. He performed in airshows all over the world before coming back here."

She eyed me. "Really? You said he flew an air

aren't you?

Have you ever been with a girl, Xavier?

That last one, especially, ran through my brain on repeat—the way she'd said it, the hidden ridicule behind it, which I'd only understood after it was all over, the thinly disguised cruelty behind everything in the whole scenario.

I ended up putting both hands on the steering wheel as I brought us to Low's yacht, missing the feeling of her hand in mine, but too consumed by the doubts inflicted by memory to trust my own read of this situation with Low.

The doubts were winning.

I wanted to think she was genuine, that she really did like me.

But what if?

God, what if?

What if this was all another hoax, another game, another dare, another bet, another tease…

It was very elaborate, if it was.

What else could she mean? What else could be behind Low's words and actions, behind the veiled hints and subtle cues, and some perhaps not so subtle, which I was too afraid of misreading to believe.

You really are naive, aren't you?

You're so dumb it's adorable.

Have you ever been with a girl, Xavier?

You like me, don't you?

Have you ever been with a girl, Xavier?

Again and again, I could hear Brittany's words. Heard the hissing mockery behind it that I'd missed the first time around. The obvious pretense I'd been too stupid and naive and gullible to see, back then.

Was I doing the same thing now, with Low?

God, the desire I felt for Low was so potent it hurt. My zipper had been tight all morning, the excitement never abating even for a moment, even as we fished. When she touched me, innocently or not, my arousal throbbed to new levels of agony. When she'd pressed her backside to me, as I helped reel in her fish, I'd been dangerously close to the threshold of mortification. Merely from her presence. From accidental contact.

Was it accidental? Could she have done that on purpose?

I drove the boat up to the larger yacht, slowed, and then stopped as we approached the garage-type enclosure. After some investigating, I figured out how to get the boat inside, and then closed the door behind us. As the door in the side of the yacht slid down, I stepped out of the boat and extended my hand to help Low.

She reached out for my other hand as well, and I helped her step from the launch to the platform. With a stumble, she landed up against me, and I instinctively caught her. She was...*so* close. Too close. God, too close. I felt her breath on my lips, her breasts flattened against my chest, and my hands were in hers and her eyes were searching mine, and her scent was almost cloyingly strong—though I knew it was my sensitivity to sensation rather than through any fault of hers.

Have you ever been with a girl, Xavier?

I backed away, choking on memory, aching from the delirium Low's proximity incited. Dizzy with a need and desire I couldn't even begin to understand. What did I do with this desire? It was so furious, so intense. More than I'd ever thought possible.

"I..." My words caught in my throat.

I ached. God, I ached.

My hands clenched into fists as I fought the urge to flap them against my thighs—an instinctive reaction to being overwhelmed. I was one wrong move away from embarrassment, and I had to recite pi in my head until the furious volcano of pressure inside abated.

"I—I must—I must go," I bit out, stepping away from her. "My apologies. Perhaps I could take a rain check on lunch and the movie."

"Are you sure?" she said, frowning, extending a hand as if reaching for me, to stop me from leaving. "Is everything okay?"

"I...yes. I am well. But I must go. Thank you for spending your morning with me, Low, it was an honor and a pleasure."

"If you're sure you have to go." She reached out, pulled me in and hugged me. "I had a wonderful time, Xavier. Thank *you*."

Her scent was heady, intense. The hug was a wreath of softness and scent and heat, her breasts squishing against my chest, her back under my palms, her hair velveteen and silken and scented against my face.

I recited pi again, and this time I didn't stop. I backed away, unable to even fake a smile. I waved, a stilted, awkward movement, and left. I was at the fiftieth digit of pi, and hit the dock running.

I was still reciting pi in my head when I got home, and locked myself in my room.

I got past the thousandth digit before I felt anything remotely resembling control of myself.

FOUR

Harlow

I STOOD IN THE DIMLY LIT SPACE, THE LAUNCH NEXT TO ME. Xavier was gone, he'd fled at a dead run.

What had happened? There had been so many moments this morning I'd been absolutely sure he was going to kiss me, but he never did. His eyes had landed on my lips several times, as if contemplating the idea. We'd gotten cozy, more than friendly—holding hands. I'd pressed my ass against him, not overtly sexually, but less than subtly—I'd felt the shockingly huge and hard evidence that he was attracted to me. And I'd been barely touching him, had never made any contact with him that could be construed as sexual, until he'd come up behind me to help me reel in the monster fish I'd hooked.

When I'd felt his presence behind me, my breath had caught. My heart had started thumping a little harder. My thighs had tensed, and my skin had tingled. My core had, well, not gone damp, exactly, but had definitely let me know that we really, *really* liked Xavier's proximity.

But he'd not even kissed me, or touched me. Except for that split second of intimacy when I'd intentionally stumbled against him as I got in the launch, I'd almost wondered if he was even interested in me. That moment, however, had convinced me beyond all doubt that Xavier Badd wanted me.

And good god, I wanted him.

Had I ever felt this kind of desire for a man? The most intense chemistry I'd ever experienced had been with Harrison, my boyfriend at NYU.

But with Xavier it was definitely different. The chemistry was different. Subtler. Deeper. Less overt, less pushy. If my attraction to Harrison had been like curling white-capped waves, my attraction to Xavier was a wickedly, deceptively powerful riptide. A riptide grabbed you as you swam, like an icy, invisible hand, and sucked you out to open sea before you knew what was happening—Xavier had that same power over me. I'd thought I just liked him, at first. He'd shown up on my boat, helped me, talked to me, had been funny and kind of awkward, and unpredictable, and unassumingly charming and devilishly sexy. His physical presence and sensuality made all the more potent by the fact that he seemed utterly unaware of it.

Today, however, the true power of my attraction to him was beginning to reveal itself—there was no overt, obvious sexual element to our interactions, but I was intensely aware of him as a male, as a physical being, and as a sexual creature. I'd seen his abs, his chest and arms, and a hint of a V-cut. I'd seen him move with unprepossessing power. I'd felt a hint of the manhood he was packing behind those tight jeans.

I *wanted* him.

I wanted *more*.

But…I also just wanted to talk to him. I wanted to know him, on a personal level. I wanted to understand him, to figure him out.

There was an element of the chase, too—how long had it been since I'd had to do any work at all to catch the interest of a man? Never, possibly. Harrison had pursued me, and I'd not exactly put up much of a fight. When fame came my way, men threw themselves at me left and right—celebrities, crew on the sets, screenwriters and scriptwriters, directors, producers, fans, cashiers, baristas, servers, and even people I'd thought were friends. A snap of my fingers, and I could have any of them. A phone call, and I could have a ripped, shredded, A-list actor—one who'd played a certain well-known superhero—in my bed; he'd made that clear more than once, and I'd thought about taking him up on it simply because I knew another celebrity would have the same vested interest in keeping our tryst quiet.

I wanted more than a quick tumble with someone who understood the pressures of fame.

I wanted more than a few quick orgasms with a guy who knew nothing about me other than what was on the screen and in the tabloids.

I wanted *more*.

I just…I'd never known how to get that.

Xavier was, possibly, the only heterosexual male in the western hemisphere who *didn't* know who I was, which made him all the more attractive to me.

Which made me feel like shit, in a certain way. I mean, if he knew, what would he do? Would it change how he felt about me?

Could I tell him?

God, how would that even go? *Oh, by the way Xavier, I'm a world-famous celebrity. Just so you know.* I mean, yeah, better to have that conversation now than after things had gotten even more complicated. But telling him risked ruining what we had, which was by virtue of my temporary presence in Ketchikan, only a temporary thing. I'd told him I was on vacation, so he had to know that whatever we were doing could not be anything but fun in the moment.

Ugh. I'd been standing in the dark, alone, lost in my thoughts for several minutes. What was Xavier doing to me?

I've met presidents and worked with the most famous actors and directors out there…and an awkward but gorgeous twenty-something Alaskan local boy was turning my brain to mush and my libido into an inferno.

What a mess.

I wondered if I was making a mistake, getting involved with Xavier? Nothing had happened, yet, so it wasn't too late to cut things off. I could recall my crew and leave. Or I could act disinterested until he stopped coming by. I could just flat out tell him I didn't want to hang out anymore. But no, the thought of doing any one of those things made everything inside me constrict in denial.

I wanted him.

He wanted me.

It was obviously a temporary situation, and was proving to be a challenge, which meant it would almost certainly turn to be even more fun and rewarding.

I was on vacation. Relaxing, spending much-needed me-time. Recharging my batteries, rejuvenating my spirit. What better way to do that than by indulging in some harmless fun with a hot guy?

If the path to getting anywhere with him was a challenge, the more the better.

I went upstairs to the main lounge, heated up a bowl of chicken and rice stir-fry, and tossed in a sappy but fun rom-com, and tried to put Xavier Badd out of my mind.

I had trouble falling asleep, that night. I was restless, antsy. My legs kept scissoring and twisting, and my pillow was too hot or too cold or too lumpy or too flat. I was hot, I was cold. Too much sleep lately, maybe? I'd had a late cup of tea, so maybe it was caffeine? My mind wouldn't stop racing, darting, flitting.

Eventually, I fell asleep, but it was a fitful sleep, and filled with dreams.

Manic, weird, intense dreams. I woke up thirsty and disoriented and flustered, but unable to remember the substance of them.

After waking up and getting a drink of water, I was once again unable to fall back asleep. And this time, remembering a session I'd had with a mindfulness therapist once, I decided to do some internal investigating. Why was I so restless? Why couldn't I sleep?

The answer became obvious almost immediately: I was horny and flush with sexual tension, and in denial of it.

How long had it been since I'd last been with a man? Months. A cute sound tech and I had spent a couple of fairly memorable nights together during the shoot in Ireland. But that had been during the shoot, before editing, and the press tour, and the premiere. Six months ago? Something like that, possibly more. Definitely longer, now that I thought about it.

A long, long time. Enough that it was difficult to remember what a man's touch felt like, what an orgasm I didn't give myself felt like.

Speaking of that, when was the last time I'd done that? Before buying the boat, I think.

Maybe it was time for self-care. Maybe if I relieved some of this ache, some of this pent-up frustration, things with Xavier would be less complicated?

Dammit, I shouldn't have thought about him. I mean, no sense dwelling, right? What would happen would happen, and in the meantime, I needed to just enjoy the novelty of stimulating conversation with an articulate, intelligent, intellectually challenging man.

Who happened to be sexy as sin.

A tactile memory assaulted me—the fishing rod in my hands, nearly tugged out of my grip by the powerful fish on the hook, and then Xavier behind me. I hadn't paid any attention to how he reeled in the stupid fish, having been more focused on him. I'd leaned back, just slightly. That's all it had taken. My butt had brushed up against his thighs and groin and I'd felt a firm, thick ridge bulging against his zipper, nudging my butt.

What would he have done if I'd turned in his arms and unzipped him? I wondered what he looked like, bare. Long and thick, I knew that much. Straight as an arrow, or curved a little? I imagined him to be slightly curved, the tip nudging his belly. Cut, or uncut? I didn't care. He'd have a thatch of curly black pubic hair, almost certainly—he didn't seem like the manscaping type. The pubic hair would be coarse against my knuckles as I stroked him.

I felt my core ache, dampening at the mental image I was conjuring. God, he'd feel so good in my hands. There'd be no rush. He'd slowly unzip my jeans and pull them down, and then remove my underwear. His lips would touch my knee, and then my inner thigh, and I would willingly let my thighs open for him.

I kicked my blankets away, spread my thighs, and brought my fingers to my clit. His tongue would be firm and hot and slithery and wet, and he'd devour me like I was the most delicious thing he'd ever tasted. Oh god, his tongue would feel so good, circling my clit, flicking against it. Maybe he'd slide a finger inside me.

Thighs quaking, I reached over to the drawer beside my bed and grabbed my vibrator, a clitoral stimulator. But…I needed more. I needed something inside me. I pictured Xavier's fingers sliding into me as I slid my giant purple vibrator inside. Immediately, I felt myself clenching around the humming silicone as the stimulator suctioned around my clit, driving me to climax within seconds.

Screaming, imagining Xavier's hands on me, his mouth on me, I came hard and fast, shaking, gasping.

Reminding myself to clean my toys later, I tossed them back in the drawer and collapsed back onto the bed, sweating, panting.

And still frustrated as hell, because even though I'd come, and pretty hard, the fantasy hadn't done anything to quench the real need I felt, and picturing Xavier had only made me want him all the more, because now I wanted—*needed*—to know if reality matched my imagination.

I lay awake for another hour at least, until sleep finally claimed me—and even then, the dreams were back, only now they were weird, intense, and sexually fraught.

FIVE

Xavier

DAWN FOUND ME ALREADY AWAKE, WIRED WITH energy, and restless. I'd stayed awake building robots until after three in the morning, and it was just barely past seven, but that was typical for me—I'd never needed more than a handful of hours of sleep a day, and I felt groggy and sluggish and irritable if I got more than six hours in a night.

Restless didn't do justice to the way I felt, though. Thoughts were cycling through my skull, a torrent, a waterfall of ideas and images and data, all tangled up with visions of Low and strange, dark, dirty desires.

At least they felt that way to me. I didn't know what to do with them. How to handle them, how to even go about feeling them.

My issues with touch extended even to myself. When I showered, I did so swiftly, with a minimum of contact with my own skin. I hated getting dressed, hated being dressed—hated the feeling of clothes against my skin. I could only tolerate clothing if it was of a certain type—usually expensive. Soft undergarments, stretchy denim without holes or rips, not skin-tight, but not baggy. T-shirts had to be of the softest cotton possible—and I tended to wash T-shirts a dozen times before I wore them the first time, just to make them softer. Ankle socks or thick cotton boot socks only, no crew length. No V-necks. No sweaters, no long sleeves, certainly nothing with a buttoned collar—ties were so completely out of the question it was almost comical—I'd tried once and hadn't even been able to keep the topmost button done for more than fifteen seconds, let alone long enough to tie the tie.

Once I was home and in my room alone for the night, I stripped out of my clothes and opened the window, liking the air on my skin, and the lack of constricting garments. Even in the winter, I kept the window open for the airflow.

Touch was a constant issue. Washing my hands required focus to get through it without cringing and wanting to stop. I hated shaving, but hated the scratchiness of stubble even more. Hugs from family, accidental contact with strangers—I didn't like any of it and couldn't handle it. Thus my tendency to keep to myself.

So, this desire, this intensity, this...*need* I felt for Low was all the more baffling, and confounding, and troublesome. I'd had crushes, of course. Girls at school I'd found attractive, whose attention I'd wished I'd known how to get. I was always too awkward, too shy. They never noticed me, and my crushes went unrequited. Fantasies of suddenly being able to talk to girls were a constant feature of my youth, none of which ever materialized.

I once got up the courage to go to a party during my freshman year. It had been so loud, so chaotic, so insane and out of control I'd left immediately.

One time, when home alone after school, I'd run out of lead for my mechanical pencil and had gone into Brock's room to borrow some—he'd been at flying lessons at the time. In my search for lead, I'd come across a stack of magazines hidden rather cleverly in the desk he and Bax had shared—those magazines had contained full-color photographs of nude women in all sorts of poses, and my raging, barely teenaged hormones had been piqued, along with my curiosity. Flipping through page after page of huge breasts and glistening buttocks and shaved groins, I'd had the natural, normal reaction, along with the natural, normal urge of what to do about the pressure I felt.

So, I'd taken the magazine in the bathroom and done what teenage boys do.

It had not gone well. The sense of my own touch had been unbearable, but the straining, aching pressure had been worse—continuing had been nearly impossible, but quitting while still engorged had been worse. When I'd finally found release, I'd vowed never to do that again, and I hadn't. I'd stolen one of the magazines, though, too curious to help myself; I looked at it frequently, and then let my mind wander into fantasies and daydreams—usually conjured while trying to fall asleep—and that, along with a sock and some grinding into my mattress, was enough to alleviate the frustration that occasionally overwhelmed me. As I got older, I learned it was easier to just avoid those thoughts and desires than to engage in the difficult process of trying to get myself off without actually touching myself.

It just wasn't worth it.

What I was feeling after my day with Low…was different. I still had that magazine hidden somewhere in my room, but it was probably dusty from disuse by this time. And my thoughts of Low…well…those were little better than the images in the magazine. I saw her, again and again, in that red and pink and white kimono, her breasts barely covered, large and round and firm and jiggly, swaying with each movement of her lush body. The hem had barely covered her buttocks—in fact, I'd seen the lower curve of her buttocks more than once as she'd moved around. When she sat, she'd been careful to cross her legs, or sit in such a way that I couldn't have seen anything between them, but that hadn't stopped me from trying to look as she shifted positions. I'd hoped, deep down, that she would move wrong and I'd see more—that I'd get to see in real life what I'd only seen in that magazine.

Usually, I only indulged in these kinds of thoughts as I was falling asleep, but right now images of Low's breasts in that kimono were all I could think of. That, and her backside against my front as I reeled in the fish. I kept wondering if she had made contact accidentally, unaware, or if she'd done it on purpose. Had she felt how aroused I'd been?

When no amount of reading or robotics could dislodge my lewd thoughts, I decided to go for a run. Intentionally I went in the opposite direction of Low's boat. No earbuds, no music, so all I had to think about were my feet and my lungs and my legs. Run, run, run. My shoes pounding the pavement, my lungs burning, my thighs churning. Mile after mile. There was no escaping it, though—no escaping *her*. No escaping my thoughts of her.

I ended up back at home after running more miles than I'd ever run at one time, shaking from exhaustion, dripping sweat, gasping for air…with images of a scantily clad Low still lodged firmly in my head, and a hard-on that wouldn't go away.

I darted up to my room, hoping no one would be awake yet. I decided on a shower.

Mistake.

The hot water did nothing to wash away the lecherous images from my mind, or force my erection to subside.

For the first time in years, I wrapped my hand around myself. I tried to imagine it was Low's hand, those small, narrow, dainty fingers instead of mine. I pictured her standing in front of me, tugging apart the knot holding her robe closed. Letting the kimono fall open. She would have perfect breasts, of course, far better than the fake ones in the magazine. Real, natural, and perfect. She would smile at me, reach for me. She wouldn't have to tell me I could touch her—I would just know. I would touch her with the confidence my brothers all possessed, which I'd always envied. As I caressed her breasts, she would wrap those small, soft, strong fingers around me, touching me.

Oh—oh god.

Within seconds of that image, I made a mess all over my hand, and the hot water mercifully washed it away, swirling it down the drain.

Immediately, I felt guilty, like I'd used Low in some way.

If she knew what I'd just done while thinking about her, what would she say? Would she be angry? Hate me? Would she think it was stupid, think I was stupid? Maybe she wouldn't care at all. Or worse yet, think it was "cute."

I washed as quickly as I could, dressed, and went back to trying to study—I was taking an online course in an advanced programming language, which, while not difficult conceptually, still provided enough intellectual stimuli that I was able to focus on it rather than allowing my mind to run away from me again.

I was scheduled to work tonight, so around four in the afternoon I changed into clothing I didn't mind smelling like a kitchen, and began my shift. After an initial dinner rush, business died away, and I left the kitchen to see who was out there.

Zane and Bast were behind the bar and Zane was trying to teach Bast how to juggle knives, using a trio of butter knives. Claire, Dru, Mara, and Eva were at the family booth, playing a card game that involved a lot of slapping the table and screaming and laughing, while Luce was functioning as bar-back, server, and busser. Joss was at the bar near the service bar, reading a book, dandling my nephew Jax on her knee as he chewed on the end of her dreadlock.

Bast saw me emerge from the kitchen, and waved me over. "Yo, Xavier. What's up with you, little bro?"

I leaned against the service bar and poured myself a glass of water from the beverage gun. "I never know how to answer that. Logically, the answer is meaningless. Everything that is not down is, clearly, up. But I know you mean it as a slang version of asking what is going on in my life. And to that, the answer is…" I sighed, not wanting to share the presence of Low in my life with anyone yet. "Not much, I suppose. Building robots, and continuing my coding class."

Bast nodded, his gaze speculative and even somewhat puzzled. "Okay…gotcha." He slapped the bar with his palms. "Hey, so I have a question. Well, more an idea I've been tossing around that I'm ready to run by you."

"All right."

He gestured at the bar. "Why don't you take a seat?" I took a stool next to Joss, who smiled at me absently and went back to reading and bouncing Jax on her knee. "I've been thinking about our staffing issues."

I mentally followed the path of his thought process to its likely logical conclusion and summarized: "You want to hire outside help. With Canaan, Corin,

Brock, and Bax having stepped back from the bar almost entirely, the strain of taking up the extra hours is telling upon all of us who are left to run this establishment. Additional resources are required, especially as you all become more involved with your significant others."

Bast chuckled. "Well, you're in a mood, aren't you, buddy?"

I blinked. "What?"

"You only talk like a walking encyclopedia when you're really deep in your head."

I sighed. "I am not ready to discuss the source of my distraction, Sebastian."

He held up his hands. "All right, all right. No big deal." He leaned his thick forearms on the bar. "So. What do you think about hiring a few people?"

"For which positions?"

He shrugged. "I dunno. I was thinking a server or two, and a cook." His eyes met mine, his gaze searching. "You've been working pretty much every single night since you came back from Stanford, and I thought you may appreciate some time away to figure out what else you want to do with your life besides flip burgers and drop fries."

"I have my robot business."

"Yeah, but if you're always here every night, you can't really spend the time on it you need to in order to really start growing it into a viable living. *If* that's what you want, I mean." Bast's gaze shuttered a bit. "And there's always Stanford. I think they'd take you back in a heartbeat if you asked."

I shook my head and shrugged. "Oh, assuredly. So would MIT or Caltech or wherever. But I am not certain a formal educational environment is right for me at this time in my life." I smiled hesitantly. "Nor do I necessarily wish to leave Ketchikan, especially now that we are all here together."

"So, back to the question at hand."

"I think hiring a few individuals would be the correct and most appropriate business decision for us." I contemplated momentarily. "Our budget can certainly handle it—business is better than ever. If you hired an executive chef with the proper qualifications, we could expand our menu during the dinner rush hours and thus draw a wider dinner-hour clientele. Additionally, if we hired two skilled, experienced servers, our capacity would increase greatly."

Bast rubbed his jaw. "If we expanded our menu, though, that'd mean actual dishes, which would mean a busser *and* a dishwasher."

"Those are hourly positions and easily filled, and also well within budget," I said.

Zane, silent on the topic until now, finally chimed in. "So, since we're on this topic, I've actually been thinking about this myself, lately. I was talking to the chief of the local PD yesterday—I bumped into him after a run. They need guys, and *bad*. He said with my skills and background, I could get rank pretty fast. But I don't want to leave you guys in the lurch, here."

Bast sighed and scrubbed his hand through his hair. "It's been fun having everyone around running this place, and it's definitely helped get it off the ropes like it was, but I guess this has been a while coming."

Zane slapped his shoulder. "I'd still put in hours, Bast, you know that. I love it behind the bar. This place is home, you know?"

"Not like it is for me, though."

"You ever want to do anything else?" Zane asked. "For real."

Bast nodded. "Fuck yeah, all the time. But then I realize I'd end up hating anything else. This is all I know, and all I've ever known."

"But you've thought about doing something else," Zane pressed.

Bast grabbed a rag and started polishing the already clean bar top. "I used to enjoy tinkering with engines, and still do, when I get the time. I've always thought it would be fun to open a little garage, do rebuilds and customs. It was always an idle daydream, though, you know? It'll never happen."

"It could happen," Zane said. "If we get this place

running right, it could happen."

"It's *Badd's* Bar and Grill, though," Bast pointed out. "There's got to be a Badd running it."

"And there always will be. We'll all still be here, helping. But we've all gotten to do our shit, live our lives and pursue our dreams." Zane clapped Bast on the back. "Maybe it's your turn, huh?"

"I would not mind a few free evenings, personally," I said. "And additional staff, at this stage, can only help. I am in favor of this plan."

Bast held his fists out, and Zane tapped his knuckles to Bast's; after watching Zane, I did the same.

"So, time for a family meeting, I guess, huh?" Bast whipped out his phone and sent a mass text to everyone, announcing a Badd clan meeting tomorrow afternoon. Everyone replied within minutes, and Canaan and Aerie said to Skype them in, as they were in Austin for a pair of shows.

The rest of the shift went smoothly, with business picking up again for the evening drinks rush. By the time we locked the door, it was after two in the morning. When the stools and chairs were up, floors swept and mopped, kitchen shut down and wiped down, bar stocked, and the bathrooms cleaned, Bast and Zane headed to their respective homes, and Luce to his apartment with Joss over The Garden.

Leaving me with nothing to do, and nowhere to

go. Usually after work I went upstairs and studied, read, and tinkered, but this evening my mind was just not in it. The thought of sitting at home, alone, in my bedroom, reading and tinkering as I did every single night just didn't appeal tonight.

I was restless again.

Truthfully, my mind was occupied by thoughts of Low. What was she doing? Sleeping? Watching TV? Reading?

I found myself heading out the back door of the kitchen and walking down to the docks. It was a brightly lit night, the moon high and full and silver, stars twinkling in their countless millions. The air was warm, the water still, and my mind and heart and body were all restless and antsy.

Where was I going? What was my plan? Well, it was obvious where my feet were taking me; my plan once I got there, however, was a different story. As in, I didn't have a plan. I was, on the surface, in denial that I was going to Low's yacht slip, even though deep down I knew that's where I was going. Once I got there…what then? Hope she was awake? Wake her up? And say what? What would be different from the last time? Nothing. My issues were the same, and unresolved.

I didn't care.

Or, I did care, but couldn't seem to stop myself

from making the long walk down the docks to her slip anyway.

When I finally reached her slip, her yacht was dark, all the lights off. For a long moment, I just stood on the dock next to the bow of her yacht, watching the pointed tip dip and rise with the lapping of the water, listened to things clinking and thumping. Willing, perhaps, her to somehow suddenly wake up and see me, and invite me aboard, and then…what?

I stood outside her yacht, staring up at what I knew was the balcony outside her private cabin—that balcony was on the forward section of the superstructure, overlooking the bow, with a low railing. Standing where I was, it was less than twenty feet from the dock to her balcony.

How long was I there? Five minutes? Ten? Long enough to know she was asleep and staying that way, and long enough to feel painfully aware that this behavior of mine could, perhaps, be construed as being creepy, or stalkerish.

I was about to turn away when I heard a sound—the sliding of a glass door. I froze, heart thundering. Now that it seemed she was waking up and would come out and see me standing here in the dark, staring up at her balcony like a lonely little puppy, I was embarrassed to have come, and afraid of what she'd say.

Rather than running like the scared little boy I felt like, I stood my ground and waited for her to emerge, and see me.

The door slid open, and I saw her step out onto the small balcony. Her hair was a tangled, messy, sweat-damp explosion of curls, sticking to her cheeks and forehead and lips. She was breathing hard, gasping for breath. Her fingers stabbed into her hair, yanking it away from her face with a ragged groan.

She was naked.

Completely, totally nude. Heavy round breasts, lifting and swaying side to side with each ragged breath. Dark areolae the size of half-dollars, and thick pink nipples. She had freckles on her breasts, in spatters and sprays. She had a flat abdomen, a six-pack of clearly defined muscles flexing and heaving with her panting breaths. Her thighs were thick and muscular, but toned. Between them? A small, narrow triangle of closely trimmed reddish-gold pubic hair.

As she emerged onto the balcony, her head was tipped back, fingers tangled in her hair, viciously tugging in what appeared to be either frustration or anger.

I backed away a step, involuntarily. I shouldn't see her like that. She didn't know I was here. She was not showing herself to me voluntarily. This was wrong of me.

Awareness flamed through me, and with it guilt, spurring me into action—I pivoted immediately, facing away.

"Xavier?" Her voice, soft, quiet, gentle, curious, hesitant even.

"I—" I had no idea what to say. "I should not have come here this way, this late, unannounced. I am sorry." I took a step away from the boat, but her voice stopped me.

"Wait."

My breath caught. "Are you okay?" I asked, not turning around.

I didn't dare turn around. If I did, I would be unable to look away from her naked body. She was the most incredible thing I'd ever seen in my life, beyond the paltry labels and descriptors of beauty any human language is capable of expressing.

She was, in every way, perfect.

"No," she said. "I'm not."

"When you emerged on your balcony, I turned around—" I swallowed hard, forcing the truth out. "Not…not soon enough, however. I should have, but I—I did not. I apologize for my inexcusable behavior."

She laughed. "Xavier, god. You're amazing."

I frowned, though she couldn't see it. "I—what? How? Why? I just admitted to you that I stole a glimpse of you in a state of undress, while you were unaware of my presence."

"Turn around, Xavier."

"I should not."

"I disagree, and it's my body."

Slowly, heart thundering loudly in my ears, I turned around. I lifted my eyes to the balcony, to her. I couldn't swallow, couldn't breathe. My jaw was clenched so tightly it was painful. My erection was so hard and urgent I was folded nearly in half against the constraint of my zipper, and I knew it was impossible to hide that, even from here.

She was still naked, standing with her hands at her sides now, gazing down at me without embarrassment or self-consciousness. "Hi, Xavier," she murmured, just barely loud enough for me to hear.

"Hi…Low." I breathed a laugh. "Let me rephrase—good evening, Low."

"Why are you here, Xavier?" she asked.

"I…I do not know. I finished work, and my feet brought me here. I was restless, and…" I shrugged. "I ended up here. I hope I did not wake you."

"I'm glad you're here. You didn't wake me up." She tipped her head to one side, shrugging. "Well, not exactly."

"I am confused."

She sniffed a laugh. "Come aboard, and I'll explain."

I trembled. "Low, you're naked."

She laughed, and it was as close to a giggle as a creature as elegant as she was capable of emitting. "I realize that. Is it a problem?"

I was drinking her in, unable to refrain from staring. "My capacity for composure is rather strained, I must admit."

She didn't laugh at that. "That's not all that's strained."

I flushed so thoroughly the heat of embarrassment on my cheeks was probably noticeable from where she stood. "I cannot help my reaction to your beauty, Low."

"I didn't say it was a bad thing." She waved me onto the boat. "Just come up here."

She turned and went inside, and even then I couldn't look away, because her backside was as perfect as the rest of her—plump and round and taut, flexing with each step, yet also shaking and jiggling in a way that left me twitching in certain locations.

Oh god. What if she was still naked when I went up there? I was barely in control now, and there were several feet between us. If she was directly in front of me, in the same space as me, and naked…how would I respond? What would I do?

What would her skin feel like, if I were to touch her? I imagined her skin would be softer than anything

I'd ever felt. Warm—hot, even.

God, no. There was no way she would allow me to touch her.

But she'd allowed me to see her, so why not touch, as well?

Before I knew I intended to, I was stepping onto the boat and moving through the lounge to the stairs I knew led up to her cabin. The door was closed; I knocked gently, twice.

"Low?"

The door opened inward, and there she was. Dressed, now—sort of—in the kimono. This time, though, it was even more loosely tied. Just enough that the silk obscured her core and nipples and that was it.

She leaned against the door frame. "Hi."

"Hello."

"You're here."

I swallowed hard, my gaze involuntarily raking down her body and back up. "I…yes. I am here." I forced my eyes to hers.

I could only hold her gaze for a moment, and then I remembered what I'd done while thinking of her—my mortification and guilt was made worse by the certain knowledge inside me that I would do it again, especially now that I'd seen her naked body.

"Here to take that rain check on watching a

movie with me?" she asked.

I felt myself drawn forward, felt my gaze drawn her creamy skin, to the round, firm, heaviness of her breasts—I forced my gaze away, to the floor. "In truth, I do not know why I am here."

I felt her palm on my cheek, fingers under my chin, tilting my head upward. "Look at me, Xavier." I did so, meeting her intense blue eyes. "Why are you looking at the floor? I'm up here."

"Because it is not, in the name of honesty, your eyes that my gaze is drawn to at this moment. Though your eyes are mesmerizing and hypnotic in their ultramarine blueness, I cannot lie and say it is to them at which I am compelled to stare."

She laughed. "I'm well aware of that, Xavier. Does it seem like I'm bothered by that?"

I shook my head, keeping my eyes on hers. "No. It does not appear to upset you."

"So, why are you embarrassed by it, if I'm not?"

I swallowed a million words, and chose the ones that seemed truest, and best. "Because…because seeing you in the glory of your nakedness felt, to me, as if I had stolen a glimpse of a goddess." I paused. "'Such knowledge is too wonderful for me, too lofty for me to attain,'" I quoted.

"What was that from? I recognize it, but can't place it."

"It is from the Bible. Psalm 139."

"I didn't know you were religious."

"I am not, but it is a quote which accurately sums my feelings on the matter."

She reached out and plucked at my shirt, using it to gently tug me closer. "I'm not a goddess, Xavier. I'm just a girl."

"No, you are far, *far* more than merely a girl, or a woman." I gazed down at her eyes, heart crashing like cymbals and tympani, hands trembling. "You are perfection clothed in feminine form."

Her gaze softened, and she leaned closer yet, a breathy laugh escaping her. "God, Xavier. You can't go around saying shit like that to me."

I blinked, puzzled. "I thought it would please you. It seemed poetic, and yet it is also the truth."

"Oh, it pleases me, all right. Too much. You're going to ruin me for all other compliments."

"You should never accept anything less than purest poetry." I lifted a shaky hand, traced the outline of a pink flower on the shoulder of her kimono.

She tugged on my shirt, pulling me forward another half inch, while leaning closer yet; I caught her scent in my nostrils, vanilla and cinnamon, this time, and felt her breath on my chin, and felt the brush of her breasts against my chest. "The things you say to me, Xavier—you make me feel…well…you make me

"And that's okay. It makes you a puzzle. It makes you interesting."

"I wish it was as simple as that for me. I wish I knew how to explain."

"You don't have to."

"You may never understand me if I don't ever explain."

She shook her head. "That's too many steps into the future, Xavier. Right now, in this moment—all I'm saying is…stay."

"You really want me to?"

"It's almost three in the morning, you saw me naked, and now you're on my boat with me. What about any of that implies anything other than *yes*, I want you to stay?"

"I often have difficulty with implication, inference, and subtlety in social situations."

"Okay, well in that case I'm not implying or inferring anything." She gazed up at me, both palms resting flat on my chest. "I'm asking you to stay with me."

Fear hammered at the walls of my skull and the cage around my heart. I wanted to believe she was being truthful and genuine. Fear tried to tell me it was the height of foolishness to trust her. The intensity of my attraction to her, the ever-growing power of my nascent crush on her—if this feeling inside could be termed anything so juvenile as a "crush"—these told me it was foolishness to reject this opportunity.

When would I ever meet a woman as beautiful and desirable, on a merely physical level, as Low? Never. When would I ever meet a woman who seemed so accepting of my…foibles, and quirks, and limitations, and awkwardness? Never.

Curiosity and attraction won, though it was hampered and stained by doubt and fear.

"I will stay."

Her smile was brighter than the moon, warm and genuine and happy. "Good." She laced our fingers together and tugged me into motion, away from her cabin. "Movie time."

She led me to the lounge, to a white leather couch with soft, thick, enveloping cushions that faced a wall inlaid with blonde wood paneling. Low sat down in the corner of the couch and I sat beside her, close but not touching. The arm of the couch had a sleek black glossy glass panel in it, and at a touch of her finger it came alive with a bright blue glow, revealing several haptic icons. She touched one, and with a soft hum, the panel in the wall parted, halves sliding away to reveal the most enormous television I'd ever seen. There was a side table next to the arm, and a large ottoman in front of it, white leather to match the couch. On the side table was a stack of antique-looking hardcover books, and she selected the topmost book, set it on her lap and opened it, revealing it to be not a book but a well-disguised tablet computer, which she used to turn on the television and bring up a Netflix account.

She glanced at me. "What do you want to watch?"

I shrugged. "I do not watch television, as a general rule. I would not even know how to begin selecting a program."

"You never watch TV?" she asked, and I shook my head. "What about movies?"

"Rarely. Sometimes I will watch a film in the company of my family."

"So you don't like TV or movies? At all?"

I shrugged again. "I am sensitive to external stimuli, and television is the definition of external stimuli."

Low blinked. "Huh. Okay." Her glance at me was hesitant. "So…would you rather do something else?"

"There is nothing I would rather do in this moment than sit here on this most comfortable sofa and watch television with you, Low."

"A simple yes or no would have sufficed, you know," she said, with a smirk.

"Oh. Um. My apologies." I pushed away the twin boulders of doubt and insecurity. "Yes. I would like to watch TV with you."

"I was teasing, Xavier. The way you talk is

growing on me."

"Hopefully in the manner of an acquired taste rather than the manner of mold growing on a wall."

She laughed. "Yes, Xavier. Like an acquired taste."

"That was a joke."

She slapped my chest. "And I laughed, didn't I, Spock?"

I relaxed a little. "Yeah, you did."

Low poked me in the arm. "You just said 'yeah.'"

I smiled self-consciously. "Would you like to know a truth about me?"

She tapped on the tablet to begin a program, what appeared to be an episodic series set in Rome. "Yes, I would absolutely like to know a truth about you."

Setting the tablet aside, she leaned forward, lifted up the top of the ottoman to reveal a stack of thick, fleece-and-fur blankets hidden in a compartment inside the ottoman. She stretched her legs out onto the ottoman and settled the blanket on our legs, and then leaned into me, resting her head against my shoulder.

"Is this okay?" she asked, tilting her face to look up at me.

Her head on my shoulder felt heavy—not from the weight but from the significance and intimacy of the gesture. The heaviness settled in my chest, on my lungs, and in my heart. I swallowed hard.

or hesitation or embarrassment. Even pride, perhaps.

As we watched, I relaxed even further. I'd started out sitting bolt upright, feet on the floor, and hands on my lap; but as the second hour-long episode began, I found myself reclining, my feet propped on the ottoman. As I relaxed, Low leaned further and further into me, which only made me even more hyperaware of her presence, her scent, her warmth.

Fifteen minutes into the second episode, she flipped open the tablet and paused it. "I have to pee, and I need a snack." She sat up, tossing the blanket aside. "You want anything?"

"Some water, perhaps?" I said.

"Boring!" she said in a singsong, leaving the couch. "You're having a glass of wine with me."

I'd tried drinking once, at Stanford, and it hadn't gone well; of course, that had been a dorm-mate goading me into accompanying him to a frat party and pressuring me into doing shots of whiskey—I'd realized later it had all only been for his own amusement, and I'd never touched alcohol again. Surely a glass of wine in a calm environment with someone I felt I could trust would be a much different experience.

Low hadn't waited for an answer, though. She'd vanished into a bathroom, and then moments later into the galley; I heard a microwave going, and then popcorn popping, the pop of a cork leaving a bottle and the glug of liquid being poured into glasses.

Returning, she had a bowl of popcorn in one hand and two glasses of wine precariously clutched in the other. I made to stand up, intending to help, but she shooed me away with the popcorn bowl.

"I've got it, I've got it. Just sit." She set the popcorn bowl down on the far edge of the ottoman, and then paused, bending over to snag a handful of the fluffy white snack and tossing it into her mouth. Bent over—robe draping open, breasts swaying, fully visible—freckles liberally dotted the upper slopes of her breast and the valley between them, and those freckles somehow seemed to taunt me, making me ache, throb. I sucked in an audible breath, and she glanced at me with a wink.

"Oops," she said, smirking around the popcorn. "Wardrobe malfunction."

I accepted the large goblet of rich red wine from her as she sat down and covered her legs with the blanket. As she settled in, tucking her legs underneath her so she was curled up on the couch, she snuggled closer to me than she'd even been before, and now my arm was pinioned uncomfortably between us. In an attempt to alleviate the awkwardness of the position, I withdrew my arm and lifted it, unsure what to do with it next. Low, however, decided that for me by scooting closer yet, so she was nuzzling into the nook created by my arm. After a moment of my arm hovering over her, I allowed it to settle onto her. My arm was over her shoulder, and my hand was resting on her waist, inches above her hip.

Was this real? Could this be happening? Why was she allowing this? Did she really enjoy my presence so much that this—snuggling, or cuddling, or whatever this behavior was properly termed—was enjoyable to her? It was unfathomable to me that this was really happening, that Low, a goddess made flesh, perfection made woman, could truly and genuinely want this with me.

Yet…as I glanced down at her to see if I could gauge her expression, all I saw on her face was what seemed to be contented comfort, and even a half-smile of something like happiness.

Low took a sip of her wine, and then made a noise of irritation. "The popcorn is too far away," she said, reaching out and grabbing at air with her hand. "Hold this," she said, handing her wine to me.

I took it, and she rolled forward, knees on the couch, one hand on the ottoman, leaning forward to snag the bowl. It was the lean forward that did it—her robe hiked upward as she reached, baring her entire backside to me.

Did she hesitate while grabbing the bowl?

After a half second, she rolled back to sit curled

on the couch with my arm draped over her again, and then settled the popcorn on my lap. Which was rather a problem, since my enjoyment of the view as she'd leaned forward had created a…ridge, one might say, underneath the blanket, tipping the bowl to one side rather obviously.

She smirked at me. "Problem, Xavier?" Her smirk was too knowing.

I eyed her carefully. "You did that on purpose, I believe."

"Did what?" she asked, sounding far too obviously innocent.

"Created that scenario, allowing a…what did you call it, earlier? A wardrobe malfunction."

She sipped her wine, a study of casualness. "And if I did?"

I had no answer for that. "Um…"

She glanced up at me. "You saw me totally nude, earlier. Why be shy, now?"

"That truly was an accident, Low. I didn't mean to pry, or spy, or intrude."

"I don't think I'd believe anyone else," she said, and then ate more popcorn. "But…I believe you."

I tried the wine, and the flavor burst over my tongue, acidic and fruity, with a barrage of undertones and hints. The popcorn, when I ate a handful of kernels, absorbed the flavor and allowed me to enjoy the way the wine exploded over my taste buds all over again.

Soon, a third episode was beginning and the wine was making my head float and my body feel light and yet heavy at the same time, and the popcorn was gone.

The sky outside was tinged with gray.

I wasn't tired, though I should have been.

Low finished her wine, and when I finished mine, she set our glasses inside the popcorn bowl, which she set on the table.

"You give amazing snuggles," she murmured to me. "I could fall asleep like this."

"Should I go, so you can sleep?"

She rolled her head against my chest in a negative gesture. "No way."

I give amazing snuggles? I had no clue I was even capable of snuggling. But this whole time, while her scent was powerful and her weight against me heavy, and her warmth was making me warm, and the contact of body against body was intense, I wasn't overwhelmed.

Because I was starting to trust her, I realized. She'd done nothing to make me think she was anything other than real, and true, and genuine.

Perhaps my discomfort with touch was mental?

Possible—or more likely, it was partly true.

Maybe it was just something about Low that put me at ease and allowed me to merely enjoy the new sensation rather than being overwhelmed by it as I typically was.

And then, during a scene in which a male and female character on the show were engaging in sex, Low twisted to glance up at me.

I turned my gaze away from the heaving breasts and flexing abs and buttocks, and down to her. The knot of her robe was all but undone, and the edges had come apart, yet her breasts weren't quite totally exposed. She had the blanket over her lap, her feet were tucked under her thighs, and she was twisted to face me.

"Hi," she breathed.

"Hi."

She shifted, pressing against me. One hand came up to rest on my shoulder, the other on my thigh. Her blue eyes hunted, darted, searching mine; was it my imagination, or was her face closer than it had been? My hand was on her hip, setting my heart to thundering, stuttering, and I was half afraid she'd notice and move it, yet she never did. In fact, as she shifted closer to me, my palm drifted further down so I was nearly touching the curve of her buttock. Which only made the hammering of my heart worse. Could she feel the tremble in my hand, on her skin?

Yes, she was definitely leaning up, leaning closer.

I couldn't breathe.

Her hand was on my chest, and then her palm was sliding across my jawline, and before I knew what was happening, what she was doing, what *I* was doing, I felt myself leaning forward.

My lips touched hers.

Her mouth was warm and her lips were damp, and pliable, and firm. Her lips softened as our mouths met, and her hand clutched my jaw, fingers on my cheek, thumb on my chin and brushing with soul-shaking intimacy across my cheekbone. I felt her tongue dance across my upper lip.

We were kissing.

Low was kissing me—I was kissing her.

My heart stopped entirely for an agonizing moment, and then pounded to life, crashing madly.

My hand was on her buttock, fully and openly grasping, cupping, clutching, tightening—and she had hers fisted in my shirt, the other caressing my jaw and cheek. It was as if I belonged to her, in some way. As if kissing me was some delirious, necessary act, as wildly crazy-making for her as it was for me. Which was utterly ridiculous.

And then, and then—I heard a voice in my head.

Have you ever been with a girl, Xavier?

That doubt.

What if Low was merely leading me on?

She can't honestly be interested in me.

There's a catch.

She'll laugh at me.

I'll take something too far and she'll stop me and make fun of me, or be angry at me for assuming someone like her could ever want me.

The doubts returned, insidious, choking the moment like vines choking a tree.

Have you ever been with a girl, Xavier?

Reality crashed down on me—I had no business being in here with Low.

This was only bound to end with me getting hurt. She couldn't possibly genuinely want this. Not with me.

You're so dumb it's honestly adorable.

Her scent was suddenly overpowering and cloying. Her hair tickled. Her tongue was wet and seeking. Her lips on mine, her hand on my cheek, the other delving under my shirt to scour the flesh of my chest and abs.

Have you ever been with a girl, Xavier?

Too much, too much, too much; panic hit me like a heat-seeking missile.

I found myself lurching up, away, off the couch and stumbling to the doorway leading to the deck. The cool air of dawn drifted against my skin, but I still

SIX

Harlow

WHAT WENT WRONG? ONE MINUTE WE'RE KISSING, and the next he's gone. I feel a thousand different things right now, but confusion is at the top of the list.

I'd never been kissed like that. So carefully, so preciously. It was a kiss that was deep with meaning and I'd never felt so special in my life.

But, god, could I have been any more obvious? I wanted him. I made sure he knew that. And damn, he wanted me. He'd been hard as a rock nearly the whole night. Watching *Spartacus* he'd been shifting during the sex scenes, as if embarrassed by them, or by his natural reaction to them.

Or by his reaction to me.

When I'd first realized he was standing on the dock outside my boat, staring up at me, my core had gone slick and wet and hot all at once, because the raw hunger in his eyes had been something incredible to behold. But then, instantly, he'd turned around, and the honesty in the gesture had made my heart melt. It was the gesture of someone without guile, without dishonesty, or self-serving desire.

My body had been screaming—*look at me, touch me, take me*!

My heart had been telling me to slow down.

My mind had been torn between the two.

When we'd settled in to watch the movie I'd made sure he got several opportunities to take advantage of my near nudity, but he never had, other than taking a few furtive glances. I thought he would untie the robe, let his hand slide down to fully cup my ass, or caress my tits. Or kiss me. Or move my hand to his cock, which had been partially hard the whole night.

He never did any of those things.

But I know he felt something. I know he wanted me. That kiss alone told me, in the brief moment it lasted, that he was attracted to me and wanted more with me. But he never acted on it.

And then, halfway through the kiss, he just utterly freaked.

My mom used to have panic attacks. She still does, but less frequently, and she manages this with medication—so I recognized the symptoms of a real, actual panic attack. And there is no question in my mind that Xavier's freak out was a panic attack.

Had it been triggered by something? Did I do something? I wracked my brain, but could think of nothing. Yet the panic had been real and undeniable. There was pain there, too, along with fear and self-recrimination.

He is hard to read, emotionally, and maybe a little closed off but, in that moment, his expression had been open, and I'd seen a frantic conflation of emotions, a whirlpool of intense mania—anger, fear, hurt, doubt, I don't even know what all, too much to read all at once.

At first I'd thought that maybe he was just a very reticent type of person, but that moment made me realize he shielded his emotions from the world behind mile-high walls. Walls of archaic, formal speech, and elaborate vocabulary, and robotic syntax. He was hiding.

When he sat, he never fidgeted, never twitched or scratched or shifted; when he stood it was the same thing, he assumed a position and held it, remaining motionless. It wasn't natural. And, I was realizing, it wasn't just a quirk of his but, like his speech, something he did on purpose, for reasons I couldn't begin to fathom.

He was gone now. He'd taken off at a dead sprint, leaving me on the deck all but naked, worked up, confused, and feeling more hurt than I had any right to be.

We'd barely kissed, so why did it feel like a rejection? I knew, mentally, he hadn't been rejecting me, that whatever had spurred his panic attack hadn't been prompted because he didn't want me, or because of what we were doing—I *knew* it was something else. But, still, his leaving hurt.

His hands had felt so good on my body—the way he looked at me had made me feel so sexy, so beautiful, so sensual, so powerful. His words, those archaically eloquent and stunningly heartfelt compliments—they made me feel things I'd never felt before, as if I really was special and worthy and valued. They weren't just pretty pickup lines, meant to impress—he really truly meant them.

And hearing those things was addictive.

He was addictive.

For the first time in my entire life, I felt like maybe I wanted someone more than he wanted me. And that feeling was scary as hell.

What was I supposed to do?

Chase him? And what would I even say if I found

him right now?

Would he come back? The thought that he may not come back sent a pang through me so powerful it terrified me. How could I want him this bad already?

It had to be just a physical thing.

Right?

It was just libido, hormones gone haywire. It had been a long time since I'd had sex, so my hormones must be out of whack. I was simply feeling a weird form of sexual frustration.

But that lie didn't scan even as I thought it.

God, what the hell was going on with me?

Maybe spending time with Xavier had been a mistake—the whole thing had been a mistake. I should never have gotten involved with him. Because now…

Now I needed to know what had happened. I *needed* to know more about him. I needed him to come back. I needed him to kiss me again. I needed to laugh with him. Tease him. I wanted to know what drove him, what prompted the panic attack, why he tensed every time I touched him, why he ignored all my obvious hints that I wanted him. I wanted to be the person to get through his walls,

I wanted to discover the way past all that.

What was it? I couldn't put it into words, but he was just *different*, and it was refreshing and exhilarating.

I couldn't figure him out, and I loved that.

I couldn't predict him, and I loved that, too.

Would he kiss me again?

Would he touch me again?

Would he come back?

I didn't know the answers…and I kind of loved that, too.

As an A-list celebrity, I'd grown used to having the world at my fingertips. "Yes" was the default answer to everything. Throw a stick, and I'd hit at least six people who didn't have the word "no" in their vocabulary, thus my microscopically small staff—Lindsey, Martin, and Emily. That was it. And even they went out of their way to make sure I got the "yes" no matter what.

With Xavier, I wasn't in control of the situation. I didn't know the outcome.

"Yes, whatever you want" wasn't the predetermined answer.

That, too, was addictive.

Everything about Xavier Badd was addictive.

Xavier

IT WAS AFTER SIX THIRTY IN THE MORNING BY THE TIME I reached the bar. I used my key to unlock the kitchen door, relocked it behind me, and headed upstairs. The light over the kitchen table was on, and Bast was sitting there, a mug of coffee in his hands, a glower on his face.

"Where ya been, Xavier?" he asked, his voice a low growl.

I was still out of breath, sweating, gasping, and the dregs of my panic attack were still laced through my brain. My response was, perhaps, less than mature.

"Out."

Bast frowned, reached over to pour coffee into

his mug, then snagged another mug and poured coffee into it for me, gesturing at a chair. "Anyone else around here and a monosyllabic answer would be no big deal. With you, not so much. So I'll ask again—where you been, Xavier?"

"I don't owe you answers, Sebastian," I snapped. "You're not my fucking father."

He blinked at me, setting his coffee down very slowly. "Well now," he drawled. "*That* ain't like you either, bro."

I heaved a long sigh, and slumped into the chair, thudding my forehead onto the table. "I'm sorry, Bast."

"You're out all night—for the first time in your entire life as far as I know. You come back looking like someone just shot your favorite cat, you're using contractions and talking like a person instead of a damn robot, you snap at me, *and* you swear at me." He smirked, amused more than anything else. "Bottle of Johnnie Walker says there's a girl in this."

I lifted my head to stare at him. "How would you know?"

He laughed. "Because only a woman can fuck us up as much as you're fucked up right now."

I took the coffee and sipped it. "She's the most beautiful woman I've ever seen. She owns a yacht that I estimate to be very, very expensive. She is cultured, and intelligent, and educated. She is comfortable in silence, and easy to talk to." I met Bast's eyes. "Her touch brings something out in me which I never even knew existed, or was even possible."

Bast stared at me. "You let her touch you? Like, close enough to make actual contact?"

I nodded, staring now into my coffee. "We have held hands. She has touched my shoulder, and my chest, and my face."

Bast's eyebrows lifted. "No kidding. Anything else?"

I swallowed hard. "We…I—there was a kiss."

Bast whistled low, a sound of disbelief. "No *fucking* way." He reached out and grabbed my hand, squeezing it. "Buddy, you're growing up!"

I narrowed my eyes at him, withdrawing my hand. "I do not find that humorous, Sebastian."

He held up his hands. "Okay, okay, sorry." A frown crossed his face. "So, this chick is hot, classy, rich, and you kissed her. What's the issue?"

"Where do I even start?" I asked. "She's…Low is out of my league, to use a popular phrase. Beautiful, hot, gorgeous—there aren't enough words to describe how perfect she is. She seems to like me. My quirks do not bother her—if anything, she seems to like them, finds them funny, or endearing, or…I don't know."

"And how do you feel about her?"

"Words fail me."

Bast quirked an eyebrow. "Gonna have to unpack that one, bud."

I struggled for words. "I have never, ever felt such an intense physical attraction. Need, desire, craving—language fails to encompass the intensity of what I feel when I look at her, or think about her."

"Damn. That's pretty intense." He swirled his mug in circles and then glanced at me again. "Is just physical?"

"No."

"Do you have any idea how she feels about you? I mean, does she seem like she's attracted to you?"

I nodded. "I believe she is. But…that's part of why I'm upset—I don't *know*. I don't trust myself. I don't trust that I understand her, that I'm reading her properly. You know how I am, socially. I miss things. I misread social cues. I want to believe she likes me, that she feels attracted to me."

"What makes you think so?"

I blushed, looking down at the table. "She… um—it's…body language, I suppose. Leaning toward me. Touching my hand or my chest when she looks at me, or laughs at something I say. What seem to be intentional physical movements designed to allow glimpses at her, in certain…um, ways."

Bast chuckled. "So she, like, leans over just right so you can see down her shirt, or bends over with her ass right front of you, or leans in real close when she's talking, like you're the most interesting person who's ever lived and she's hanging on your every word?"

"Yes, precisely."

"She's into you, dude."

"But...why?"

Another chuckle. "Every guy asks himself that when a girl who's out of his league is into him. Don't ask why, just go with it."

I shake my head. "I am not capable of not asking why, for many reasons."

"She likes you. Why does anyone like anyone? Something just clicks, man. You interest her." Bast tossed back his coffee and poured us more. "And dude, Xavier, you're a fascinating guy, okay? You are by far the smartest person I've ever heard of, let alone met. You're funny when you want to be. You're a good listener. And plus, you're a Badd. Which means you're a damn good-lookin' motherfucker, all right? You got Mom's eyes, and Dad's height, and you're shredded—what's not to like?"

I blushed. "Thank you for the motivational speech."

Bast snorted. "I was bein' serious, douchebag."

"So was I. Thank you, I mean it." I sighed. "But

for reasons I'm not prepared to explain, that does not alleviate my doubt, and my inability to trust that she could actually like me."

"Someone hurt you, I'm guessing?"

I nodded, not looking at him. "Yes. Very badly."

"So, what happened?"

I shook my head. "I can't...I can't talk about that."

"Fair enough." Bast tapped the side of his mug with his wedding ring. "So what happened with your girl? What'd you say her name was? Lola?"

"Low."

"Low. Cool name," he said. "So, what happened? Why're you here all pissed off and crazy?"

"We...we were watching a show. She was very close to me all evening, what one might term cuddling, I suppose. That was nice, and as long as I didn't think about it too much, it was okay. Extraordinarily pleasant, and yet overwhelming at the same time." I swallowed hard. "And then...we kissed. She was wearing a robe, and—and not much else. Nothing else, to be truthful. My desire for her was...it was out of control. I felt crazed. Even now it blinds me, makes me dizzy, unable to think straight. I had a panic attack."

"Because of how bad you wanted her? She was kissing you, so clearly she was into it. I don't think she'd have minded if you took it further."

myself to daydream about Xavier, and maybe even indulge in a little…ahem…doodling. Meaning, I'd be tracing the letters of his name onto my clit with the tip of my two middle fingers.

I forced my attention back to the screen of my laptop, which had gone to sleep while I was talking myself out my unscheduled daydream. I dropped myself back into the story, channeling my friend Janelle's voice as I wrote.

Once into the flow, I lost myself in it for a good hour. But then my characters—the hero who saved my heroine from her villainous ex-fiancée—started messing around in her kitchen, which sent my own my mind racing down a rabbit trail which led, inexorably, to Xavier. Last night. The intensity of his kiss. The slight tremble in his hands.

The hunger in his eyes as he stood on the dock, staring up at me. I wondered if he'd been able to see how my nipples had puckered under his scrutiny. If he'd been able to see how I'd clenched my thighs together. Surely he'd been able to hear my heart pounding in my chest as I forced myself to stand with a confidence and boldness I only partially felt.

I imagined him standing on that deck again; I would be naked, and he would be shirtless and barefoot in a pair of those tight jeans he liked. He'd leap onto the yacht and scramble up the deck, too impatient to get his hands on me to bother with stairs. His mouth would devour mine, and his hands would be everywhere…

My fingers delved under the laptop, dipping under the waistband of my bikini bottom. I exhaled shakily, thoughts of Xavier's heated, hungry gaze and wandering hands and firm strong lips making me tremble before I even started touching myself. The thought of his zipper straining brought my finger to my clit, and an image of him sliding down the zipper—or better yet, me tugging the zipper down—to reveal a thick hard cock, the bulbous head slick with precum…

Oh fuck.

Fuck…

I was moments from orgasming when I heard a footstep on the deck, a shuffle, and a throat clearing. My eyes flew open, and there he was, in the flesh.

Standing at the bow, dressed in a plain white crewneck T-shirt, the front of which was tucked behind a thick black leather belt with dark-wash blue jeans, and a pair of faded, well-loved Converse All-Stars. Those fiercely green eyes were locked on me.

My cheeks flushed as I tried to subtly withdraw my fingers from my bikini bottom, hoping it hadn't been obvious what I'd been doing.

I closed my laptop and rested my hands on it,

noticing with no small amount of embarrassment the telltale sheen on two of my fingers. I wondered if he'd notice that.

"Hi," I said.

He gave an odd, abbreviated wave of one hand. "Hello." He cleared his throat. "May I come aboard?"

I smiled. "Yeah, of course. No need to ask."

He stepped onto the deck and crossed to lean against the railing next to me. "I would not want to assume I would be welcome," he said, staring at the deck between his feet. "Especially after my…abrupt departure last night."

"Of course you're welcome here." I twisted to bring my legs over the side, facing him, and set my laptop to my left. "And about last night…Xavier, I hope I didn't do anything—"

"I know this is a horribly cliché thing to say, but it was not you, Low. It was me. You were perfect, and I was…I am…" he sighed, trailing off. "I was me."

I tipped my head to one side, puzzled by that. "Well, yeah. You're you. And I like you."

"But what happened, my panic attack…that is a part of who I am."

I set my laptop underneath the chaise lounge and patted the cushion next to me; Xavier sat down nervously, leaving a good two inches between us.

"My mom gets panic attacks," I said. "She's

learned to manage them through medication, meditation, and exercise, but she still gets them. So…panic attacks I understand."

"At the risk of sounding as if I think I'm some special case…the source of my panic attacks is not something any of those remedies will help."

I wasn't sure how to respond to that. "Oh?"

"Perhaps you've noticed, and perhaps you haven't," he said, staring out at the water, "but I have difficulty with physicality."

"Like being touched?"

He nodded. "It is partly a sensory issue. When a person touches me, and I mean even basic, everyday physical contact, such as shaking hands or bumping shoulders in a crowd—the physical sensation of the touch overloads my senses."

"What do you mean?" I asked. "How does that…I don't know—how does that manifest, I guess?"

"Have you ever come in contact with a live electrical current? Even a small one. Like something not grounded properly, or shorting out."

I thought about it. "As a kid, I used to go grocery shopping with Mom. We always went to the same store, and we went every week. We'd go through the aisle at the back where the cheese and lunchmeat and all that stuff is, right? The cooler section. Well, you know those little grates at the front of the coolers, where the cold air comes out? I would run my fingertips across those grates or openings as we walked down the aisle, and there was this one spot, right in front of the blocks of cheddar cheese, where I'd get shocked when I ran my fingers over it. Not bad, just like…a zap."

He smiled, nodding. "I know exactly what you mean." He rolled his hand in a circle. "Well, for me, someone touching me feels much like that. I feel it throughout my whole body. The contact…I don't know how to describe it—it sort of briefly but intensely short-circuits the part of my brain which registers touch. I've always got so many thoughts running through my head—which, incidentally, is why I sometimes seem out of it or distracted—and then adding touch is just one thing too many for my brain."

"So…does it hurt?" I asked, glancing at him.

He shook his head. "It does not register as pain, exactly. Well, it does, but—" He broke off with a sigh. "It is difficult to accurately describe. I mean, pain is pain, so if I bump my knee or break an ankle, it would feel exactly as it does for you. It is not a heightened receptor issue, on a physiological level. It is mental, neurological, but it manifests physically." He was silent for a moment. "So, last night…"

I followed where he was going. "So if even shaking hands or bumping someone accidentally in a crowd is overwhelming, I suppose that means something like hugging, or holding hands," I met his gaze, "or kissing..."

"To describe the sensory experience as intense would not be even remotely accurate." He held my gaze, and I saw a silent plea for understanding in his eyes, which were unusually open in terms of emotional transparency. "I do not mean to say unpleasant. I...the time I have spent with you, I have been able to tolerate and enjoy the physical aspect of our...relationship, or—or however one would appellate it."

"Tolerate?" I swallowed hard, more upset by that word than I should have been.

He sighed sharply. "Low, please. You must understand. Tolerating physical touch is, for me, a victory. My own brothers know not to touch me, because it is something I typically cannot handle. You—" he glanced down, and we both watched his hands find mine, a gesture I now found more significant than ever, "—there is something about you. I don't have the words to encapsulate it. I imagine you would find the word 'tolerate' in reference to the physical aspect of what is occurring between us as an insult, or painful. But from my perspective, toleration of physical affection is an enormous step forward."

I stared down at our hands, our fingers laced together. When was the last time I'd held a man's hand?

Just held hands, like this, innocently? Harrison, most certainly. And he was not, generally, a physically demonstrative person, at least in terms of nonsexual affection such as holding hands.

"So, last night, your panic attack, that was because you were just overwhelmed by…everything?"

He nodded slowly. "Yes." A pause. "Mostly."

I looked at him, then, my head swiveling sharply to pin him with an inquisitive gaze. "Mostly?"

He sighed again. "I shouldn't have said that," he muttered, more to himself.

"But you did, and I heard it, so…what does that mean? What else is there?"

He shot to his feet and paced away to stand at the bow of the boat, hands fisted at his sides. He was ramrod stiff and straight, shoulders hunched as if to ward off a blow.

"Xavier?" I stood up and followed him, standing beside him, close but not touching. "What is it?"

He was exuding anxiety and angst and pain, every line in his face etched into a rictus of unease and agony. "To explain would mean telling you a story I have not told another person since it happened."

"Not a good story, I'm guessing."

He shook his head, laughing bitterly. "Assuredly not."

"Do you want to go inside?" I hesitated, and then

put my hand on his forearm—noticing now how he tensed immediately, and then slowly relaxed. "And… you know you don't have to tell me, right? You don't owe me any explanations. I mean, I'll be honest and say I would like it if you did tell me, and I would obviously hold your confidence in me as sacred. But…you don't *have* to tell me."

"I would be more comfortable outside, I believe," he murmured. "Perhaps it is time I shared this. It has haunted me for several years, and it does affect you, or at least concern you, so…yes. But I would ask you to not interrupt me until I am finished, because the telling will not be easy for me."

"Not a word, I promise." I pivoted to put my back to the railing, leaning against it facing Xavier. Our hands remained laced together, and he spoke with his gaze on our joined hands, my fingers twined with his.

"As you can probably guess, I was not what you'd call popular." He laughed, as if the very idea was so preposterous as to be comical. "I had little to no control over my tendency to lecture endlessly on whatever topic I was interested in at the time, and I was obviously just…different, in every way. I would finish assignments in a quarter or an eighth of the time as everyone else. I would correct teachers frequently. If we were assigned a book to read, I would finish it in that class period, while the teacher was still talking—and

I'd be able to recite the entire thing verbatim, as well as everything the teacher said."

He waved a hand.

"I only say this to exemplify my oddity. In high school, this behavior set me apart, obviously, and I'm sure you're familiar with how cruel high school students can be. Well, when you're as vastly different as I was, that marked me as a target for cruelty of every kind imaginable. I was beaten up regularly, locked in lockers, made fun of mercilessly even by the unpopular kids…I was set on fire in chemistry class, once. Imagine a torture devisable by teenagers, and I experienced it. Rocks were thrown at me on the way home from school, and bricks even, a few times. I was attacked with paintball guns in drive-by shootings." He glanced at me, seeing my horrified expression. "I survived it, clearly, and developed mental and physical toughness because of it. I learned to fight back, until the bullies didn't dare approach me except in large groups."

"Jesus, Xavier." I whispered it, choking back tears at what he'd endured.

He smiled at me, nudging me with his shoulder. "None of that, if you please. I am stronger because of it."

I smiled back. "What doesn't kill us makes us stronger, huh?"

He nodded, exhaling a deep sigh. "Exactly." He traced the back of my hand with a fingertip, following the blue veins up to my wrist, sending thrills and chills racing through me. "So. The story is this. When I was fifteen, almost sixteen, I was walking home from school when I was approached by a girl who lived in the same neighborhood. Her name was Brittany Delany-Price, and she was a senior from a well-to-do family, the most popular girl at the school, beautiful, captain of the cheerleaders and the dance team, and prom queen and all that. Every guy in the school had a crush on her, including me. I never even bothered to pretend to myself that she would ever give me the time of day, because I simply knew better. Being a senior, she had a car and a license and usually left school with all her friends. So, when she walked up next to me that afternoon, I was surprised."

He was silent a while, and then he continued.

"She told me some story about getting her car fixed and all her friends having other appointments, necessitating her walking home. Being wary, I didn't say much. We walked a few blocks, until we came to the place where she would turn to go to her house and I to mine. She grabbed my arm and asked if I wanted to come over and hang out with her. I was… apoplectic with disbelief. I mean, she was being *nice* to me. Showing interest. I was fifteen, and she was the hottest girl in the school, the girl every guy had fantasies about, and she was talking to *me*. Asking me to hang out at her house. Instinctively, I would have said no. But I told myself I had to at least try stepping out of my comfort zone. I told myself to act like my big brothers—be bold, be confident. Step out of my comfort zone and see what happens."

My heart constricted at the bitterness in his voice, at where this story was going. I didn't say anything, though, and continued to listen and hold his hand.

"So I accepted her invitation, and we walked to her house together. Being the only child of busy, wealthy parents, the home was empty. She fixed us a snack—soda and pretzels and homemade brownies. She told me she'd always thought I was, quote, 'cool and chill, if a little weird,' end quote. She told me she'd always wanted a chance to hang out with me, but just never got the opportunity. She chatted with me—*at* me, really—and then asked if I wanted to see her room. It felt unreal, you know? Was this happening? She wanted me to see her bedroom?"

Oh, no. No.

He continued. "So up we went. She invited me to sit beside her on the bed." His voice dropped to a barely audible murmur, his words tense and hard with remembered pain freshly felt. "She asked me if I liked her. I nodded. She asked me…if I thought she was pretty. Even looking at her was difficult, in that moment, because my nerves and fears and desires were so overwhelming. All I could do, again, was nod."

He paused here, his breathing rapid, his hands clenched, the hand holding mine squeezing so tightly it hurt, but I didn't dare let go.

"Her next words…I hear them in my head…I can hear her voice, even now, as if she had just spoken to me. She looked at me, her expression…sultry, I suppose is the correct word. I didn't know that, then. Reading people and situations is even more difficult for me than touch. Anyway. She looked at me with this weird expression on her face, and said, 'Have you ever been with a girl, Xavier?'"

Another pause.

He shook his head, laughing bitterly. "Once more, I could only shake my head." He swallowed hard. "She was wearing a sweater, a thin, soft sweater, stretchy. Pale blue. V-neck. She twisted to sit so she was almost but not quite facing me. She said, 'You know, I've always thought you were cute, Xavier. I've always known you have a crush on me.' And then she reached up and drew down the neck of her shirt, and her bare breasts emerged, propped up when she released the sweater. I was…I could not breathe, could not believe what was happening. I could not look away." He closed his eyes, speaking through clenched teeth. "'You can touch me, if you want,' she said. 'I know you want to. Go ahead.'"

I didn't want to know the rest—I could guess. But he continued, and I listened.

"I was fifteen, a virgin in every way. Seeing breasts for the first time—well, you can imagine how immediate my natural hormonal response was. I reached up one hand, which was shaking like a leaf. I put my hand on her breast. I remember it being soft, and heavier than I'd expected—" Here he broke off with a fierce blush, stammering. "I—I—um. That is irrelevant, my apologies."

I squeezed his hand. "It's fine. It's your experience—and your observations are not irrelevant."

"But I do not wish for you to think—"

I cut him off. "Xavier, it's *fine*. It's okay. Don't worry about it, please."

He nodded, breathing out sharply. When he started again, it was haltingly, his gaze on the deck between his feet. "Brittany…touched me, then. She reached out and put her hand on my…on my crotch. Over my jeans." He swallowed hard, several times. "I…the touch was—it was far, far too much for me. No one had ever touched me there, in that manner, and I…you know. Um. I lost all control over myself, right there, in my pants. Words like embarrassment or mortification are not nearly sufficient."

"Oh...my god," I breathed.

He laughed bitterly. "I wish the story ended there, but unfortunately it does not." He sighed. "So, with my embarrassment complete, a very visible and obvious wet stain on the front of my jeans, sticky and wet and horrible, Brittany jumped up off the bed, laughing as she righted her sweater. Her bed faced a computer desk, you see. The screen was dark, which I had assumed meant it was off. It...was not. She shook her mouse to wake up the screen, laughing hysterically. 'I did it, bitches!' she shouted, looking into the webcam. 'I made the little twerp come in his pants!' And then she turned back to me, pointing, laughing. 'Oh my god, you're so dumb it's honestly adorable,' she said. 'You actually thought someone like me could *want* someone like you? You really are naive, aren't you?'" He choked, but continued. "She had live-streamed the entire encounter. The whole situation had been on a dare, a bet. The whole school saw. I went to school the next day and everyone was pointing, laughing, calling me 'preemie' for reasons you can extrapolate."

My heart hurt for him. How could anyone be so cruel?

He glanced at me, and his expression softened. He reached up and his thumb brushed my cheek, swiping at a tear I hadn't realized had slipped out. "Such a tender heart."

I shook my head. "I don't understand why she would do that. That's…so vicious, so vile. So cruel. You were so innocent, so genuine."

"We must account for the caprice of human cruelty, Low," Xavier said.

I moved closer to him. Met his eyes with mine. "That probably scarred you pretty badly, huh?"

He nodded. "Trust was already difficult for me, and what Brittany did to me made trust nearly impossible. Especially when it comes to women. So, while I truly want to believe, and *do* believe you are nothing like Brittany, it is difficult for me to overcome my instinctual defensiveness."

My heart squeezed. "Xavier, you have to—you *have* to know I'd never, ever do anything to hurt you."

"I…I desperately want to believe that." He was barely breathing, then, as I moved to stand in front of him, wanting to be closer to him, to comfort him.

His gaze on mine was searching. "You have questions, I believe."

"I don't want to push, or sound…insensitive. I just want to understand."

"Ask, then, and I'll answer to the best of my ability."

"Didn't she give off any clues that she was being disingenuous? That she was leading you on?"

He lifted one shoulder, and dropped it again.

"Perhaps, but I missed them if she did. Subtleties, clues, hints—I almost never read these correctly, if I notice them at all."

"What do you mean?"

"Social connectivity, awareness, and sensitivity are things I struggle with. Being around people overwhelms me. Crowds overwhelm me. Excessive noise or visual stimulation, being jostled, all of this triggers that sense of too much. And people are largely a mystery to me. I have read hundreds of books on human psychology, sociology—and I can recite them all. But…understanding people in situ?" He shook his head. "They say and do things I don't follow, or understand. So when Brittany asked me if I wanted to come over, I doubted her motives, and I doubted her sincerity, since my experience thus far was that cool kids never liked me. That *no one* ever liked me, or wanted to be around me. But I wanted so desperately for her to like me that I ignored my fears. What would a clue of disingenuousness have looked like? A facial expression? I still don't know what that would look like. If she was lying, how would I have known? She was speaking in a tone of voice which seemed nice and sounded interested."

I frowned. "So…you never even suspected she was tricking you?"

Xavier shrugged. "Of course I did. I doubted it

was real the entire time. But I forced myself to follow through, hoping against hope that it was genuine. At first I thought I was dreaming, and then I thought it was too good to be true. Which, of course, it was. So…was I surprised? As in I couldn't believe it had happened, that she'd turned on me like that? No." He sighed. "I absolutely believed it. I castigated myself afterward. Even now, it is difficult to think about or speak about that event, because the pain and shame and embarrassment are just as potent as they were then. But no, I was not shocked. What Brittany did? That is, to use a phrase from the popular vernacular… par for the course, in my life."

My heart broke even further. "Par for the course?"

"Yes, meaning the common average."

"I know what it means," I said. "That's just *horrible*. How could anyone be so cruel?"

He only shrugged. "Other than my brothers, and their respective significant others, my experience with the majority of people is that in their treatment of someone they do not understand or feel inferior to, cruelty is the norm. And nearly everyone misunderstands me and feels inferior to me, so…nearly everyone is cruel to me."

"God, Xavier. I'm so sorry."

He smiled, shrugged, and shook his head. "Such is life."

I inched closer staring up at him, our bodies flush. His gaze was intense and inscrutable.

"You talked about not being able to read clues and hints correctly."

He nodded. "Yes. I often miss even blatant sarcasm."

"What about flirtation?"

"What about it?"

"Can you…I don't know…read it? See it for what it is?"

He frowned, wobbling his head around in a gesture of uncertainty. "Somewhat. But I don't trust it."

"You don't trust the person flirting with you, or your understanding of the flirtation?"

"Both. I don't trust my own ability to detect whether a girl is flirting with me, or mocking me like Brittany, drawing me out for nefarious purposes. I do not trust, because Brittany taught me—no offense meant to you—that women cannot be trusted. I've learned that even when a girl seems interested in me, or appears to like me, it's not real. It's not true. If it seems too good to be true, it most definitely is."

"So, when I flirt with you—" I said, tangling both of our hands together. "You don't trust that to be real? You don't believe that I actually mean it?"

"Well, flirtation is such a subjective thing, is it not? What counts as flirtation? Is it a particular look

hand to hold a lock of my red-gold hair that had come out of the loose chignon. He ran it through his fingertips, following the spiral.

"Low," he said, tentatively, "I hope I'm being clear, here, that this is an issue of mine, and my distrust of your intentions is not meant as a reflection of my assessment of your character."

"Can I be honest?"

"I hope you always have been, are, and continue to be, in all circumstances, honest with me, even to a fault."

That stung, a needling dart piercing my knowledge of the fact that he had no idea who I was and that I continued to keep that information to myself.

I slid my hands around his waist to his back, pulling him up against me, relishing the hardness of his body and the heat of him, his masculine scent and virulent green fire of his eyes on mine. "It's kind of hard not to be a little hurt that you don't trust me." I spoke over his objection. "I know you have painfully good reasons not to, and that you can't help it. I just...I wish there was something I could do to prove to you that I'm really, truly interested in you."

"Why, though?"

I tilted my head, confused. "Why what?"

"Why are you interested in me?"

I couldn't help a laugh, a gentle, disbelieving huff

as I slid my fingers through his hair. "Why am I interested in you, Xavier Badd?"

"Yes."

"Because I like talking to you," I said, leaning closer, inching my face gradually nearer and nearer to his. "You're funny, and weird, and unpredictable in the most delightful and fun way. You're smart—the smartest person I've ever known, and that challenges me. I don't feel inferior to you, because I know myself, and I know my skills and talents, and I'm comfortable and confident in them. I know I'm smart. So, I'm not threatened by how intelligent you are, or jealous, or anything. I just feel challenged by talking to you and being around you, and I like that."

His chest swelled, and the corners of his mouth tipped up in a smile, as if he was daring to believe me. "I see."

"I have fun hanging out with you. I never in my life thought I would ever enjoy fishing, but I did. Watching the eagle catch that fish was one of the most exciting things I've ever seen. Watching that show with you was fun and relaxing—and to be honest, I don't relax well around other people."

"Nor do I." He made an odd face, somewhere between a smirk and frown. "And to be honest, I cannot say I was especially *relaxed*, although I did enjoy the experience immensely."

"Why couldn't you relax?"

He hesitated over his answer. "I was...distracted. Focused on..." He blinked, swallowed hard. "On the sensation of...cuddling with you, to use a word one might label emasculating."

I smiled up at him. "It's not emasculating at all, Xavier. There's nothing unmanly about a guy cuddling with a girl. It's just showing affection, demonstrating that you enjoy each other and enjoy being close, touching, being together."

His smile returned, and had gained confidence. "Thank you for that clarification. So, yes. The physical sensation of cuddling with you precluded my ability to relax, but nonetheless, it was an experience I shall treasure always." His expression darkened. "At least, until I freaked out."

"A hiccup, that's all," I said. "All of which leads me to the other reason I like you—you're sexy. I'm just crazy attracted to you on a physical level."

His frown was adorably befuddled. "Sexy?"

I couldn't help laughing. "Yes, Xavier." I feathered his hair away from his eyes, and then slid my fingertip down his temple to his jawline. "Sexy. Hot. Gorgeous." I leaned closer yet, so my lips brushed his. "You need more? I've got more. *Sinfully* sexy."

I wasn't sure he was breathing. "Please do not say things you do not mean, Low."

I dove my hands under his T-shirt, untucking it from behind the belt, finally getting my hands on his bare skin, on those steely abs. "Oh, I mean it, Xavier. I mean every single word."

He sucked in a sharp breath. "Your touch is setting my skin on fire."

"Should I stop?"

He shook his head slowly. "No. Please…don't stop."

"Good, because I like touching you."

He released the lock of my hair he'd been toying with, and his hands drifted downward to alight, like nervous birds, on my waist. "The thrill of my hands on your body is electric. It sends a strange, manic energy through me."

"I like it. The feel of your hands on me, I mean."

"You do?"

"Of course. Quite a lot."

"May I ask you a question?"

"Anything."

"Is this flirting?"

I touched my lips to his cheek, not quite a kiss, really, just a brush of my lips across his skin, just beneath his cheekbone. "No, I'd say this is quite a bit more than just flirting."

"Oh." He swallowed hard again, and his hands moved down to rest on my hips—he was taking liberties, exploring a little, and it made my heart beat like a tribal drum. "Another question, then, if I may—when I showed up here, the last time, and you were naked…you put on your kimono, and we watched that show." He blinked, his fingers tracing around the waistband of my bikini bottom. "More than once throughout that evening, you bent over or otherwise moved in such a way as to allow me a glimpse at your bare flesh. Was that intentional? If so, why?"

I took a huge risk, then, and pushed his shirt up, gently easing it off his head and tossing it onto the chaise lounge. I touched a kiss to his jawline, next. "Yes, Xavier, it was intentional."

He tensed again as I dragged my fingernails down his chest. "Why?"

Once again, I couldn't help laughing. "I was hitting on you, Xavier."

"Which is like flirting, but more aggressive or intentional."

"Yeah, exactly." I pressed our torsos together, flattening my tits against his chest, wrapping my arms around his neck. "You want me to break that down for you?"

He nodded, his palms exploring my back, roaming from shoulders to waist to hips in random patterns; the warmth of his touch sent shivers down my spine, and had my thighs clenching. He was touching my back, innocently enough, and I was responding like this? God, what was it about this man that affected me so potently?

"It feels weird to explain this kind of thing in so many words," I said, laughing, "but here it goes. Basically, when I bent over so my robe opened, or when I crawled across the ottoman to get the popcorn, that was an invitation."

"To what?"

I lifted an eyebrow. "What do you think?" His hands stilled on my back, his eyes hunting, darting, as if he was nervous to say the answer wrong. I laughed again, and kissed another spot on his jaw. "This isn't an exam, Xavier. I honestly want to know what you think the reason would be behind me doing that."

"Because you like me."

"Well yes, but I've said as much. Try again." I tugged at a strand of his hair. "Why do you think I would intentionally expose my naked body to you, Xavier? Just say what you think, the first answer that pops into your head—go."

"Because you want me to touch you."

I grinned. "See? You understand more than you think."

"It's not a matter of understanding, but one of believing you really mean that."

"Why wouldn't you believe it? What reason have

I ever given you to think I wouldn't mean it, or that I don't truly want it?"

"It just..." He sighed, eyes closing momentarily. "It falls under the umbrella of 'if it seems too good to be true, it probably is.' I want so badly to touch you, Low, to be allowed the glory and wonder and privilege of touching you—an angel made flesh—and I do not believe myself worthy. Just being near you is a privilege. To be your friend, to spend time with you is a privilege. To be allowed physical intimacy with you? How can that be real? I would never, could never presume that someone as...as incredibly, stunningly, blindingly, perfectly lovely as you would want *me* to put my hands on you."

"I'm not just *allowing* it, Xavier," I said. "I *want* it."

"Truly?" he breathed.

Rather than answering in words, I slid out from between him and the railing, led him by the hand inside and up to my room.

The sliding door to the balcony was open, letting in a cool breeze off the water, and the sound of squawking gulls and the gentle lap of the water against the hull.

Xavier stood in the middle of the room, shirtless in his jeans, belt, and sneakers. He was a vision of lupine male sexuality, all hard muscles and planes and curves and ridges, with that messy dark hair and those vivid green eyes. He was staring at me as if he'd never seen me before, his gaze raking over my body hungrily. His hands were at his sides, rubbing up and down his jeans, a gesture I don't think he was aware of.

I was nervous too, for some reason. My heart was pounding, and my skin was tingling as if his gaze had a physical effect on my flesh, and my thighs were clenched, my core throbbing.

I wasn't sure how much longer I could hold back my desire for Xavier—his body tempted me, called out to my hands, my lips. I wanted him naked, and I wanted him beneath me, above me, behind me. I wanted to hear his voice crying out in guttural pleasure; I wanted to feel his hands on my skin, possessive on my curves.

I bit my lip, the mental images I was torturing myself with making my core clench and throb and seep the liquid essence of desire.

I tugged my hair loose from the knot and shook it out, combing my fingers through it. I took a step toward Xavier, who was standing frozen in the middle of the room. Reaching behind me, I untied my bikini top—a halter that tied at my neck and at my back; I used my elbows to keep the cups pinned against my breasts, drawing out the moment. I paused like that for a moment, watching Xavier's reaction: he shifted his weight from foot to foot, his jaw clenched, and he swallowed and licked his lips, hands clenching and unclenching then rubbing his palms against his legs.

My smile was lopsided and shaky—as if I'd never taken my clothes off for a man before. But somehow, this felt different. His gaze, the intensity of it, the hunger in it, the need, the utter self-control he displayed as he stood stock-still, waiting, watching, not allowing himself to move—this was unlike anything I'd ever experienced. Xavier made it that way, just by virtue of who he was.

Desperate to feel his touch and to feel wanted simply for who I was, I dropped my arms and let the halter fall to the floor at my feet, standing topless in front of him.

He took a step toward me, and my heart raced in anticipation. "You are…" He shook his head, as if unable to finish the thought.

I closed the space between us, stopping when my nipples brushed against his bare chest. "What, Xavier? What am I?"

"Perfect," he breathed. "Fucking perfect."

I palmed his abs with both hands, ran my palms up his chest, down his biceps. "So are you."

"Your skin…it looks so soft."

"Touch me and find out," I murmured.

"Where?"

I laughed at his question. "Anywhere you want. Just touch me."

"You're always laughing at my questions."

"Not at you, not in the sense that I think you're stupid for asking. It's just...no one has ever said things this way to me before."

He reached up, and my nipples hardened in anticipation of his touch, but his hand went instead to my face, cupping my cheek, his thumb brushing my cheekbone. His fingertips traced the column of my throat, and then his palm skated over my bare shoulder. My whole body trembled under his touch, and yet he still didn't reach for the obvious fruit. He glided his hand down my arm, to my forearm, and then to my hand—his fingers interlaced with mine, and his eyes locked on me.

"Low, my attraction to you is...it's more than I know how to process. If you're not...if this is a game or a joke, please—tell me now. Because I can't handle—"

I lifted up on my toes, silencing him with a kiss. A brief one, meant only to shut him up, to prove my desire.

Only, it morphed into something more.

I felt him tense at the contact of my lips, as he always tensed at first touch, but then he relaxed, shifted forward to tower over me so I had to tilt my face up.

He made a low noise in the back of his throat, and he let go of my hand, pressing his hands to the small of my back and deepening the kiss.

I moaned—an unaffected noise of genuine surprise at the power of his kiss, at the hunger of it. He went from zero to sixty in an instant, and my tongue instinctually slid out to seek his. Slowly at first, but with increasing fervor and confidence, Xavier kissed me. I felt him hardening behind his zipper, felt his breathing hitch.

I buried my hands in his hair, lifting up onto my toes to kiss him harder still, deeper yet, and then let my hands wander down the strong expanse of his back. I cupped his ass, moaning again at the firmness of it, the hardness, and then—god, yes, finally, his hands left the small of my back and drifted up and around to my front. They alighted at my diaphragm, just beneath the low hanging swell of my breasts, paused, and he broke the kiss, his forehead against mine.

I waited, my breath caught in my throat. I wanted to beg for his touch, but I didn't—not yet.

What was he doing to me? He made me feel as if this was as new to me as it seemed to be to him. His reverence, his hesitation…he wasn't a hard-charging, take-whatever-he-wants super dominant alpha, and yet he was still utterly male, intensely masculine, and totally himself. He made me feel like what he'd said I was—the most beautiful woman in the world. And this feeling he gave me, it meant more to me than all the attention the media could give me—because it was about *me*, about who I was, about how he saw me, absent of any guile or pretense or ulterior motive.

The tremble in his hands brought me out of my thoughts and back to him, to us, to the moment. He slid his hands upward, gently taking the weight of my breasts into his palms, and his thumbs grazed over my nipples.

I gasped audibly at the blazing thrill of sensation that shuddered through me, and he froze.

"Don't stop," I murmured. "That feels amazing."

He lifted my breasts, ran his palms over my nipples, and then let their weight fall, swaying and bouncing gently. I hooked my fingers in the front pockets of his jeans, pulling him against me even as I leaned my upper torso away so he could keep touching me. His gaze was locked on my tits, on his hands moving over them, watching himself caressing and exploring their weight and shape, and I felt his cock hardening with each passing moment until he was surely so hard it had to be painful.

Keeping my fingers hooked into his pockets, I walked us backward until my knees hit the bed, and I fell to my back, laughing at his surprised expression as

and then swept his gaze downward, to my core. I was so wet with arousal, the fabric of the bikini bottom stuck to my nether lips, outlined and obvious. Blushing, I resisted the urge to cross my thighs, to cover up the evidence of my need.

He bit his lip, his eyes narrowing, nostrils flaring, chest swelling with a deep breath. I caressed his chest and stomach, letting him get used to the feel of my hand on his skin before I dared do anything any further. I was on my side, facing him, propped on an elbow, leaning most of my weight onto Xavier; his fingers trailed over my breastbone, down between the valley of my breasts, to my stomach, hesitating at the waist of my bikini. His eyes met mine, looking for demurral or disapproval; I rolled to my back and let my thighs splay apart.

He followed me, rolling to his side now, and his palm spread over my navel and carved down my left leg, fingers exploring the delicacy of my inner thigh. My breath caught when he dragged his middle finger up the seam of my core, over the fabric of my bikini bottom.

"Another gasp," he noted. "You enjoy that."

I nodded. "Keep going. Please."

His gaze flicked to the loose bowknots at each hip, all that was keeping my bikini bottom fastened. Moving his hand maddeningly slowly, he reached out and captured one loose end of the ties at my left hip-bone, tugged, and the knot came undone, the strings falling open; his fingers danced across my belly, low, following the waistband to the other knot, which he untied. I forced myself to keep breathing, to let him go at his own pace. But god, I wanted his touch. I wanted an orgasm I didn't give myself. I wanted his fingers, his mouth. His tongue.

He drew the small triangle of cloth away from my core, and I lifted my butt up slightly so he could pull it free and toss it over the side of the bed. I lay naked, flushed with desire, aching, trembling, I waited for his touch.

His gaze widened as he stared at me, his eyes roaming my core—the tiny inverted isosceles triangle of reddish gold hair over my core, which I'd recently trimmed and shaped. His hand, once again, spread over my navel, his palm centered over my belly button. His breathing hitched, and he slid his hand downward, fingers first.

Please, please, please, I thought.

His middle finger covered my seam, and then slid with delicate gentility upward, eliciting a whimper from me. I drew my legs further apart, spreading my pussy open for him, letting him see all of me. My heart was hammering, nerves slamming through me as if this was my first time doing this. Was it his? I somehow thought it might be, but I wasn't sure and wasn't going to ask, not in that moment; selfishly, perhaps—I just wanted him to touch me. His touch was beautiful, soft, gentle, exploratory, strong…and I needed more of it. So much more.

I covered his hand with mine, placing my fingers over his. I guided his middle finger into me, inhaling a sharp whimpering gasp at the feel of his thick, strong finger inside. When he drew it out, I guided his finger, slick with my essence, to my clit. Showed him how to touch me—slowly, in wide circles around the hardened nub, occasionally flicking it or brushing side to side. He caught on rapidly, mimicking what I'd shown him.

Within seconds, I was gasping, and my hips were flexing, and my core was spasming and clenching around nothing.

He gazed down at me in concern. "Low? Are you…are you okay?"

I laughed breathlessly, burying my hands in my curls, whimpering at his touch. "Fuck yes, I'm okay—I'm *so* much more than okay," I said, writhing against his fingers—he'd added a second finger to the first, smearing my leaking juices around my clit. "So good, *so* good. Don't you dare stop."

"You're having an orgasm?" he asked, watching me carefully.

"Almost—almost. So close. Keep doing that—just like that, and I will."

"I won't stop."

I laughed again, through a whimper, and grabbed at his face, pulling him toward me. "Kiss me while you make me come, Xavier."

He bent over me, fingers circling, and his mouth claimed mine. His tongue hunted for mine, and the kiss stole my breath, the hunger in him, the power of his kiss, the intensity and the passion of it. He kissed as if kissing me was more important than his next breath, as if he could die if he didn't kiss me.

I knotted my fingers in his hair, and when we broke to gasp for breath, I shoved his head down to my breasts. "Kiss me there," I breathed, "taste me."

He took me literally, kissing the side of my breast, and then again in a different spot. His fingers were still busily circling, bringing me closer and closer to the edge, and I didn't want to get there—not yet. God, not yet. I wanted this to last forever, his weight on me, his fingers on my clit, his mouth on my tits.

"You taste amazing," Xavier said. "Like salt and… and something else I can't name."

"Taste more of me," I said, meeting his eyes. "All of me. I want your mouth on me."

I sucked in a sharp breath as his mouth centered on my nipple and his tongue flicked it, and then lapped at it—when I whimpered, he repeated what he'd done to make me whimper. The other breast, then, and I was a writhing mess of need, gasping, whining, my hands tangled in his dark locks.

I was close, so close.

Heat shattered through me, pressure subsumed me. Need ran through my veins in place of blood. The orgasm that was building inside me was going to be nuclear, I knew.

But I still wasn't ready for this to end.

I caught at his wrist. "Slow—slow down."

"Is something wrong?"

I shook my head. "If you stop for a second and let me catch my breath, let me back away from the edge of coming, when I do get there it'll be all the more intense for me."

He busied himself kissing my tits, his lips and tongue paying homage, again and again, his kisses covering them all over. He lapped and licked, teased and flicked, and then suckled one nipple until I shrieked.

"Holy—holy shit, Xavier," I gasped. "*More*."

I guided his mouth to my other breast, and he suckled my nipple into his mouth again until I wrenched away, half screaming, half whimpering. The need to come was so sharp now it felt like a knife inside me. I lifted my hips.

"Touch my pussy again," I whispered. "Make me come."

He started over, gingerly delving his finger inside my channel, drawing my essence out of me and smearing it onto my clit, and then beginning small slow circles. When I started moaning and driving my hips into his touch, he sped up.

In moments, I was riding the ragged edge again, and I knew I couldn't draw it out any longer—if I didn't come right then, I'd go mad.

I needed to touch him, now, needed to make him come as hard as he was about to make me come.

I clung to his shoulders and let my knees splay apart even wider, heels driving into the mattress to provide leverage for the gyration of my hips into his touch, which was fast now, speeding up as I finally felt myself about to fall over the edge.

"Oh—oh fuck, Xavier, I'm—oh god—I'm *coming*, holy shit I'm coming! You're making me come so hard, Xavier…don't stop…faster! Yes! God yes!—fuck!—just like that!" I let go completely, let myself scream and thrash and chant his name, unable to stop myself, coming harder than I had in years.

He milked me through the climax, not stopping or slowing as I pumped against his fingers, whimpering and moaning as I came back down. Finally, I had to stop him, too sensitive to bear being touched any more.

I caught his hand, brought it away from my pussy. The rush of the orgasm made me crazed, made me daring—I brought his essence-slick fingers to my mouth and slid my tongue up his digit, tasting my own essence on him.

He sucked in a harsh breath. "What—what does that taste like?"

I smirked coyly. "Find out for yourself."

He slid his finger into his mouth, eyes widening at the sudden assault of flavors and scents from my pussy. "Wow—*wow.*" His gaze slid down to my core. "Not what I was expecting."

I'd thought I was done—unable to take any more touch, any more stimulation—but the heat and hunger in his gaze put the lie to that.

"Taste me," I invited.

"Down there?"

I nodded. "If you want to."

"You taste good," he said, palms cupping my breasts as if he just couldn't help himself.

"You could make me come again, if you did."

"Do you want me to?"

"I want you to do what you want, Xavier." I brought his mouth to mine for a slow but brief kiss. "But yes, it would feel amazing if you went down on me."

"Then I shall go down on you." He suited action to words without hesitation, sliding down my body to wedge his shoulders between my thighs.

I hooked my knees over his shoulders, propping myself up on my elbows to watch. His bright green eyes were focused on my slit, flicking briefly up to mine and then back down. Hesitantly, his tongue slithered out and drove up my seam; he made a surprised noise in his throat, and licked my slit again.

"Oh—oh god," I murmured, the feel of his tongue and rasp of his stubble beyond heaven, beyond nirvana, beyond anything I'd ever felt. "More. *Please*, more."

He gave me more—so much more. I didn't have to tell him or show him anything, he seemed to know instinctively what to do, following the sounds I made, the way I writhed, to make me repeat the moans and movements. He stiffened his tongue, circling my clit with it like he had with his fingers, and then when I broke apart into gasping pleas for more, he lapped at my clit, faster and faster, in a vertical swiping of his tongue.

"Oh fuck—fuck, *fuck*!" I screamed. "God, yes! Oh please, God, Xavier—right there, just like that—"

I cut off with a wordless scream, coming even harder than the last time, shattering into a million spasming shards.

When I came back down from the orgasmic high, he was still eating me out, devouring me, and I pulled his face up to mine, wiping at the smear of wetness on his cheeks, laughing at his awed expression.

"Making you come—" he murmured, wiping at his mouth, "it's—it's the best thing ever."

He fell to his back, staring at me sideways. I was gasping, still, limp and lifeless.

"You just gave me two incredible orgasms," I said, rolling toward him. "I think it's time to return the favor."

NINE

Xavier

I COULDN'T BELIEVE THIS WAS HAPPENING. IT FELT UNREAL. Surreal. But it was real, and it was the best day of my life. Beyond any dream or fantasy I'd ever had. Her naked body was…it was the stuff of dreams. A fantasy made real. That I got to see her, touch her? How could it be real? What had I done to deserve this?

My senses were on overload, everything inside me screaming. But—it felt *good,* beyond good, the feel of her skin like silk or velvet, the salt of her skin on my tongue, her hands in my hair, the wet slickness of her pussy around my fingers and against my mouth—so much, too much, and I didn't want it to ever end. Everything was heightened. My entire body tingled and throbbed.

And now she was reaching for me.

I had a flashback of being at Brittany's house, her cruel eyes and vicious laughter—I shut it out, pushed it away and focused my attention on Low, on her heavy round breasts, the damp curls of her pubic hair above her womanhood—what did I call it? What did she call it? I resolved to avoid calling it anything until I could figure out how to ask that question without sounding stupid.

She was leaning over me again, hooking two fingers into the elastic of my underwear. "I want to make you feel as good as you made me feel," she said.

I swallowed hard, trying my best to shut out the flashbacks piling behind the walls I was frantically erecting in my mind.

"Okay," I whispered, unable to say another syllable.

She drew my tight gray boxer-briefs away from my body, away from the throbbing shaft of my erection, and tugged them down. I lifted my hips, a knot in my throat, my pulse crashing in my ears. She slid them down past my butt and drew them off, tossing them aside.

I was naked. Lying on my back, my eyes on hers as she stared at my erection. I couldn't breathe. Everything tingled and ached and throbbed. My senses were so far overloaded it felt like I was seconds from a total meltdown. My erection was so painful it felt like a white-hot spear stabbing and throbbing.

"Holy *shit*, Xavier," Low muttered in a soft voice.

I frowned at her, teeth gritted. "What?"

She ran her palm down my stomach, giggling. "Your cock is *huge*."

"I…oh. It is?"

She met my eyes as she hovered her hand over me. "I mean, I knew you were probably pretty well-endowed just from the size of the bulge behind your zipper, but this thing is…" She shook her head, laughing again. "Seriously the most incredible cock I've ever seen."

I didn't want to think about her seeing other cocks, but her words made something inside me swell. "Really?"

She leaned over me, her plump soft damp lips brushing my cheekbone. "Absolutely the fucking truth," Low whispered. "And now…I'm going to touch you. Okay?"

Couldn't breathe. She was going to touch me.

Bare.

Have you ever been with a girl, Xavier?

So dumb it's adorable…

As if someone like ME could ever actually want someone like YOU…

I shut the voice out, focusing on the present, on Low's voice in my ear, murmuring I wasn't sure what, my head buzzing, my pulse too loud in my ears to hear anything. I watched as she settled her hand onto my erection, cupping me, and then her thumb and fingers wrapped around me. Explosive urgency rose inside me.

The feel of her hand on my cock was…god…oh god.

I forced my eyes open, staring down at her small pale hand around my cock, and then to her eyes, watching me.

"You're so sexy, Xavier," she said.

I couldn't breathe. Couldn't manage words.

It was going to happen again. I would embarrass myself.

Too much, too fast.

Too soon.

I gritted my teeth, tried to hold back, but her touch was too perfect too soft too warm too smooth, and then she was sliding her fist down and back up.

She leaned close to me again, her lips brushing my year. "Don't fight it, Xavier."

"I—I can't…" I gasped, gulping. "I'm…it feels too good, Low."

"It's supposed to feel good." She nibbled on my earlobe. "It's *okay*. Let it happen. Let go."

I didn't want to let go. It wasn't okay. The last time that had happened in front of someone, it had been the most pivotally, fundamentally scarring moment of my entire life. I knew—mentally—that Low was very likely rather familiar with what would happen when I let go, and that my hang-up with this issue was unique to me, and probably ridiculous. I *knew* this. But I couldn't fight it. Couldn't stop the panic. Anxiety ruled me. Embarrassment owned me. Fear crashed through my skull, pulsed in my veins.

I felt her touch like fire on my skin. My breathing was ragged, and my hips were flexed upward as far as they would go. Her fist slid down my cock with exaggerated slowness—or perhaps my awareness of time was distorted, drugged by her touch.

I was a living dichotomy of sensation—

One half was chanting in a frenzy: *touch me touch me touch me don't stop god it feels so fucking good please never ever stop—*

And the other half, just as manic: *oh god it's too much I can't take it, it hurts don't make me go there don't make me embarrass myself in front of you like this I don't want this where can I hide from this where can I hide from myself it's too much too much too fucking much I can't stop this—*

I heard my breathing and a soughing and rasping in my throat as if I was having an asthma attack. My voice, groaning as if in utter agony. Her small warm strong delicate soft fingers traveling the length of my organ, swirling and twisting around the top before plunging down to the base, stroking there.

How long had it been going on?

Seconds.

Perhaps three full strokes of her fist.

And I couldn't hold back. Already.

Please no, please no—

Have you ever been with a girl, Xavier?

That laughter.

The cruelty in her eyes.

It's not her, Low is *not* Brittany—I told myself this, again and again with every firing of each synapse, but it made no difference.

I was fifteen again, in a bedroom with the popular girl, her cruel voice in my ear.

I opened my eyes, forced them to stay open, gazing at Low.

"There you are," she murmured.

"Low—"

She leaned over me, and the soft weight of her breasts against my chest made me throb and ache and pulse closer to the precipice, so close I was riding a razor's edge between control and embarrassment.

"I love the way your cock feels in my hand,

Xavier," she whispered in my ear. "Does it feel good for you?"

She nipped my earlobe. Her fist twisted around the head of my cock, and her lips skated over my cheek, and her tongue traced my lips, and her thumb smeared over the clear wetness seeping from the tip.

"Low—*shit*!" I grated past clenched teeth. "I can't—I can't—I fucking *can't*—"

Weight behind my eyes, pressure in my skull. Pressure in my chest, in my balls. A furious maelstrom in my heart and brain and body, all aflame, all a roiling chaos out of my control, all centered on the slow slide of her hand around my cock.

I heard a whimper escape me, a small, helpless sound—and then a growl.

Low's forehead nudged against mine, her eyes locked on her hand and my cock. "Yeah?" she whispered, a sultry, provocative breath. "You're about to come, aren't you? Let me have it, Xavier. Give it to me. Don't hold it back."

She didn't understand—she didn't understand.

This moment, this sensation was irrevocably and inextricably tangled with embarrassment and humiliation.

I focused on sensation—her hand, the soft gentle affectionate slow grip of her fingers around my cock; her breasts crushed against my chest, her nipples hardened; her thigh draped over mine, the tickling rasp of her pubic hair against my thigh as she ground her center against me; the scent of her skin, of her sex; the scent of her sex on my face, on my fingers; the taste of her sex on my lips, her essence still tangy and sweet and musky and intense on my tongue and lips; my cock, aching throbbing pulsing, balls boiling with a raging need I could no longer deny.

I'd held out as long as possible.

Thirty seconds?

She sat up, breasts swaying. She guided my hand to her breasts, and then used that same hand to cup my balls, which she massaged while stroking me.

The silken weight of her breast in my hand, her touch all over me, her beauty on display in front of me, sensation coursing through me—I was undone in that moment. She was my undoing—all of her, all that she was.

I exploded with a ragged cry. I felt myself release, choking back another moan of humiliation.

I watched—I had to watch. She wrapped both hands around my cock and stroked me slowly as I climaxed. My seed rocketed out of me with unbelievable force, striping up my belly and chest in a hot wet line, and over her fingers. She didn't stop as I came, watching with what appeared to be sensual delight, lower lip caught in her teeth. More and more and more thick white viscous spurting cum, dripping all over her hands, both of them, trickling down her knuckles and the backs of her hands, still seeping out of me as she continued to stroke me.

She giggled. "Oh…my…*god*—you came *so* much," she said, trailing a fingertip through the mess on my stomach and chest.

My heart stopped.

Lungs froze.

Brain short-circuited—going haywire, showing me Brittany and feeding me her voice in my head even as I saw Low and heard her.

I was there, yet again, in that bedroom, that cruel laughter ringing out.

I'd humiliated myself yet again. In front of and all over the hands of a woman I liked and admired and was attracted to more strongly than any other human being I'd ever met.

Panic is what I felt.

She saw it.

"Xavier, it's okay. It's okay." She scooted closer to me, leaning over me. "Breathe, Xavier. It's okay."

"I'm sorry—I'm sorry—"

Her lovely features scrunched up in confusion. "Sorry? What the *hell* are you sorry for? That was amazing!"

"No, no—" I shook my head, sitting up and

scrambling away, trying to escape the mess on my stomach and chest. "I—it's all over me. It's all over *you*. I can't—I can't—" Words refused to emerge coherently, because my brain was a hurricane of a million thoughts and emotions, overlapping and colliding and smashing and exploding, recriminating, shredding through my logical understanding.

She moved with me, reaching for me. "Xavier, wait! Just breathe, okay? It's okay!"

"It's *not* okay!" I shouted. "I'm not okay. This is not okay. I can't handle this."

"We can handle it together—"

"No, no, you don't understand, you don't fucking understand—I keep seeing *her*. I know you're not her, but that's all I see, it's all I feel." I was off the bed, flattened against the wall, the mess from my orgasm dripping down my body, a sensation I couldn't stand. "God, get it off, get it off. I'm sorry—I'm sorry!"

Low, unashamedly still naked, hurried into the en suite bathroom and grabbed a hand towel and then returned to me with it.

"We can clean you up, Xavier. I'm sorry, I should've realized the sensation might be—"

I snatched the towel from her and grabbed her hands in mine. "No, god—no, get it off *you* first," I snarled, scrubbing and wiping my cum off of her hands with panicked, clumsy movements. "I'm sorry,

I shouldn't have—shit, shit, shit!—"

Low took the towel from me before I could finish cleaning her hands. "Xavier, stop—*stop*," she snapped, firmly but not unkindly, and my eyes whipped up to hers. "I *like* your cum on my hands."

She lifted her right hand, the one I hadn't cleaned, up to her face, to her mouth, and her tongue flicked out and licked away a smeared droplet of my seed.

"I'm not embarrassed, or upset or grossed out—I'm *happy*," she said, her eyes not wavering from my own incredulous gaze. "I'm ecstatic. I'm *turned on*. I've never been more attracted to *anyone* than I am right now, to *you*."

"*I'm* embarrassed," I said, closing my eyes as the truth emerged, involuntarily, from my lips. "I'm humiliated. It happened again."

Her eyes widened. "It happened again? You mean—the story you told me about that nasty girl from your high school, that cruel trick she played on you?" Low pressed her face closer to mine, so all I could see was her fierce blue eyes. "That did *not* happen again, Xavier. I wanted to touch you because I'm attracted to you. I *want* you. I *want* this. I *wanted* to make you come, and I'm so fucking turned on by how hard you came that I could come again in a heartbeat. Watching you come, just from touching you with my hands—that was *so* fucking hot I can't even—"

She grabbed my hand and guided it to her center, between her thighs, and guided my finger through the hot wet pink center, just beneath the apex of the triangle of reddish-gold curls. "Feel how wet I am? *You* did that to me. Watching you come, making you come did that to me." She gestured around at the room. "It's just you and me. No computer, no phone, no camera, just you and me. Just this moment we shared. You made me come. You made me feel more incredible than I've ever felt in my whole fucking life, Xavier! You! With your hands and your mouth, the way you touch me, the way you kiss me. *You* did that. And I want *more* of that with you. Do you understand?"

I jerked my hand away, rude and frantic from the welter of panic and doubt and confusion and sensory overload. "You don't *understand*, Low."

"What don't I understand? Please explain it, because I'm confused." For the first time since I'd known her, there was a hard note of anger in her voice.

"I hear everything you're saying," I started, closing my eyes, knowing I was about to unload a truth on her no one else knew about me. "But it doesn't change the way this is processing for me."

"Why?"

I forced my eyes open, forced myself to meet her blue eyes with mine as I dropped the bomb. "Don't you get it? Haven't you been listening?" I knew I was being unkind, being unfair, but I couldn't help it. "Sensory overload, difficulty with social situations, tendency toward involuntary physical tics, combined with unusual mental capacity in one or more areas—do those *symptoms* mean anything to you, Low?"

She shook her head slowly. "What—what are you saying, Xavier?"

"I'm not just really smart, Low—I'm fucking *autistic*!" I paced away, stomping, gasping for breath, as I said out loud for the first time the diagnosis I figured out for myself more than three years ago. "High-functioning autistic with savant tendencies."

She blinked, stammered. "I—I…what? Autistic?" Low inhaled sharply.

"I've never seen a doctor for an official diagnosis, but I've read dozens of case studies, and I've memorized everything modern neurology, psychology, and biology knows about Autism Spectrum Disorder, and I know without a shadow of a doubt that I'm on the spectrum." I returned to where she was, and slid down to sit on the floor, back to the wall, facing her again.

"On—on the spectrum?"

"Autism is—it's not like most disorders, where you either have it or you don't, where it displays largely the same way in everyone. It's a spectrum, meaning a broad range of potential ways it can present. Low functioning would be on one end of the spectrum, what you'd think of when you hear the word 'autistic'—" I was in lecture mode, now, retreating into facts to get away from feelings. "You know, slapping and flapping and nonverbal and all that. The farther to the other end of the spectrum you go, the less obvious it becomes."

"But you're—you're normal."

I laughed, a sarcastic bark. "No, I'm *not*. I'm *far* from normal. I've gone through hell my entire life to hide how abnormal I am. I have physical tics. Difficulty verbalizing things. The worst of it for me is social and physical. I get caught up in my own world; I get lost in my thoughts and obsessions and forget about the people around me. I get overwhelmed easily, and when I do, it's impossible for me to get out of it. If I count or work through an equation, or distract myself mentally somehow, I can slow down the process of getting overwhelmed, but doing so marks me out as…a freak or whatever."

Low breathed out a sigh, fidgeting with the towel. "You're *not* a freak, Xavier. Don't you *dare* say that about yourself."

"Low—" I began, but she cut in impatiently.

"No, I won't hear it. Different, yes, sure, okay—and that's a huge part of what I like about you, everything that makes you different." She glanced down, gently and gingerly wiping at the mess on my torso with the towel, folding and wiping until I was clean. "More to the point, though—you're on the spectrum…so what? What does that have to do with—with us? With me? With what happened in high school and everything we've done together?"

Her proximity was too much, her scent, her heat, the tactile memory of her touch, the pounding need for more of everything she was despite my mounting panic and anxiety. I was counting the freckles on her skin in an attempt to fight my panic, but the fact that the path of freckles across her shoulders and throat led down to her breasts didn't help.

I swallowed hard and closed my eyes against the manic press of humiliation at the answer I knew I had to give her. "What happened with—with that girl, whose name I don't even want to say ever again—that was the single most painful and humiliating moment in my life. It—it fucked me up, Low." I choked on my words but kept going. "Part of the disorder is a tendency to fixate, and to…to sort of equate a significant emotional trauma with a particular physical sensation. Everyone does this, but because of my heightened sensitivity and tendency toward sensory overload, it's just…worse for me."

Low's eyes closed as she followed the logic. "So when she did what she did to you, humiliating you and sharing it with the school—you equated that humiliation with coming."

"Yes. But even before that, masturbation was difficult for me, simply because my issue with touch extends to myself, and the process of getting myself to orgasm despite my sensory issue was frequently just…too difficult to be worth it, so I tended to avoid arousal, keeping my mind occupied in other ways. I took to sports and exercise to alleviate the physical aspect of it, resulting in a need to push harder and harder to evade and avoid my natural hormonal responses and inclinations."

I retreated yet again into the factual realm to avoid the emotional one, which put me back into the more formal pattern of speech. "This is all still true. But when that event occurred, any hope of enjoying climax was erased. The approach to that sensation is wrought with emotional landmines. I see her face, hear her voice, her cruel, mocking laughter. It is more like punishment than pleasure, because I remember how she made me feel. Touching myself was impossible—*is* nearly impossible, even still. And reaching any kind of rapport with a female has always been equally impossible. Compound my social difficulties stemming from ASD with the trauma of what she did to me, and women are usually impossible for me. I don't trust people in general and women in particular, and I trust myself even less. It's not just psychological, but neurological as well."

She blinked hard, sucking in a deep breath and letting it out slowly. "So what happened with Bri—with *her*..."

I nodded, understanding her underlying question. "It was the closest I have ever come—until today—to any kind of sexual encounter."

She didn't answer immediately. "*Any*thing? Ever?"

I attempted to regain my dignity, such as it could be. "Anything, ever." I met her eyes with mine. "I am a virgin, Low. In every possible way. When we held hands, it was the first time I've held hands with a girl. When we kissed, it was the first time. Aside from the encounter with Brittany Delaney-Price, I have never, until you, seen a naked woman in person, touched a woman's body, or been touched by a woman in any way."

"Jesus." She turned away, pacing to the sliding glass door, arms crossed over her chest, one hand lifted to toy with a curl of hair.

I couldn't help the way my eyes followed the sway and bounce of her buttocks, the way one cheek tilted and shifted as she leaned her weight on one leg, the other slightly bent.

"You can't be all that surprised," I said. "Surely it was obvious in everything I did that I was either a virgin or very, very inexperienced."

"No, I'm not surprised." She turned around, eyes blazing. "And I don't care. Does that make me a horrible person? Did I…do you feel like I took advantage of you? Did I pull you into my web of seduction? Did I defile you?"

I stepped toward her. "*No*, Low! You didn't take advantage of me. I knew exactly what I was doing, and I made every choice at every step of the way out of my own free will. You didn't defile me. You didn't seduce me—well, at least, not in a way that I would view negatively." I swallowed hard, a knot in my throat. "This is…it's on *me*, Low. It's *my* issues causing this. Not you."

"Why does there have to be an issue?" she asked.

"Because—" I broke off, had to start again. "Because I still don't understand you, or what you want from me, or how you could like me, or how you could enjoy anything that's happened. How someone like you could want to be with someone like me. An awkward autistic virgin, more interested in robots and quantum physics and Shakespeare than people or TV. I'm difficult and complicated—I'm a freak. And you're—"

She cut in again, that note of anger in her voice once more. "Xavier, you're *not*—"

"I *am*!" I shouted. "It's exactly what I am! I've

come to grips with that, and for the most part, I'm okay with it. Then I met you and—I finally understood what I've been missing out on all these years... and what we just did—what I let you do to me and what I did to you? I finally understand what desire really is. I know I'm weird, and hard to understand and be around. I want to believe you when you say you understand, but I just...can't. Most people would be able to get past something like this, see a therapist, or give themselves time and just eventually let it go. I can't. I've tried and I *am* trying, but I just...can't."

She moved closer to me. "You *can*, Xavier. Did you think you could ever get through something like what we just did together?"

I laughed bitterly. "Not in a million years." I gestured between us. "And I'm not exactly *getting through it*, am I?"

"You are—we are...*we* are." She sounded...upset. Hurt. Confused. Anxious, scared—I couldn't parse it all, couldn't perform the emotional calculus to understand her. "Just...*try*, Xavier. Keep trying."

I shook my head, backing away from her. "I can't. I can't." I jammed my feet into my jeans and snagged up my shoes, and socks. "You're too much. You're perfect, and you're incredible. You've given me—more than I can express, but I—I just can't do this." I moved past her, through the door, jogging down the stairs and onto the deck.

She followed me, the bedsheet wrapped around her torso, the edges flapping in the breeze as she stood on the deck mere inches behind me. "Don't run from this, Xavier. Please."

I was breathing heavily, not daring to turn around, not daring to look at her. "I don't know how to do this."

I smelled her behind me, felt her behind me. "Xavier—"

"I'm sorry. For everything." Then I left…again.

But not before I heard her answer, "I'm not."

Harlow

ONCE AGAIN, I STOOD WITH MY HEART BLEEDING IN MY throat, watching Xavier literally run away from me. He had his shoes and socks in one hand, running down the docks at a pace so punishing it seemed impossible he could sustain it, yet he did sustain it until after he was out of sight.

When he was gone, I sank onto the chaise lounge, loosely wrapped in a bed sheet, the cool wind off the water pebbling my skin.

Autistic.

A virgin.

The virgin part wasn't a surprise. It didn't bother me, either. He was within a couple years of my own age and he was an adult both cognitively and legally. He was clearly capable of making his own decisions. He was a man, just…a sexually inexperienced one. In some ways his inexperience made a physical relationship with him all the more fun and exciting and different and unique, in ways he was probably embarrassed by. When he forgot to be overwhelmed and just indulged in his senses, he exuded wonder and awe and appreciation and passion and desire. He kissed like he'd been created for that singular purpose. When he touched me and went down on me—which he'd done without hesitation or qualm—he was hesitant at first and then increasingly masterful and dizzying.

I didn't regret a single thing I'd done with him—and I didn't feel bad about any of it. I just wish I'd been able to understand how deeply he'd been affected by what that bitch had done to him, so I could be more…I don't know…better at helping him past the trauma to a place where he could simply enjoy sex.

The autism aspect was more concerning. I'd had no clue autism was a spectrum until he'd told me and explained it. Did it mean he was handicapped in some way? Not from my perspective, no. He'd always seemed one hundred percent self-aware, aware of me, and capable of and willing to make decisions for himself with total understanding of risk versus reward. He was just…*different*. Superior, in many ways, to anyone I'd ever met. Socially, sure, he didn't quite fit into the average or normal boxes. But that was part of what made him so fresh and interesting and attractive. Yeah, he was awkward at times. Hard to understand at times. Impossible to predict, always. But talking to him, being with him, being around him—it was a blast of fresh air to someone like me, having spent so many years among a crowd of a certain type.

At NYU, in the fine arts program, you could reliably expect everyone to be smart, well educated, sophisticated, creative, artistic, difficult, mostly wealthy—with all the usual foibles and quirks of being all of those things. Of course there were outliers and the different; as you get everywhere you go, whatever you do. And then in Hollywood everyone is an actor, or has a script they're working on, everyone is waiting for a callback or script approval or for the right producer to discover their material. In the industry, people fall into predictable camps and cliques and circles. In the A-list world, things get even smaller despite having the entire world at your fingertips—you trust few people, allow fewer still into your inner world. Even seeing the world is done through a filter, through the screen of wealth and celebrity, dodging fans and crowds and anticipating recognition, and being catered to and fawned over. Those are good things, amazing things which few will ever have, making me absurdly fortunate, and I know it. Yet, it is a closeted way of life and it eventually gets old.

Xavier…he fits into none of the molds or archetypes I've seen anywhere, he fits into no group, no clique. To him, I suppose, that made him a freak, but to me…it was as refreshing and exhilarating as being in the fresh air and natural beauty of Alaska after living in the smog and urban chaos of LA.

I was…

He'd been gone less than five minutes, and I missed him.

Still sitting on the chaise lounge wrapped in a sheet, I glanced to the deck and saw his T-shirt, forgotten; I picked it up, sniffed it, inhaling his scent. I shrugged into it and discarded the sheet as I snagged my laptop and went back inside and connected to the Internet. I began researching Autism Spectrum Disorder and the high-functioning end of the scale, and what it looked like, what it meant psychologically and socially, emotionally and physically.

A million questions assaulted me as I researched and read, and began to understand a bit more of what made Xavier tick in terms of ASD, and how that related to the situation I found myself in with him.

Was the touch and sensory issue connected? That led me down a whole new rabbit hole of research and articles and websites, and what I learned once again made more sense because of my experience with him.

He'd never been officially diagnosed, he'd said. How had this been missed his whole life? Could anything have been done to help him learn to cope and function, if he'd had a proper early diagnosis? According to what he'd said of his childhood, he'd sort of raised himself, with his older brother helping out as much as he could. Which was how it had been missed, clearly. He'd figured it out himself while trying to understand why he was so different.

I imagined a young Xavier, isolated, lonely, feeling trapped in his own head, unable to form normal friendships, without the love and support of either mother or father—he seems to love and look up to his eldest brother, but no matter how good an elder sibling does at playing parent, I doubt it could ever be the same. I imagined him trying desperately to figure himself out, to find a way to fit in, to be normal, or at least understand why he didn't…wasn't…couldn't.

If he couldn't form a basic friendship because expressing emotions was difficult or impossible, if he was hypersensitive, if he had suffered emotional trauma at the hands of cruel high schoolers, if he already had difficulty trusting his own judgment let alone trusting another person…how could he ever have a normal relationship?

My heart squeezed, twisted, cracked.

And I'd been angling for a casual sexual relationship. Jesus.

I know I had no way of knowing. But still.

Clearly, that wasn't going to be possible.

Was a romantic relationship even possible?

I still had no idea how he felt about me. Was he mad at me for pushing a physical relationship on him? I didn't think I'd intentionally manipulated him, or seduced him in any kind of malicious way. I just...I wanted him. I'd seen evidence that he wanted me, but he'd been hesitant to follow that desire.

Guilt and shame hit like a lightning bolt. I'd been assuming, either consciously or subconsciously—or a bit of both, really—that he was hesitant because of who I am, because of what I look like. I'd been approaching him the whole time as the woman who'd literally been told her whole life how gorgeous and sexy and desirable she was, as the woman used to being pursued and ogled and pestered and desired and obsessed over, as the woman chased by paparazzi hoping for a single photograph of me which would be sold for thousands of dollars, as the woman who could have any man she wanted with a snap of her fingers.

Xavier had no interest in any of that. He had no idea who I was, what my background was. He was just...attracted to me. Physically, obviously. But also for who I am…

He was attracted to *Low.*

Not Harlow Grace, movie star and sex symbol.

Low, just a girl.

Worse yet, he'd left hints and clues all along that weren't just weird or a little different, they were the source of uniqueness that went beyond simple personality quirks. The way he'd occasionally pat the sides of his legs, or seem to get lost in his thoughts while staring at a wave or a bird or a pattern on the floor, the way whenever he looked directly at me, it seemed…forced, or difficult for him. As if direct eye-to-eye contact was something he'd learned would make him seem more "normal" so he'd learned to fake it. There were so many things, now that I knew what to look for.

But I'd been selfish. Seeing only what I wanted and not really ever taking into consideration, truly, what he was saying. What he meant. How everything I said and did affected him.

Had I pushed him too far?

God, what a mess.

I put the laptop aside and sat on my private balcony, cocooned in the warmth and masculine scent of his T-shirt.

I should just go back to LA. Forget all this. Forget him, forget us.

Which was ridiculous, because it was now late at night, at least one in the morning—I'd spent countless hours researching and reading online. But yet, sunglasses at night were the norm in my world, and I felt more secure with them on, so I wore them despite the darkness of the night.

It only took a quick Google search to come up with an address for Badd's Bar and Grill, about a mile and a half away straight down the docks. Firming up my resolve to do what I could to fix the mess I'd made, I started walking, following the water.

It was dark, with heavy clouds blocking out the sky and a thick fog hanging low, sprinkling my face with cool mist as I walked. I was the only one out at this hour, and my footsteps echoed loudly on the wood of the docks, making my walk that much lonelier, somehow.

Halfway there, panic hit. What if his whole family was there? What if the bar was full of patrons and I got mobbed without security or a car or a driver or even Emily around to shield me?

What if Xavier didn't want to see me?

...and the way he'd taken off, that wouldn't surprise me.

God, I'd made a damn mess of things.

I stopped, a hand on a wooden pylon, equal parts fear and ridiculous hope warring within me. Fear that he'd turn me away, fear that I'd hurt him too much, that I'd pushed him away, fear that I'd get recognized. Hope that he might still want to talk to me, want to see me, or at least give me a chance to explain.

What I'd say, I had no idea.

On impulse, I pulled my phone out of my pocket and turned it on—I'd snagged it on the way out, just in case. I dialed a number.

"Hello, Miss Grace," the pleasant male voice on the other end answered on the second ring despite the late hour. "How can I help you?"

"I need the crew back on the boat as soon as possible. I would like to move on." I swallowed hard. "As soon as possible."

"Certainly, ma'am. I will alert the crew. They'll be ready to cast off within twenty-four hours."

"Thank you."

"My pleasure, Miss Grace."

I hung up, switched the phone back off without checking emails or calls or messages or social media, and resumed my walk.

There.

Now the decision was made—I would say what I needed to say, and I would leave Xavier in peace. This whole thing had been stupid in the first place, and has all been my fault. He had a status quo before he met me, a life that, from everything he said, he was content resting on the backs of two chairs, both of which were occupied by women, both on the shorter side, and blonde. Another man, younger than the others but perhaps older than Xavier, his long hair in a ponytail, also sat at the bar, and beside him a dark-skinned woman with thick black dreadlocks. There was a redhead, a woman with thick, loose, straight black hair, another man with longish, messy brown hair, his arm around yet another stunning blonde.

I stood in the middle of the bar—empty except for them—and realized this was Xavier's family. His brothers and their wives and girlfriends.

And they were all looking at me.

The tallest man, who also looked to be the oldest—making him Sebastian, I thought—waved at me. "Come on in and grab a chair. Don't mind us." He sidled away from the group as I approached the bar. "What can I getcha?"

I took a chair well away from the group, sitting down nervously, trying to figure out what to do next, now that I was here. "Um. White wine?"

He withdrew two bottles from a small cooler under the counter and thudded them in front of me at an angle, eying the labels. "We got Kendall Jackson, and…however the fuck you pronounce this French bullshit."

I smiled despite my nerves. "I'll take the French

bullshit. Thank you."

He popped the cork, flipped a stem glass around a finger with a practiced flourish, and poured a generous amount. "There ya go. Pay now or start a tab?"

I swallowed hard. "I—actually…um…"

He frowned slightly, waiting, and then laughed when I came up empty. "Need a minute to decide? No worries. Just don't try and run off past Bax without paying. That big motherfucker is *fast*." He said this with a wink, moving back to the cluster of his family.

One of the women was looking at me hard—Claire, the diminutive, exhibitionist girlfriend of Xavier's brother Brock, who I recognized standing behind her. I'd met them both, sort of, when we'd borrowed their fishing gear. And now Claire was eying me.

She got up off her chair and took the one next to me. "Hi. You're Xavier's friend, aren't you? Low? We met the other day."

I nodded, keeping my eyes on my wine. "Yeah. That's me."

She wasn't very friendly, at the moment. "I don't know with happened with you two, but he came back here at a dead run, half-naked, and acting more upset than I've ever seen him."

"I know." I took a fortifying sip of wine. "I…I'm actually here to—"

Someone else came up to stand between Claire and me—she was tall with platinum blonde hair done in a neat twist, wearing yoga pants cinched at the knee with an off-the-shoulder sweatshirt, looking effortlessly elegant.

"Hey, I'm Aerie," she said, extending a hand to mine, which I shook without making more eye contact than necessary.

"Low," I offered, still hoping to make it out of this without a scene.

Claire was still staring hard at me. "Not to be rude or whatever, but would you mind taking off your sunglasses for a minute?"

I hedged. "I'd rather not."

She snorted. "You ashamed of yourself for hurting poor sweet innocent Xavier and can't look me in the eye?"

"Is he here?" I asked, my voice barely audible.

"I dunno," Claire said, her voice razor sharp. "That depends on why you're here…and what happened to upset him."

I breathed out shakily. "What happened is kind of between him and me, but just…I didn't mean to hurt him, and I just want to talk to him."

Aerie was now staring hard at me, but in a different way. "You look familiar."

I took another long drink. "You must be mistaken."

She shook her head. "No, I don't think so. I know you, somehow." Her eyes flicked over the explosion of curls springing out from the back of my cap. "I'm certain I've seen you, or met you somewhere."

"We've never met, I can guarantee you that." The truth, at least.

Why was I drawing this out? I was here to make peace with Xavier, wasn't I?

I sighed, realizing it would be better in the long run to just get it over with.

Slowly, I drew the hat off and removed the sunglasses, and shook my hair out. I didn't say my name—I didn't have to.

Aerie's breath caught. "Harlow Grace," she breathed.

Claire's jaw dropped. "*You're* Xavier's friend?"

I tossed the hat and sunglasses on the bar. "Yeah."

"Holy shit." She laughed, then. "He was hanging out with *Harlow Grace* and never told any of us?"

Brock, her boyfriend or husband or whatever, heard that. "Who was hanging out with Harlow Grace and didn't tell us?" he asked, pivoting to join the conversation; then, he saw me. "Holy shit, it's Harlow Grace. In our bar."

"Goddammit," I muttered under my breath. "Here we go."

Brock howled in laughter, as if something

hysterical had happened which I'd missed. "Yo, Bast! Come get a load of this!"

The bartender, who was indeed Sebastian, the oldest, ambled over, eyeing me warily. "What?"

Brock gestured at me. "You know who she is?"

He frowned. "Seen you in a few movies I think, but..." The penny dropped, then. "Harlow Grace. That's you, yeah?

"Yes," I said, a little too loudly and with a little too much irritation—but these weren't random fans, these were Xavier's family. "I'm Harlow Grace."

"She's also the *friend*—" here, Claire sarcastically emphasized the word, "Xavier has been hanging out with lately."

Bast's intimidating gaze turned scary. "*You're* his friend? Low?"

I nodded. "Yeah."

"He showed up all freaked out a while ago. Care to explain that?" Bast demanded.

"We're all pretty protective of our boy, you see," I heard from behind me—Bax, the bouncer, had appeared.

"I—um. It was...a misunderstanding," I said.

Lucian, the long-haired brother, spoke for the first time. "Does he know that?"

I couldn't answer. I just kept my eyes on my wine.

"Oh *hell* no, bitch, you did *not*," Claire snapped;

apparently she was the one with the fewest shits to give.

I jerked my head up to glare at her, my eyes blazing. "Now just hold on a damn minute—you don't know me, or our situation, and you certainly do not get sit there judging me and calling me names!"

Claire crossed her arms over her chest. "I sure as fuck do get to sit here judging and calling names, *bitch*—that's my brother-in-law we're talking about and he's…Xavier isn't the kind of person you can just go and fuck with his head and his heart and think he'll be okay with it. He's not like that."

I felt my eyes prickling and burning, a knot in my throat. "I know. I know that…now."

"Yeah, *now…after* you fucked with his head." This was from Aerie.

Bast, as they called him, had his arms crossed over his massive chest, thick forearms tensed and ropy, tattoos shifting, dark brown eyes glinting. "Like Bax said, we're all pretty protective of Xavier. He's… unique."

"You think I don't realize that? Why do you think I'm here? You think I'd risk my privacy and anonymity showing up at a bar when I'm on vacation and under the radar for just anyone?" I was standing up, gesturing angrily, my voice raising. "I fucking *know* he's unique, and I get exactly why you're protective of him, but I—"

"Carried on whatever you had going on with him, in secret, when he had no idea who you were, or what getting involved with you might mean for him," the redhead pointed out. "Which is kind of shitty."

"It wasn't secret," I protested. "I just...I value my privacy, okay? I doubt any of you would understand." I blanched as I realized how that sounded. "I don't mean that as an insult to any of you, I just... being famous can be hard, okay?"

"Oh poor you! Poor Harlow Grace," Claire snarked. "You can't just go fucking around with the hearts of sweet, innocent, precious local boys just because you're rich and famous."

This girl was gonna get smacked in a second.

"You need to back off. It's not like that." I stabbed a finger at her. "And you're all acting like Xavier is incapable of making decisions for himself, like he's some helpless child or something. He's *not*."

"I'm not sure you're in a position to make that judgment call," the redhead said. "He's *our* family, and you've known him for what, a matter of days?"

"Maybe that's exactly why I *am* in a position to make that call," I said. "Because I'm seeing him more objectively than you. You're protective of him, and I get that, but just because he's high-functioning autistic doesn't make him helpless. It just makes him different."

The silence following my pronouncement was icy and fragile.

"He's *what*?" Bast asked, leaning toward me, suddenly so scary-quiet I might've peed a little. "Repeat that."

I was confused; did his family not know? "High-functioning autistic with savant tendencies." I blinked, swallowed. "Did he…I thought—"

There was a deafening chorus of questions then, all shouted at me from a dozen different directions.

At that moment, I happened to glance to my left, where Xavier was standing in the doorway of the kitchen, paper baskets full of fried food in his hands, his eyes on me.

I shot out of my seat and pushed through the shouting crowd of his family, who went silent again when they saw him. I stopped a foot from Xavier, wanting to reach for him but not daring.

"Xavier, I—"

"You are here," he said, his face and voice giving nothing away of his emotions as he set the baskets on the service bar and returned to stand in the doorway of the kitchen, as if that felt like a safe space for him. "Why are you here?" This last part was flat, a question spoken as a statement.

"I'm—I hate how we left things, Xavier."

He glanced past me at his family. "I heard the last part of your conversation with my family. My autism is not something I speak of to anyone. None of them knew. I had hoped to keep it that way."

I blinked back tears. "Xavier, I'm sorry, I'm *so* sorry—I didn't know they didn't know. I didn't mean to betray your trust."

He breathed in deeply and let it out slowly, his gaze flicking to mine briefly and then away, then back, taking in my clothing. Once more, his eyes flitted past me, this time to Claire. "Claire."

The tiny but explosive blonde came over to stand by him, putting herself between me and Xavier. "Hi, Xavier."

"Hello, Claire." He spoke without quite looking at her directly; I had a feeling he was keeping his emotions, whatever they may have been, on total lockdown; his hands were at his side, fisted, as if it was taking every ounce of willpower not to pat them against his legs. "You said several things I do not understand."

"What's that?"

He looked at me, then at Claire. "You called her Harlow Grace. Who is Harlow Grace? Her name is Low." He held up one finger. "That is the first thing. Second, you said, quote, 'you can't just go around fucking with the hearts of sweet, innocent, precious local boys just because you're rich and famous,' end quote." He paused for almost a minute. "How is she fucking with my heart? Why am I a sweet and innocent and precious local boy? Those words make me sound like…like an anime character with wide, shimmering eyes. Like a boy. Like a child. Is that how you see me?" He paused again, and then continued, his voice still hard and flat. "The third item of my confusion is related the previously quoted statement—the word 'famous.' Rich I understand, given her ownership of a large yacht. But…famous? Please elucidate that claim."

His eyes went to me again, not looking at me directly, but rather looking at me as if trying to see me differently. His jaw was flexing, and his hands, fisted, were beginning to knock against his thighs, and he was staring at me without blinking, as if the whirlwind in his head was howling so loudly his control was shredding.

It took everything inside me to hold back the tears. "Xavier, I—"

"Allow Claire to answer, if you please," he interrupted.

Claire sighed. "Her name isn't Low, Xavier. That's a nickname. Her real name is Harlow Grace, and she's a movie star. Like, a really, *really* famous one. And…I don't know what's going on with the two of you, but the chances of her intentions regarding spending time with you being totally innocent are… practically nil. Which is what I meant about fucking with your heart. I've never seen you interested in a woman, Xavier, and I've always just kind of assumed you're a…well—a virgin, which makes you innocent. And you're sweet, and you're precious to me. I don't mean any of that as an insult, Xavier. You know I love you like a brother, right? I'm just trying to look out for you."

"You are a famous movie star?" he asked, his eyes shooting toward me, but not looking *at* me, like he sometimes did.

I sighed. "Yes, I am."

"Which is why you asked with such close interest about my television watching habits." He blinked at me, his expression still blank. "You wanted to know if I knew who you were."

"Yes."

"Which means you intentionally kept the truth of your identity a secret from me."

I blinked back tears, which trickled down my cheek. "Yes." I reached for him, but he backed away. "I'm sorry, Xavier."

"Why?" he asked. "Why lie, even by omission? Do you not trust me with the truth? Am I not worthy of the truth?" There was a tremor in his voice on the last sentence, and that, more than anything else, broke my heart.

"It wasn't about any of that. It was…" I breathed deeply through my nose, trying to keep some kind of control over myself. "It was selfish, I admit. People look at me like…like a commodity. Like they know me, like they own me, like they have a right to me. Anywhere I go, whatever I'm doing, I'm photographed and watched and pointed at. Anyone I meet, they only see me as Harlow Grace, the celebrity, the movie star, the sex symbol. They see me for my net worth, for my filmography. They want to know if…" I shook my head, brushing tears away. "*You* didn't look at me like that. You just looked at me like…like a guy looks at a girl he's interested in. And I wanted that."

He didn't respond, even facially, so I had no idea if he'd even heard me.

Eventually he did speak. "There are so many things I am confused about, so many things causing me to feel…a great many intense emotions. Hurt, I believe, foremost among them. Betrayed, perhaps. Used, possibly. I also understand the logic of your reasoning, so I cannot entirely fault you, but my ability to trust is…a rather fragile thing, I am afraid."

"Xavier, you have to know that I…" I swallowed a hot hard knot in my throat; the swirl of emotions inside me baffled me with their intensity. "I kept my celebrity status from you, yes. But everything else I said, everything we did, every moment we spent together…it was all *real*. I meant everything. You have to believe me."

"I want to." He unclenched his fists and shook them out. "I am trying to."

"This whole thing with us, Xavier—it's…it's more than I ever thought it was."

"I do not know what that means."

"She means she started out looking for a quick and easy hookup with a local," Claire said; I'd become so focused on Xavier that I had forgotten we had an audience. "But now she's realizing she has actual feelings for you."

Claire's man—her husband, boyfriend, fiancé, whatever they were—stepped up behind her, pulling her away. "Claire, babe, I think maybe we let Xavier handle this from here."

"Hookup?" Xavier asked. "Meaning a sexual encounter devoid of emotional investment, intended from the outset to last for a limited timeframe."

"Yeah, buddy," Bax said, "that's a pretty good definition."

Xavier's gaze went to me, direct this time, for a moment or two at least. "Is that what you intended?"

I let out a shaky breath. "Yes, and no. When we

met, all I knew was you were a hot local guy who was a little…different. And yeah, I'm on vacation so I'm only here for a temporary stay, which meant whatever we ended up as, it'd be temporary."

"I am not capable of such a thing. Even if I was not a virgin, I do not think I could engage in a sexual encounter with someone I was not invested in, to at least some degree."

"I didn't know that then."

Claire glanced between Xavier and me. "Wait, so are you still a virgin?"

Brock huffed in irritation. "Not our business, Claire."

"No," I said, shooting a glare at her. "It's really not."

Claire just rolled her eyes. "Whatever. Bite me."

I frowned. "Why are being so nasty to me? What did I do to you?"

"We all care about Xavier a lot, and we all just want to protect him from getting hurt," Brock answered for her; he shot a meaningful glance at Claire as he continued. "Claire is just expressing her protectiveness in a less than helpful way."

Claire whirled on Brock. "You better watch it, bub! I can speak for my fucking self." She turned back to me. "When someone I love is hurt, I turn into Mama Bear. And you're just lucky Mara's not here, or she'd have already kicked your ass."

"Word," Zane, the other scarily enormous bartender said.

"Can we back up for one second?" Bax said. "I feel compelled to point out that Xavier has been hanging out with and possibly messing around with *Harlow Grace*, and I for one would like to just take a moment to bow down to your game, little brother, because *damn*." His action suited his words, bowing at the waist toward Xavier, arms extended in a deep, pantomime bow. "Also, Claire, you *are* being kinda salty. You know I love your skank ass, but Harlow *did* come here, apparently, to make things right, so maybe...you know...cut her some slack?"

"I'll cut your slack dick off, is what I'll cut," Claire snapped.

The woman with jet-black hair left her stool for the first time. Until now, she'd watched the proceedings in silence. Now, she took Claire by the shoulders and spoke in a soft, gentle tone. "Claire, honey, no one is faulting you for being protective. But there's no need to be antagonistic toward Miss Grace."

"I just...I get so *mad*, Eva," Claire said, deflating. "All the boys are special to me, you know that, we've talked about it. But Xavier is just...he's *Xavier*. And the thought of some big-shot Hollywood superstar waltzing in and messing with him when he's such a gentle and special soul, it just…I just get—"

"I know, I know," the other woman, Eva, said. "But Brock was right when he suggested we let Xavier handle this in private."

"There is nothing to handle," Xavier said, shoving his hands into his jeans pockets and heading into the kitchen. "I am leaving, now. I have to think."

"Xavier, wait," I said, following him a step. "Can we please talk in private?"

"There is nothing to talk about," he said, not turning around or slowing down. "You said yourself that you are leaving, so whatever may have happened between us is done, I would think."

"It doesn't have to be, though," I said, choking back that stupid knot in my throat yet again. "I don't want it to be."

"Why? You are a famous movie star, and I am just…me. An awkward local boy."

"I never said that," I protested. "And I never acted like that toward you, did I?"

He stopped, then, facing a counter in the kitchen, toying with a pair of tongs. "No, you did not. You always seemed to be genuine."

"Because I *was* being genuine. I was never pretending. I meant everything I said." My voice dropped to a whisper. "What happened with us today, Xavier… that meant more to me than you know."

withdrawn, or weepy, or clingy; in a role I could be trashy or elegant, wild or reserved. I could be what I didn't know how to be in real life.

In my relationship with Harrison, I was the affectionate girlfriend, as much the instigator of sex as him, as prone to needing a night out with my friends away from him as he was; loyal and fun, not jealous, eager to please…but not deeply emotionally invested. I had cared about Harrison, and I had enjoyed our relationship, but…

Wherever this intensity toward Xavier was coming from, whatever it was, whatever it meant, it was coming from a much deeper place, a raw, unfiltered, primal place.

So, I cried.

I sobbed.

In front of strangers, in front of his family, in front of him, I sobbed.

Because I couldn't do anything else.

ELEVEN

Xavier

EVER SINCE BAST MET AND MARRIED DRU, I HAD BECOME used to the presence of women in my life. Until then, women were something that happened to other people. There were professors at Stanford and teachers in high school, and bus drivers and waitresses and strangers, but no one that penetrated the veil of my daily life.

Until Dru.

Since then, I've seen Dru cry, but only once—she cut herself cooking and required a large number of stitches to her left hand, and she cried as I held a towel around her injury while Bast guided her to the truck.

I've seen Eva cry, and Aerie, and even Claire—but

I wasn't supposed to, and she made me promise not to tell anyone.

I've seen them cry. But none of it was connected to me. They weren't crying to me, or for me, or because of me, or about me.

Low was crying in all those ways right now.

And not just crying, but sobbing. As if the pain was simply too great to fathom, and the great shuddering racking sobs were the only possible outlet for them.

Her tears made me panic.

What was I supposed to do?

I glanced at Bast, and he just inclined his head toward Low in a gesture whose meaning eluded me. Go to her? But do what? Hug her? Apologize? Ask her to stop? What did one do with a woman you'd made cry?

Why was she crying?

She'd wanted a hookup. Something temporary. I understood how that worked—I'd seen my brothers carry on hookups by the dozen; they met a girl they were attracted to, used their "game" to bring them home, had sex with them, and then that was it. That was the whole of it.

I couldn't do that.

Even if I wasn't a virgin, such behavior was anathema to my personality.

People were either just people—outside my world, outside my life, and ephemeral—or they were inside my world, inside my life, and I was fiercely attached to them. I didn't hug as my brothers liked to do, but I loved them all ferociously, in my own way. I could never walk away from them, never leave them. Not now. If I'd stayed in California, perhaps it would be different, but living here with them and having this ever-growing tribe of family members who knew me and loved me and accepted me despite my aberrant behavior…it wasn't something I could ever do without.

Meaning, in my mind, in my heart, you were either family—inside, close, needed and necessary and mine—or you were no one.

And sex? How could I casually do something I'd never done before? How could I give her something like that, something important and precious to me, and then just watch her leave? I couldn't. Even now, after what we'd shared, it was cutting me to pieces to know there could be nothing else, because I could feel an attachment to her forming.

Or, more correctly, it had already formed.

She was already inside me, wrapped around my mind and heart and soul like tangling vines of ivy.

She was still sobbing, and I had no idea what to do.

The panic was growing, mounting—*do* something! Make it stop. Her pain was palpable, knifing into me, merging with and becoming my own pain.

I felt my body moving forward.

She had her face covered with both hands. Shoulders shaking. Her whole body was stiff and tense and shaking. She was turned away from me, toward a wall, as if to hide her brokenness.

I wanted to comfort her and to stop her tears.

Not wanted to—I *needed* to. I had to.

I caught her wrists in my hands, pulling them gently away from her face. "Low, stop. Please…please stop crying. It hurts me too much to see you crying this way."

She pulled out of my grip and turned away, crying harder, saying something the force of her tears made unintelligible to me.

Panic had me in its grip, and the need to comfort her, to stop her crying was total.

I moved up behind her, wrapped my arms around her shoulders, breathing past the initial sting of discomfort at the touch. Clasping her shoulders in my hands, I turned her around to face me. Her hands dropped, and she looked up at me, tears streaking down her cheeks.

"No more crying," I whispered, brushing tears away from her cheeks with my thumbs.

I kissed her, then.

It was desperation, both as the only thing I could think of to quiet her, to calm her, to comfort her, and desperation of my own to simply feel the dizzying electric thrill kissing her gave me. That thrill was a drug, and I was addicted.

I knew better.

I knew she was going to leave.

But I had to kiss her anyway.

I heard shocked exclamations from my brothers and the women, but I tuned them out and focused on her, on her waist in my hands, her lips on mine, moving now, seeking mine, seeking more, on her hips nudging against mine, her hands lifting to bury in my hair, sobs escaping into the kiss, the salt of her tears on my tongue.

"Holy shit! It's Harlow Grace!" a voice I didn't recognize shouted, and the shout was accompanied by a flurry of smartphone camera clicks.

The moment was shattered.

A cluster of tourists had stumbled in, at least fifteen of them, all looking well on their way to inebriation.

"Bax, you lousy fuck, you forgot to lock the door," Bast snarled.

"Hey, there was shit going on, okay?" Bax snapped back, moving toward the tourists. "And

noise and commotion.

"Come on," I murmured to her. "This way."

I led her to the stairs, trying to ignore the shouts and questions, the photographs. The noise physically hurt, making my head swell and slam and throb, making my skin feel too tight, making panic swirl in my head like a fireball.

Away, away—I had to get away.

Low was in my arms, shaking, and I yanked open the door, ushered her through, and closed the door behind us. Not realizing we were in a staircase, Low tripped on the first step, and I caught her, my hands on her hips, pulling her upright. She jogged up the steps, eager to get as far from the din as possible.

I didn't stop, but led her to my room, closing the door behind us and locking it. Low crossed to my bed and sank down onto it, leaning over her knees, burying her face in her hands, and heaving a shuddering sigh.

"That's why I came to Alaska," she muttered, "to get away from *that*."

"You go through that often?" I asked, incredulous.

She barked a laugh. "That's nothing. I get swarms of hundreds of people on a daily basis. If I go out in public in LA, I need security and a getaway driver to deal with the crowds."

My heart flipped. "That must be awful."

She shrugged. "It's part of the job. Usually I'll

stop and take a few selfies and sign a few autographs, but today I just…I couldn't."

"You really are famous," I breathed. "Those people knew you by sight. They were…crazy. Rabid, almost."

She laughed again. "That's how it is, Xavier. Welcome to my life."

"Those men…they acted like you should want to date them simply because…I don't even know. I cannot fathom their thought processes."

"They think because they saw me in a movie, I'll just…I don't know, fall in love with them and bring them into my glamorous movie star life and buy them sports cars and service their sexual desires day and night."

"That is patently absurd," I said.

"Yes. But that's how most men treat me." She sighed. "That's not true. The vast majority of my male fans are content with a selfie or an autograph. Sometimes guys will cop a feel, or make a bad joke, but I've got security for that. But guys like that, back there?" She shook her head, her eyes going to mine. "*That's* why I didn't tell you who I was, Xavier. Because I was afraid of *that*."

"I would never treat you like that—or anyone for that matter."

She nodded, tearing up again. "I know. I know

that now." She breathed out shakily. "And then it was just...it was so...so amazing, so wonderful to just be *Low*, to be no one special, just a girl with a guy she liked, and I just couldn't...I couldn't tell you."

"You *are* someone special," I said. "But not because you're famous—just because of who you are."

She laughed through tears. "There you go again with that shit."

"It's not shit, Low, it's the truth."

"I know, I know." She smiled at me as I stood facing her, hands shoved into my pockets to keep them from ticking or spasming or flapping or patting. "I only call it shit because I get so melty and weak when you talk to me like that."

"Like what?" I asked. "Like I care?"

"Yes," she laughed, through a quiet sob. "Exactly. Like you care."

"But I do."

"And so do I."

The silence between us was no longer easy or comfortable but filled with a million questions, none of which seemed to have an answer. For me, at least.

"You're still going to go back to Hollywood," I said, eventually, sitting on the bed next to her.

"Yes."

"So what are we supposed to do? What can this be?"

She didn't answer. Instead, she toed off her sneakers and lay back on the bed, horizontally across the width. "I'm exhausted, Xavier. I hate crying."

"Sleep, then," I said, standing up. "I can sleep on the couch."

She sat up abruptly, catching at my sleeve. "Don't. Please—don't leave."

"Then I will sleep on the floor."

She stared at me. "Sleep with me."

"I—we—" I stammered.

"I mean *just* sleep."

"Won't that only serve to confuse the issue of our emotions?"

"Probably. But I don't want to be alone." She lay down on the bed, on the far side, against the wall, on top of the blankets. "Please? Just...be here with me. Just for tonight."

Has anyone ever been so torn as I was in that moment? Half of me wanted nothing more than to climb into that bed with her, to know what it felt like to simply hold her in my arms, to smell her lush, comforting, feminine scent and feel her warmth and the weight of her body against me; the other half wanted to run and hide, because that half knew if I got into that bed, I would become even more attached than I already was, which would make her departure all the more agonizing for me.

My hesitation was obvious, and Low's face fell. "If you don't want to, I'll understand," she said, sitting up again.

"It isn't that I don't want to," I said.

She inhaled deeply, closing her eyes and holding her breath, and then sliding forward to rise up from my bed. "I'll just go." She moved across the room, grabbing her sneakers and pausing to stand beside me in the middle of the room, reaching up to lay her palm on my cheek. "I never meant to hurt you, Xavier. And I certainly don't want to hurt you, or confuse you, more than I already have."

She made it to the door, her hand on the knob, before I found my voice.

"Wait," I whispered, my voice rasping. "Stay."

I sat on my bed, unlaced my shoes, slipped them off and set them aside, I removed my socks and tossed them into my hamper, and then rose again, returning to where Low was still hesitating by the door.

I took her by the hand and led her to the bed, turned back the blankets, and sat down on the edge.

Low resisted my tug, standing by the bed in front of me. "It was a bad idea. I should go."

"I would like you to stay. As you said, only for sleep. Nothing sexual, only mutual comfort."

She hesitated a moment more, and then sighed

as if she'd just let down a heavy weight. "Mutual comfort."

Low sat beside me. "You want the inside or the outside?"

I wrinkled my brow. "I do not know. I have never shared a bed before."

"Well, where on the bed do you usually sleep?"

"The middle."

She laughed. "Oh. Well, it's not a very big bed, so I'm not sure we'll both fit in the middle."

"I will take the outside," I said. "I do not think being between a body and the wall would be restful for me."

Low nodded, smiling. "That's fine with me. I actually tend to prefer the right side of the bed anyway. It's where I always end up even when I'm alone."

My mind supplied unhelpful images of her in bed with other men, and those images made my stomach roil and my heart contract painfully. "Have you shared a bed frequently?"

Low frowned. "Um…I mean, just for sleep?"

"Yes." I studied the floorboards under my feet.

"No…actually." She glanced at me; I felt her gaze, but avoided looking at her, until she ducked so I had to meet her eyes. "Does the idea of me sharing a bed with someone else upset you?"

I left the bed and went to my desk, where I had

a handful of robot creations I had recently finished, which only needed a few finishing touches; I sat down, opened a crate of parts, and began tinkering.

"Yes," I said, after a moment.

"You feel jealous?"

I added a few little LED lights to one robot, creating the impression of a face. "I feel jealous of you, yes. My understanding of social boundaries informs me that to feel this jealousy of you when we have known each other for such a short time, and have not committed to any kind of relationship…is probably not acceptable."

I felt her watching me work. "I've only ever had one other serious relationship, with a guy named Harrison. We dated for a couple years while I was at NYU, but we never lived together, and rarely spent the night together." She hesitated. "And…none of my other relationships, such as they have been, were of a kind that we would sleep together."

"They were based on a physical relationship, you mean."

"Yeah." A pause. "Does that upset you?"

"It causes an uncomfortable amount of jealousy, yes. But I cannot logically feel jealousy in relation to your life before you knew me. And even now, I do not think jealousy is appropriate, considering the inherently temporary nature of our relationship…

such as it is."

I heard her leave the bed; felt her beside me, kneeling on the floor next to my desk chair. "You're back to talking to me in the Spock voice."

I finished adding the last pieces to my creation, plugged it into my desktop computer and tested the programming. "Which is upsetting to you."

"Yes, it is," she said. "I like it when you look at me and talk to me like yourself."

"The Spock voice, as you call it, *is* me. It's just..." I trailed off.

"A way of expressing yourself when you're uncomfortable with a situation, don't know how to connect to someone, or don't understand a social situation."

I eyed her with interest. "Yes. Precisely."

"After you left, I spent several hours researching Autism Spectrum Disorder, high-functioning autism, and tips for dealing with and forming relationships with someone on the spectrum." She sat down cross-legged on the floor beside my crates of parts, picking up a piece and examining it.

"Why?" I asked.

"To try and understand you better." She rose up on her knees, peering over the surface of my desk at the little robot. "What is this thing? What's it do?"

It was a prototype of a new model I'd been

working on, with slightly more complex movements and programming; this one featured four appendages, which had hinges in the middle. It was a small box approximately four inches to a side, with the legs at the four corners on two axes, and LED lights in the front to give it a facsimile of a face, making it look, when perched on all fours, somewhat like a very tiny dog.

I unplugged the cord, set it on the floor, and pressed the power button, which activated its simple programming loop. The four-legged box sank back on its "hind" legs, the hinges folding, and it paused, then sprang forward so the "front" legs rotated at the hinge, essentially performing a flip so it was upside down and on all fours again. It hopped forward a few steps, flipped again back the other way, and then repeated the loop.

Low watched, mesmerized, giggling. "Oh my god, Xavier! That thing is adorable!" She lay down on her stomach to watch it go through the loop again. "You made it?"

"Yes. I create them and sell them. I have a website." I plucked one of my business cards from a pile on my desk and handed it to her.

"Procrastination Creations: robotic diversions, distractions, and eccentricities," Low read, "A bespoke robotics boutique by Xavier Badd."

I had never felt embarrassed by my little business before—indeed, I have always been proud of it. But now, knowing Low was a world-famous movie star, it felt a little silly.

"It's just something I do in my spare time, for fun."

She fiddled with the other unfinished bots on the desk. "I think it's amazing. So they're meant to just be fun, for a quick distraction?"

"Yes," I said. "Most of my clients keep them on their desks, and when they need a break from work, they turn it on and watch it go, and just let their minds relax."

I began finishing another prototype, this one a gimbal-based creation—it was a hollow disc about three inches across, thicker at the middle than the edges, like an old-timey representation of a UFO. It had been tricky to engineer, and I was rather proud of it. I added LED lights in strips of alternating colors in a concentric ring on the top and bottom, with the lights programmed to sync to the speed of its rotation, so the faster it spun, the faster the lights blinked, creating what I hoped would be a fairly mesmerizing spectacle. Once the programming was checked and tested, I unplugged it and turned it on to begin rotating on my desk.

"This is a brand-new model as well, and very

her blue eyes, and finding a wealth of emotions in her expression. "I can't escape you, Low. You throw my whole world into chaos. You create feelings and thoughts and desires I have no experience with, no capacity to understand, and no mechanisms for dealing with. Being around you, being with you—it sometimes feels like being thrown from an airplane and told to fly. And I do not know how to fly, nor do I have wings or a parachute."

"I don't know how to fly either, Xavier."

"But you have wings," I said. "You understand emotions. You understand people."

"That doesn't make dealing with something this new and this…this *strong* any easier for me." She reached for my hands, and I let her take them.

I searched her face again, saw tear tracks on her cheeks, sadness in her eyes, exhaustion. "Do you still want to share my bed for sleeping, Low?"

"Yes," she whispered. "Very much so."

I went to my bed and lay down, fully clothed in jeans and a T-shirt. Low stayed on the floor, a puzzled expression on her face.

"You sleep fully clothed?" she asked.

I laughed. "No. I typically do not wear anything to bed. But to be naked with you would be to invite temptation I do not think I am strong enough to deny, and I think we are not emotionally prepared for…

anything physical."

She moved to sit on the bed near my feet. "I sleep naked too. But I think you're right." She paused, and then glanced at me. "I don't know if I can sleep fully clothed, though. What if we compromised on partially clothed?"

I nodded. "That is an agreeable idea."

"So can you sleep in a pair of shorts, and I'll sleep in a T-shirt?"

I nodded, leaving the bed to find a pair of running shorts. I hesitated, then chastised myself for being shy when Low had already seen all of me. The chastisement didn't stop me from blushing, or my heart from hammering as I stepped out of my jeans and tossed my T-shirt aside, and then slid the shorts on. Low's eyes raked over me as I changed, and I wondered what it meant when her tongue slid along her lower lip, or when her teeth caught at that lip and her nostrils flared, and her fingers tangled together and tightened into a white-knuckled knot.

"You have a T-shirt I could borrow?" she asked, her voice strangely hoarse.

I opened a drawer, hesitating, and then gave her my second-favorite shirt—a faded gray one of thin, worn cotton, with the logo of a servomotor manufacturer on the right breast—the company had gifted it to me as a thank you for ordering so many parts from them, and it was the most comfortable shirt I owned, only second favorite because my first favorite was a Badd's Bar and Grill T-shirt of Dad's, which I'd stolen from his drawer immediately following his death. That shirt, however, I never wore, and kept out of sentiment.

Low's eyes stayed on mine as she unzipped her jeans and stepped out of them, she took off her sweater, and peeled out of her T-shirt, standing in front of me, then, in nothing but a matching bra and underwear, deep indigo in color, lacy, revealing, provocative. My hands fisted at my sides and my heart thundered at the sight of her clad thus, tantalizing, lushly beautiful, dizzyingly perfect, a vision of pale cream skin and freckles, delicacy and strength, curves and softness. I wanted her. My hands yearned to slide over her skin.

"Put on the shirt, please," I whispered, my throat clogged. "Before my ability to resist you is depleted."

Moving slowly, as if reluctantly, Low slid the T-shirt over her head and it dropped into place, the hem hanging at the tops of her thighs, only just hiding the indigo lace of her underwear.

Once changed, Low sat on the edge of the bed. "You ready?"

No. I wasn't. I was worried my control would slip. My desire was an inferno inside me, my need for her a volcanic pressure inside me. We both wore so little—mere moments and we could be naked together. Touching.

I swallowed hard, tried to pretend I wasn't hard as a rock inside my shorts—which was clearly visible, something I knew Low saw. I sat on the edge of the bed, swung my legs over, and lay down on my back, stiff and tense. My feet nudged against Low's thighs, and my hands were pillowed under my head.

She sighed, and crawled across the bed to lay beside me.

A foot separated us.

My heart was beating so loudly I was certain she could hear it.

After only a moment, she sat up with a hiss of irritation. "I can't sleep in a bra."

I watched, unable to help myself, as she slid her arms out of the sleeves and let the shirt hang loosely around her neck, reaching up behind her back to unclasp the bra, shrugging out of the undergarment and tossing it aside onto her pile of clothing. For a moment, then, her breasts were bare, hanging heavy and pale and spattered with freckles I longed to count and to kiss. Then she threaded her arms through the sleeves, and the shirt fell back into place.

She lay back down with a sigh. "Better."

I could only swallow, teeth grinding, and work furiously at ignoring my erection.

More moments of silence.

"Xavier?" Low asked, her voice not quite a whisper, hesitant, questing.

"Yes?

"Can I…?" She rolled to her side and shimmied closer to me, lifting her head and settling it onto the hollow between my shoulder and chest, one her hands resting on my chest near her face. "Is this okay?"

Her scent filled me; her warmth billowed against me, the silk of her skin brushed against mine in a dozen tingling points of contact. Something inside my chest expanded—a metaphysical expansion, a swelling of some nebulous but fiery emotion I had no name for.

"Yes," I murmured, wrapping my arms around her, one at her shoulders and the other around her waist. "As long as this is okay with you."

"It's perfect," she whispered.

Even beyond watching the show with her, beyond being naked and exploring her body and tasting her and exploding from her touch, this moment, merely holding her…

This was a golden moment—

It was one of those memories that seem limned in a golden light, shimmering and perfect forevermore. My most potent golden moment was a memory of being three or perhaps four years old, with my mother, walking on the docks. It was raining and we were both soaked, but we were laughing and splashing in puddles. I remember her black hair wet against her spine and her green eyes dancing with laughter, and her hand in mine. I was wearing red fireman rain boots.

This, holding Low in my arms...whatever happened next, I knew I would remember this always. A golden moment, more perfect than any other.

Slowly, her breathing evened out, and she went limp against me, fingers twitching against my chest now and then.

I lay awake long after she was asleep, inking as much of this memory into my soul as I could. Unwilling to sleep, or miss any of this feeling. Unwilling to face reality, which awaited tomorrow. Wanting only to abide in this perfect affectionate warmth as long as possible, Low's breath on my chest, a soft girlish snore, her breasts smushed softly against my ribs, a thigh over mine.

"You *have* to leave tomorrow," I whispered, "because if you don't, I'll fall in love, and then you'll break me completely."

TWELVE

Harlow

I didn't want to wake up. God, I felt so comfortable. So warm. Every molecule in my being felt…perfect. There was a golden warmth on my face, something solid and warm and smooth under my cheek. A heartbeat thumping gently, rhythmically, steadily.

But now that I was enveloped in this warm beautiful floating happiness, I didn't want to fall back asleep either. I just wanted to float here, enjoying this.

Had I ever been this perfect?

Sensations intruded into my awareness, one by one: the solidness under my cheek and the heartbeat in my ear melded with an arm across my shoulders, and then I felt a hand on my left buttock, resting naturally, easily; I heard a breath, a low sound from somewhere above my head, and then I felt a faint touch of that breathing on my hair; my thigh was draped casually over a muscled leg.

A man.

Strong. Gentle. Warm, and solid. Holding me in his arms, cradling me in a protective cocoon I never, ever wanted to leave.

Full awareness slammed into me like a lightning bolt—Xavier. His family. Crying. The tourists, the photographs.

Of me.

Kissing Xavier.

Hiding behind him.

Probably with puffy eyes and swollen lips.

Posted on the Internet.

I heard a familiar sound, then, and my heart sank and went cold at once—I heard voices, a thunderous din of them, shouting questions and recording clips.

The pap were here.

I've brought them down upon Xavier and his brothers and their women.

I wonder if they have any idea what's about to hit them, now that the world at large has gotten a glimpse of those eight men, each more gorgeous than the last.

I slipped out of Xavier's arms and tiptoed to the

window, which looked out over the street and the docks beyond it. Standing to one side of the window, I edged carefully around the edge of the frame until I could peek out.

Fuck.

It was a full-court press, at least a hundred of them, photographers and reporters and video camera teams, all clustered around the entrance to Badd's Bar and Grill.

I rolled away from the window and put my back to the wall, buried my face in my hands, and groaned.

"Low?" Xavier's voice, sleepy. "What is it?"

"The paparazzi are here."

"The what?" he asked, sitting up and rubbing his eyes.

His hair was mussed and sticking up in a million directions, his eyes were half-closed, and he rubbed them with his fists, then stretched, feline and languorous, making a moaning sound that shot straight to my core.

I forced my eyes away from his abs and turned away from him to hide the hardened nubs of my nipples protruding against my thin borrowed T-shirt.

"The paparazzi. Reporters. Photographers," I answered, and began gathering my clothes.

"Why are they here?" He was still half-asleep, and adorable and delicious and sexy all at once.

"Because those tourists last night posted photos of me, and now everyone knows I'm here."

He blinked twice, and then seemed to hear the noise for the first time and padded on bare feet over to the window.

"Stay to one side," I cautioned. "Don't let them see you."

"Why?"

I laughed, somewhat bitterly. "You don't want them to get any more photos of you than you can help. The less they see of you, the less they know of you, the better."

He glanced at me, and then turned his gaze out the window, standing to one side as I'd suggested. "I don't understand."

I sighed. "They're going to ask questions. They'll get your email address, your phone number. They'll stand out there asking questions and taking pictures and blocking the entrance and scaring away customers. They'll write speculative stories about you full of lies. They'll make up stories if there aren't any to find. By now, those photos of me and you, from last night, will have sparked a hundred different articles. Probably speculating that you've gotten me pregnant, or that we secretly eloped, or…who knows. They come up with the craziest shit." I was sitting on the side of his bed, my clothes in my lap, idly toying with the strap of my bra. "Now that they know who you are, things won't be the same. Eventually, if you keep your head down and don't give them a story, they'll forget about you. But in the meantime, things are about to get a little crazy for you guys."

He didn't answer, just stared out the window at the crowd of paparazzi.

"Xavier..." I started, but didn't really have anything to say. Or at least, nothing I knew how to say.

He turned his eyes to mine. "Yes, Low?"

I shook my head. "I don't know. Just...I guess I'm sorry I brought this on you."

"They will go away, won't they?"

I shrugged. "I mean...eventually? But how long can I hide in here? I have to leave eventually."

He sighed. "I suppose you do." He moved away from the window, began withdrawing clothes from his bureau. "There is a back door through the kitchen. We can sneak out that way and hopefully get you onto your boat."

I nodded. "Okay."

There was a huge weight in the air, an unacknowledged tension; if I was leaving, this was the beginning of goodbye. The end. And, as he'd said it would, having slept together, having woken up in his arms, had only confused my heart.

Or, rather, not confused, but...intensified the

feelings I had for him.

Shit, I couldn't afford to have feelings for Xavier. I barely knew him. We hadn't even had sex. We were from different worlds, and he had said in so many words that he couldn't handle a relationship with me—and that was *before* he knew I was a celebrity… and he still had no real understanding of what that meant. Not really.

He stepped into tight black jeans and shrugged on a black T-shirt emblazoned with a logo of some kind—some obscure company I'd never heard of. Socks, combat boots, and a quick finger-combing of his hair, and he was ready.

I laughed. "Boys. Throw on whatever, messy hair, and you still look sexy as fuck. Wish it was that easy for me."

He moved for the door. "I will give you privacy to change."

"Why? You've seen me naked already, and more than once."

He stood with his hand on the knob, not turning to look at me, his voice low, almost a growl. "Because nothing has changed, Low. You're leaving. There is no us. And if I don't leave right now, I will do something which will only make this even more impossible than it already feels."

"Like what, Xavier?" I asked, knowing the answer,

onto a side street.

We moved to the mouth of the alley where I pulled him to a stop. "Check and see if they're looking this way," I said. "Sometimes they'll post lookouts."

Xavier snorted. "This feels like *The Great Escape*. Next thing I know, we'll be dodging Nazi bullets."

"You should see what I go through to give them the slip in LA or New York," I said. "Decoy cars, sneaking in and out of delivery doors, getaway drivers, disguises."

"Does it work?"

"Usually. I can't avoid them all the time, though."

"What do you do when they catch you?"

I shrugged. "Pose for selfies, hug my fans, and give autographs."

"It must be strange, is it not?" he asked, leaning around the corner to look.

"What?"

"All the craziness you go through. People chasing you just for a picture of you. Standing in line for hours for your signature." He waved toward the crowd of paparazzi around the corner. "Objectively speaking, the notion of fame is...just strange. You are just an average person. You are more attractive than most, and you have a facility for acting, but to translate that into millions of people around the world knowing you and craving your attention? It is...it's just strange to me."

"Fame is weird," I agreed. "And it's even weirder how fast you get used to it, while at the same time never getting used to it."

"I do not understand that statement." He turned back to me. "The coast is clear, as they say."

I rested against the wall, wanting to delay the moment I had to go out there, knowing we wouldn't get away clean.

"Being famous is fun at first. After my first big role, I loved the attention. The star treatment, you know? Private jets, limousines, photographers everywhere I went, everyone catering to my slightest whim. You get used to *that* shit *real* fast. You start to expect it, in a way. Even if you do your best to stay grounded and down-to-earth, you always just *know*, you know?

"But then, the reality sets in. I can't go to Starbucks for a latte or I'll cause a riot. I can't hit up the mall with my friends, because number one, my friends are famous too, and if we went together we'd shut the place down, and number two, if I get photographed buying something it becomes accidental marketing for that company, which could piss off the companies I'm a spokeswoman for and cause publicity problems. Just leaving a hotel and getting a Lyft becomes a major event. The driver wants a photo and picture for his daughter. The bathroom attendant wants to talk about that one scene she loved so much. Everyone wants something. Random guys think because they saw me in a movie in a bikini that they have a right to grab my ass in public. And you never get used to that, even as you learn to expect it."

He frowned at me. "What is a bathroom attendant?"

I laughed. "Fancy bars or restaurants often have someone that works in the bathroom. They hand you towels and toothpaste and perfume and whatever."

"Why?"

I blinked. "Um. I actually have no idea. It's stupid, and they make me feel awkward, because, like, I can get my own paper towel, and why would I use random toothpaste or perfume?"

"People are strange."

"They really are," I said, sighing.

He tapped his palms against the sides of his legs, staring at me, but I couldn't read his expression. Abruptly, he fisted his hands and then shoved them into his pockets, ripping his gaze away.

"Why do you do that?" I asked.

"Do what?"

"Put your hands in your pockets like that."

"To stop the tic." He withdrew his hands and tapped his thighs again, looking past me. "It's a compulsory movement I'm unaware I'm doing, especially when I get lost in my head."

"I know that part—what I mean is, why do you stop yourself?"

"It's embarrassing. It marks me as…as what I am."

"And what's wrong with that?" I asked, looking at him sidelong. "You're an amazing person, and you should be proud of who you are."

"All I ever wanted, my whole life, was to fit in. To be normal. If someone had offered me a pill that would take away the tics and the staring into space and the social awkwardness, but also took away my above average intelligence, I would have accepted it."

"But then you wouldn't be you."

He blinked hard, not looking at me. "Precisely."

I swallowed, my throat hot and thick. "Xavier… no." I turned to face him, trying to get his eyes on mine. "Who you are is *amazing*, Xavier. You're…you shine like a star. People call me a star, but I'm not. I'm just an actress. *You're* the star. Never be ashamed or embarrassed of who you are. Let yourself tic. Let yourself stare. So what? It's part of you. It's not bad, or weird, it's just different."

His jaw clenched, and his breathing halted. His eyes fixed on mine so directly and so intently it felt like he was seeing into the very fabric of my soul, of my heart, a stare so open and direct and intense and unfathomable I couldn't look away, but to endure it was almost painful.

"If…if I could be near you all the time, I might have the courage it would require to do that. Because you make me…you make feel…whole, in ways I never knew I could feel." He blinked, three times, rapidly, and then turned away, taking my hand and pulling me into a fast walk. "The coast is clear. Baxter and Eva have them distracted. Let's go."

There wasn't time to protest or think, then. We were out of the alley in a few steps, and there were flashes going off and voices shouting questions and the sound of shutters clicking, and then we were in the street, and then on the dock.

"Hey! There they are!"

"Shit." Xavier pulled me into a run, and I felt them behind us.

Good thing I was in shape—Xavier could *run*, and run we did. The paps chased us, shouting questions, begging us to wait, just answer one question, *Harlow, Harlow, Harlow—*

We reached my boat out of breath and sweating, and yet somehow, despite carrying cameras and gear, they weren't far behind. The crew of my boat was onboard already, and when they saw me approaching there was a bustle of activity. I heard the motor snarl to life, a deep, throbbing, guttural rumble, and then Xavier was hopping from dock to deck and I was right behind him.

And so were the paparazzi.

"Harlow! Who is your new boyfriend? How long have you been seeing each other?"

"Harlow, are you and Xavier engaged?"

"Why were you crying, Harlow?"

"Xavier, how many brothers do you have?"

"Why are you in Alaska, Harlow?"

The questions were fired nonstop, a barrage. Xavier froze, barely breathing, stopping in the middle of the deck.

"Just go inside, Xavier," I murmured to him. "Ignore them."

"All they had was a photograph of me," he said. "How do they know my name?"

"It's just how they are."

"Why do they want to know all these things?"

"Xavier! Can you pose for us? Put your arm around Harlow! Give us a shot!"

"Why did you leave Stanford, Xavier?"

"Can you comment on the video that surfaced of you a few weeks ago, Harlow? Who was the man in the video? Were you drunk? Were there drugs involved?"

"Kiss him for us, Harlow!"

I put my hands on his shoulders. "Just go inside. The boat will get going in a minute, and we'll be away from them."

He shook his head. "I can't breathe."

I moved around in front of him. "Just take a step, okay? One step forward, toward the cabin."

His eyes locked on mine, and I realized then what Bast had meant. "Too much—Low, it's too much."

I took his hands in mine. "Just look at me, okay? They don't matter. Ignore them."

"Can't." His eyes were darting everywhere, panicked.

I palmed his cheek, and his eyes fixed on mine, desperate. "Breathe. Deep breaths."

He sucked in a breath, as if he'd come up from under the water.

"Good," I murmured. "Keep looking at me, and just breathe."

"Harlow! Look at me, Harlow! Over here! How do you know the men from the bar?"

Cameras were flashing like strobe lighting.

Walking backward, I pulled him forward a step, and then another, and then we were in the saloon and a crew member was closing the door, shutting out the noise.

The quiet was abrupt, and total.

"Why we aren't moving yet?" I snapped to no

one in particular. "Get us out of here. Anywhere, just get us away."

We were alone again, and Xavier was sitting on the couch, bent forward with his head in his hands, sucking in huge lungfuls of air.

"Sorry," he breathed. "I'm sorry. I—"

I palmed his cheek again, threading my fingers in his. "Hey, it's fine. It's overwhelming. Trust me, I get it. You think I didn't freeze the first few times I got mobbed? I broke down crying and screamed at them to leave me alone the first time I got trapped by a mob."

He exhaled shakily, and then glanced around as the ship juddered. "We're moving."

"The captain will get us away from here and we'll figure something out."

"The captain?"

I laughed. "You didn't think I operated this thing myself, did you? I can barely make coffee on my own." I put my nose in the air and affected a posh British accent. "I *am* a star, you know. I can't be expected to do these things myself."

He smirked and rolled his eyes. "Silly me."

Except for the faint rumble of the engines and the sound of water skimming past the hull, several minutes of silence enveloped the saloon. Ketchikan receded behind us, forested hills sliding past on either side.

"Xavier, about what you said—"

He shook his head, standing up abruptly. "I'm going to call Brock. He can meet us in a channel somewhere and pick me up."

"I want to talk about what you said, though."

He faced the rear of the boat, watching our wake. "Why?"

"Because—you…I…" I trailed off with a sigh, and moved to stand beside him, leaning a shoulder against the sliding glass door, looking at his beautiful profile, his strong jaw and intense green eyes. "I care about you, Xavier. You make me feel whole and brave, too. You make me feel like…more like just Low than I've ever felt, especially since becoming famous."

He let the silence breathe before answering. "So what does that mean for me?" He turned his head to meet my eyes, with that piercingly, disconcertingly direct gaze he only gave me rarely. "What does that mean for us?"

My heart skipped several beats. "For…*us*?"

He smiled sadly. "Yeah? See?"

He tugged open the door and stepped through onto the rear deck, the wind blowing his hair backward. He reached into his pocket, withdrew his cell phone, tapped a speed dial, and held the phone to his ear.

Rather than listening in, I closed the door and returned to the couch, my heart twisting, my mind screaming, my body shrieking.

I felt stupid for allowing this situation to even happen—I should have known better. I *did* know better. I just ignored my better sense and thought I could indulge myself. I thought I could get away with it.

But…the way he'd panicked, the fear on his face at the barrage of questions, the way his family had reacted…none of it was fair to them.

This whole thing had been a mistake.

I should have just rented a villa in Italy or something.

For Xavier's sake, for his family's sake—for my heart's sake—I had to go back to LA. Before this got even more out of hand.

I remained inside, and Xavier stayed outside. Long minutes passed, and I tried not to think about Xavier leaving, tried to pretend I was okay with this, that I was doing the right thing for him, for me.

He didn't need the kind of attention being around me would bring. It would only hurt him, and the last thing I wanted to do was hurt him any more than I already had. He was leaving, and so was I. But it was for the best.

This had been a temporary vacation.

And had never meant to be anything more.

My heart was just going to have to get on board with that.

Several minutes later, I heard the sound of an airplane overhead and behind us, and Xavier came inside.

"Will you ask your captain to stop the boat, please?" he asked.

"Sure." I went up, explained the situation to the captain, and returned to Xavier.

"One last request: will you ferry me from here to Brock's plane in your launch?" he asked.

"Sure." I tried a smile. "Let me get someone to operate it for us."

His smile was as unconvincing as my own. "Because you can't be expected to do things for yourself."

"Exactly. Glad you're finally understanding how we world-famous superstars operate."

The joke fell flat, and Xavier just lapsed into the expressionless stare into nothingness, dismissing the subject.

I saw the emotions in him, though; in ways I'd have missed when we first met.

His hands were at his sides, but his palms were moving imperceptibly, tapping rhythmically and steadily against his thighs. Occasionally he'd squeeze his hands into fists, and his shoulders would hunch and become tight, and his jaw tensed.

I wanted to ask what he was thinking about.

But I didn't.

Best not to know.

"Right. The launch." I found a crew member, a young man with blond hair and an absurdly perfect jawline and effeminate mannerisms.

Within minutes, we were in the water in the little wooden boat, speeding across to where Brock's seaplane was bobbing, propellers slowing. The crewman piloting my boat brought us up to the float and stopped us in a neat little maneuver, and Xavier caught the strut and stepped from the boat onto the float immediately.

"Is this goodbye?" he asked, gazing at me but not making eye contact.

"I don't know," I said, standing up and catching hold of the strut for balance. "I don't want it to be."

I stared up at him, longing for one more kiss, one more taste of his lips, his breath, but lacking the courage to take it—I was afraid he would deny me the kiss, in preservation of his feelings. Selfishly, I wasn't sure I could handle that rejection, not at that moment.

He exhaled a sharp, short breath, almost a hiss of frustration. "Harlow, I—" His jaw tensed, flexed, he blinked rapidly, and then shook his head. "Fuck it."

And then he leaned forward, bending low over

me, one hand on the strut was all that kept him balanced as he swayed way out over the boat and over me. His hand curled around the back of my neck and his fingers buried in my hair, tilting my face up to his. His lips slanted across mine, claiming a kiss, and his breath shot through mine, and his tongue lanced through my teeth and tangled with my tongue, and then the kiss became hot and hungry and wild, demanding, furious, intense and crazed. I moaned, lifting up on my toes. I laced the fingers of one hand in his hair and knotted my other hand in the front of his T-shirt, smashing up against him.

And then, just as I was starting to shake from the need of his kissing, he released me, abruptly and completely, so I fell backward and sat down hard on the bench of the boat.

He wiped his fingertips across his lips as if tracing the remainder of my kiss, his eyes searching me.

And then, without a goodbye or a single word or backward glance, he leapt into the open doorway of the seaplane. The door shut, and then after a moment the engines coughed and snarled to life, and the propellers began churning up to speed, buffeting me with wind. I watched, heart cracking and throbbing, throat thick and hot, as the seaplane inched away, turning in place, and then bounced across the waves with increasing speed, the engines ratcheting into a roar as it picked up momentum, and then it smoothly left the water and angled skyward, and I was alone in the middle of a channel.

"Are you all right, ma'am?" the crewman asked.

I watched until the aircraft was out of sight. "Yes," I said, eventually.

"You're crying, ma'am."

I dashed a wrist against my eyes. "Take me back, please," I said, in lieu of trying to explain.

"Yes, ma'am."

Back aboard *The Lola*, I found the captain waiting in the saloon.

"Do you have a destination in mind, ma'am?" he asked.

I spoke without looking at him, heading for the stairs to my cabin. "LA."

THIRTEEN

Xavier

THE PAPARAZZI WERE STILL CAMPED OUTSIDE OUR BAR when Brock and I returned about two hours later. We had to plow through the crowd just to get in the front door. I did my best to keep breathing and to ignore the barrage of questions.

"Xavier! Xavier! Where's Harlow?"

"Did you guys fight?"

"Did she leave you?"

"Xavier, did Harlow break your heart?"

"What's it like dating a celebrity, Xavier?"

Just before closing the door on them, I paused and looked back at them, "Harlow is not here anymore," I said, "so…go away."

This only resulted in a fresh onslaught of questions, but once it became clear that nothing else exciting was going to happen, they eventually trickled away. We had to close the bar for three days, but eventually they all left town. Business reopened, and life went back to what it had been. Sort of.

I couldn't get Low out of my head. At first I tried ignoring the thoughts of her when they cropped up—which was every thirty seconds, roughly speaking—but that only made me distracted and clumsy. At work, I cooked the wrong food, forgot what I was doing, burned food, and burned my fingers. At home, I was tense, stressed, irritable, and prone to snapping at everyone, even Dru who was one of my favorite people.

They all tolerated me as best they could.

Things should have returned to normal.

Cook food.

Read books.

Build robots.

Run, workout, sleep.

Repeat.

Repeat.

Repeat.

Now, though, nothing was the same. I couldn't run down the docks without imagining Low's yacht berthed at the end. When I slept, I dreamed of her.

When I worked out, I saw her eyes on me, her gaze raking over me like I was something she wanted to eat. When I took a shower, I fantasized about her. I fantasized about her naked body, about her in a robe, in my room...untying the robe and letting it fall to the floor, and then crawling across the bed toward me. I would touch myself, trying to relieve the pressure and the ache, but I couldn't.

It didn't feel right.

It wasn't *her* touch. My touch still felt alien and wrong, whereas her touch had felt perfect and right.

Her touch had brought me to life.

Set me on fire.

My own touch just...grated on my nerves. I always gave up without finding release, which meant the only way I had to vent that frustration and pent-up energy was through exercise.

Which I did to an unhealthy level.

I punished myself, is what I did.

I ran until my legs gave out, until my lungs burned as if I'd breathed fire. Until I couldn't run anymore and had to literally hobble home in agony. I hit the free weights until one day Bast found me trapped under the bar, unable to finish the last rep, and banned me from the free weights until I could "figure my shit out," as he put it.

I stopped sleeping almost entirely, except for two

or three hours here and there.

Everywhere I went, everything I did, Harlow was on my mind. In my heart.

On my skin.

After almost a month of this, Bast caught me as I was heading out for another brutal run. I intended to run until I passed out, because I literally could not stop thinking about Low, couldn't get her hair and her eyes and her skin and her kiss and her body out of my mind, couldn't erase her voice from my heart, couldn't stop craving her presence.

"Yo, Xavier. Hold up," Bast said. "I'm coming with you."

I stared at him. "No offense meant, brother, but I do not think you could keep up."

"So slow down for my big carcass."

"This is an intervention, I take it," I said.

He laughed. "Yeah, actually."

I sighed. "Say your piece, and then I will run."

It was just past dawn, my favorite time to run.

Bast only shook his head. "You need to really listen. Not just wait for me to finish talking."

I exhaled in irritation. "I do not want to listen." I kicked my foot up behind me, grabbed my toes, and stretched my quad. "I want to run."

"You can't escape how you're feeling, Xavier."

"I'm not trying to escape it, I'm trying to quiet it.

I'm trying to…" I sighed. "Fine. I'm trying to escape it."

Bast laughed. "Trust me, I know." He clapped me on the back with a huge paw, and guided me back inside the darkened bar, all the stools up on the tables and bar. "Come on. Just sit and listen, okay? How often have I ever asked you to hear me out, Xavier?"

"Rarely, if ever."

"Exactly. So just give me this, okay? And try to give me the real you, not the encyclopedia-professor-robot you."

"Spock, Low calls it," I said, before I could stop myself.

Bast laughed. "Exactly. No Spock."

"I'll do my best," I said, following him back upstairs to the apartment.

He poured us both coffee, and we sat at the kitchen table, facing each other. "Okay, bud. What I have to say is pretty simple: you're being a pain in the ass, man. You're fucking up orders in the kitchen, you're snapping at everyone, you're damn near killing yourself physically, and it's clear you're not eating or sleeping. I clearly have no fuckin' idea what happened between you and that actress chick, but you need to find a way past it. Because this shit has *got* to stop."

I stared at him, disbelieving. "Wow. That's… spectacularly helpful."

"I wasn't trying to be helpful. I was trying to say what I had to say, for the sake of all of us that gotta live and work with you."

"I thought you were going to come to me with some kind of sage, brotherly advice."

"I'd have to know the situation to do that," he said, and sipped coffee, eyeing me across the rim. "All I know is, you had some sort of a thing with Harlow Grace, but you didn't know it was her, and now she's gone, and you're a fuckin' disaster. And, oh yeah, *she* mentioned that you're fuckin' autistic or some shit, but you never told any of us? The fuck is that about?"

"You are upset."

"I'm your big brother. I damn near raised you by my fuckin' self. So yeah, I'm upset you didn't bother sharing that little piece of information about yourself." He sighed, rubbing his eyes. "But then, you're a Badd. We're not exactly known for our tendency to share personal shit with each other."

"It never seemed to matter," I said.

Bast slammed his mug down so hard coffee sloshed out over his hand. "*Bullshit.*"

I blinked at his anger. "Excuse me?"

"That's bullshit! You're my baby brother. How the fuck you think that doesn't matter?" He wiped at his hand, wincing. "How long have you known?"

"I began suspecting my junior year. I spent the

summer between my junior and senior year researching and self-examining for markers and symptoms, and I was one hundred percent convinced by the end of the summer."

"A doctor officially diagnose this?"

"No. But there's no need. I am as certain as medical knowledge will allow." I quirked an eyebrow at him. "Have you ever known me to be in error when I claim to know something with certainty?"

He sighed. "No, I guess not." He shook out his hand. "Fuckin' burned my hand, goddammit."

"That's what you get for outbursts of anger."

"Shut up, dork." He grimaced again, and then seemed to dismiss the pain, returning to sipping his coffee. "What's it mean, then? This autism thing."

I spent the next half hour explaining what I knew about myself and about the disorder, the effects and ramifications, how I displayed it, everything.

He was quiet a long time, thinking. "So, there's no cure or anything?"

I actually laughed. "It's a disorder, Sebastian, not a disease. I am different, not sick."

"Right, sorry." Another long silence. He finished his coffee and poured more. "So..." Bast started, hesitated, and started over. "Would it be weird if I said it's hard for me to feel like this changes how I see you?"

"I hope it does not. I'm still just...me. The same

as I've always been. Nothing is changed. You merely have a term now which encapsulates what makes me different from most people."

I finally remembered my coffee, but it was cold; I dumped it out, poured fresh, and made a new pot. When I sat down again, I could tell Bast had things to say.

"What happened with you and Harlow?" he asked.

I sighed. "A lot, and not enough, and too much."

He laughed. "Oddly, I think I get that. Care to elaborate?"

"No. Not really."

He frowned. "Come on, Xavier. You never talk about yourself. And in this case, I think you really need to get this shit out. I know I'm not as smart as you, but I may actually have some sage brotherly wisdom to impart. I've been through some shit myself, you know."

"I wouldn't even know where to begin."

"Why are you being such a dick? Start there."

"Well, by all means, don't mince words, Sebastian," I laughed. Sobering, I sighed, scrubbing both hands through my hair. "It's…everything."

"Helpful."

I sipped coffee for a moment, trying to find the words. "I seriously don't know where to start.

Discussing emotional issues is…very hard for me."

"How do you feel about her?"

I shook my head. "That's not a great place to start."

Bast laughed, a sarcastic snort. "Dude, you're being *so* difficult right now." He leaned back in his chair, hand curled around his mug, resting the bottom of it on his chest. "How about this—the day you came running back here half-naked, carrying your clothes, freaking the fuck out…what happened?"

I took a long drink of my coffee, tuning out my innate dislike of talking about myself, instead focusing on making sense of that day. "I suppose what you'd have to understand first, in order for that day to make sense to you, is that my relationship with Low was, from the very start…unlike any other interaction I've ever had with another person. I've never felt anyone to be as…interested, I suppose, in me. I don't mean that as an indictment of you or any of the guys, but you're my brothers. I've never had friends, not really. I've never trusted anyone enough to allow them close enough to develop a friendship, and I wouldn't know what to do in a friendship anyway.

"All the people I went to school with were… well…I loathed the large majority of them, and the rest simply didn't register on my radar. So when I met Low—which happened by accident, by the way—from the very start she just seemed fascinated by me. Curious. Interested. And all of that felt very nonjudgmental. Which was totally new to me, considering the way most people treat me, given my predilection for highfalutin syntax and verbal formality, and my tendency to wax eloquent on any number of topics. I suppose I've always just assumed everyone is judging me, because I always feel judged."

"That's not fair to a lot of the people who meet you, though, bro," Bast said. "Not everyone is judging you."

I shrugged. "I know that logically, but try telling that to my emotional experience."

"Fair enough." He rolled a finger. "So, she was interested in you."

"At first, I wondered if she was interested in me merely as…a curiosity, you know? But she kept looking at me in odd ways, and trying to sit close to me, and touching me."

Bast's eyes rose. "And you let her get away with that?"

I nodded. "I still have no idea why, but yes. There's something unique about my physical and neurological reaction to Low touching me. And I mean any kind of touch, not just…you know."

"No, I don't know."

"I mean innocent, platonic, friendly physical

contact, not sexual touch."

Bast covered a grin behind his coffee. "I see," he muttered, into the mug.

"If you make me feel embarrassed by the things I'm saying, I'll stop talking," I warned.

He held up a hand palm out. "Not my intent, bud. But this is new territory for me, hearing this outta you."

"Trust me, it's new for me, too." I gathered my train of thought. "So, she would sit close to me, which by itself is hard for me. But as much as it felt weird and uncomfortable and made me anxious to have her that close, there was another part of me that liked it. I deeply, desperately enjoyed the way it felt to sit next to her, even if it was just her leg only sort of brushing mine, or her hip, or whatever. It…excited me."

"I know that feeling," Bast said. "Like…you love how it feels, and it's exciting and exhilarating, but you're also scared of how it makes you feel, and scared she'll realize all of a sudden what she's doing and stop doing it."

"Exactly," I said. "I also am very untrusting of women."

"Why?"

I sighed. "That is a long story, one which I do not have the emotional wherewithal to share at this time." I sipped coffee, continued. "Suffice to say, I experienced the cheerfully vicious cruelty of high school students at the hands of the most popular girl in the school, in such a horrifically embarrassing manner as to scar me for life and turn me against all women."

Bast blinked. "Dude. The fuck did she *do* to you?"

I groaned. "Short version—she tricked me into thinking she liked me, lured me to her house, and then secretly live-streamed to the entire the school as she tricked me into admitting to having a crush on her, and then caused me to…er…prematurely ejaculate into my pants. Which, I emphasize, she live-streamed to the entire school. After which she mocked me in the most cruel way possible, making it brutally obvious how pathetic she found me."

Bast growled. "That fuckin' bitch."

"Yes, well, I was naive."

"No excuse. Even *less* excuse, if anything."

"Thus the reason I don't trust women. That was my one experience with a girl telling me she liked me, and it was a sick, cruel joke."

"Yeah, I don't blame you."

"So, when Low demonstrated interest, it was difficult—meaning, nearly impossible—to believe her. To trust her. To feel as if she was being genuine."

"She give you any hint that she wasn't genuine?"

I shook my head. "No. And I knew that logically.

But emotionally, I was too scared. To distrusting. And plus, the closer we became as friends, the more she pushed our friendship into a more physically...affectionate, shall we say, sort of realm, the more uncomfortable I became. I just...I wanted to be able to enjoy the touch of a woman who seemed to genuinely like me—and not just any woman, but the most beautiful woman I've ever seen, let alone met or spent time with. And at that time, I had no clue she was famous. All I knew was that she was clearly wealthy, and so beautiful it was hard to breathe or think around her."

Bast shook his head, chuckling. "Fuckin' hell, man, I do *not* blame you there. And listen, my wife is the absolute center of my universe, okay? Just so we're clear—I love her with every single goddamn molecule inside me, and there's no one in the world who can compare to her in my eyes. But...Harlow Grace? Man, that woman is fine...as...*fuck*."

"Indeed she is," I said. "So, yeah. She overwhelmed me. Being interested in me, wanting to spend time with me, touching me, overwhelmed me. And then I told her the story of what happened with Brittany, and that sort of led into...um...it's hard to remember exactly how it happened. I told the story to her, and then she was upset about it, and upset that I didn't trust her. She said she liked me, that she was interested in me, and somehow that led to her...

flirting with me, I suppose. Speaking in a low voice, getting very much inside my personal space, up very close, putting her hands on my shoulders and chest and stomach."

"She wanted you, man," Bast said.

"I wanted to believe exactly that. But I never know what a person's true intent is by their body language. Sometimes I think they mean one thing, and they really mean another. I often misread social situations, and take what people say literally—you know this about me."

"Yeah."

"So when the most beautiful woman in the world—to me, and perhaps literally, now that I know she's famous—seemed interested in me and was flirting with me, and when my one experience with a woman turned out to be a cruel prank…I doubted my own interpretation of her intent. But she made it clear to me that she meant it. That she was attracted to me."

"And how did you feel about that?"

"Disbelieving, but longing to believe. So attracted to her it terrified me, and this…this…*need*. Like… when you haven't eaten all day and you're so hungry the idea of a delicious meal makes you feel very literally mad? As in crazy mad, not angry mad. That kind of manic, desperate hunger, but for *her*. For her to

what she enjoyed about my body. Showing me how she wanted to make me feel good in return. Being touched, for me, in any capacity, feels somewhat like...an electric tingle or shock. I'm struggling to find an appropriate metaphor...if my body is a campfire, someone touching me at all, for a handshake or a hug or an accidental contact, it's like tossing a piece of paper on the fire—a brief but intense flare-up. The way Low was touching me? Sexually? It was...her touch to my most intimate, sensitive places was like...like pouring the highest octane rocket fuel on the fire."

"Damn, dude," Bast muttered. "Sounds intense."

"It consumed me." I was still speaking with my eyes closed, focusing on the flow of memory via my words. "*She* consumed me. The experience just utterly devoured me. I lost myself."

Silence, as I prepared the next phase of the story in my mind.

"Then, as I reached release from the fury of her touch, I became overwhelmed completely by the sensation. I *was* the rocket blast of sensation, it was all that I was, in my body and my mind and my soul. It was an unsustainably intense thing, Sebastian. My mind retreated. I don't know how else to put it. I couldn't endure it. It felt so intense it was painful, but a...a beautiful pain. Beautiful like a sunrise is beautiful—no, more than that—beautiful like...analogy and metaphor fail me. It was beautiful in the way a nuclear explosion is beautiful, in its way—a perfect maelstrom of power, utterly consuming, utterly and maximally destructive. But also beautiful and hypnotic at the same time, and beautiful and hypnotic *because* of its destructive power. That is as close as I can come to explaining how it felt for me." I paused to think, to gather my thoughts. "My mind's way of retreating from the intensity of it, I think, was to fall back into remembering the last time anything like that had happened."

"Meaning the thing with that bitch from your school?"

"Yes. That was the last time I'd felt such a release." I saw and felt the surprise on Bast's face, and explained. "To provide the sensation for myself, the way I imagine most other men do on a regular basis, is nearly impossible for me. The momentary burst of pleasure at the end is not worth the discomfort and frustration of getting there. So yes, what happened with Brittany was the last time, until I met Low, that I'd reached orgasm, not to put too fine a point on it. I was content living asexually for the most part—outside of the world of those thoughts, needs, and sensations. But Low brought all that out of me, and with a furious, explosive, fiery vengeance. And it was just...too much. My mind couldn't cope. My heart had been so hurt and so scarred from Brittany's prank that as I reached that peak of sensation, I fell back into that moment. I knew, in some part of me, that I wasn't there, that I was panicking from the overload of sensation, but it didn't matter. I freaked out. Had the worst panic attack I've ever had, and ran. Literally ran. It was just too much. And I tried to explain it to her, tried to work through it. But I couldn't. I just couldn't."

"Shit, dude, I don't think anyone would blame you for that, not with the way you're explaining it."

"I do, though. I blame myself, and I hate myself for it. I should have been stronger." I huffed a self-deprecating laugh. "It's embarrassing. I lasted literally moments under her touch, before making an embarrassing mess of myself, and her. I had the most beautiful woman in the world wanting me, wanting more both *from* me and *for* me, wanting to be with me, wanting to do…everything. Wanting *me*. But I'm so…so…just *me*…that I couldn't handle it, and I ran."

"There's nothing embarrassing about that, Xavier. I mean, in terms of not lasting very long, that's just natural and normal. You think I lasted for hours my first time having sex? Hell, no, dude! I blew my load in seconds the first time I got with a girl. And even now, despite being pretty experienced, Dru can drive me so crazy that I just can't hold out for more than a few seconds. So…speaking as an older, more sexually experienced guy, let go of any preconceived notion of what you think it means to be manly or whatever when it comes to lasting during sex. Porn and movies and pop culture and all that makes it seem like you're a pathetic dweeb if you can't fuck for hours, right? But that's not real. That's just not how it is.

"You connect physically and emotionally with a woman, someone you really enjoy being with, in every way, when she just *gets* you and knows how to touch you and knows what drives you wild? You don't stand a fuckin' *chance*, bro. You're gone—you're done. She's got that power over you. And, newsflash—that doesn't make you any less. It makes you *strong*, Xavier. Showing a woman you trust her with your vulnerable side, showing her that you can be all emotional and touchy-feely, that you can give her and allow her that power over you, Xavier, brother—*that's* real strength."

"It's hard to feel that way."

"I know. It takes time to work up to that kind of vulnerability. But it starts with trusting her."

"How?"

"By just…accepting the risk, I guess." He paused, eyeing me. "And dude, there's nothing embarrassing about her making you come, okay? Get rid of that stupid idea. Sex is messy, my man. It just is. And that's part of the fun. Embrace it and learn to love it. Her

she means it. And shit, she was here in hiding, and she came out to find you, to explain, because she didn't like how you got upset. That shows that she gives a shit, Xavier. She essentially sacrificed her privacy for *you.*"

"She wouldn't have had to if she'd—"

"Xavier, stop," he cut in, calm but firm. "Yeah, she should've told you, but at the same time, give her some slack. Show some understanding. You don't know what it's like to be her, any more than she knows what it's like to be you. You want her to show understanding and patience? You can be difficult, man. Just being honest, here. You're hard to read, hard to understand. And if she's willing to try, and wants to, you owe it to yourself and to her to let her try, which means offering her the same understanding in return."

"She's gone, though. She went back to wherever she lives."

He laughed, then. "And? You're just giving up? She's gone, oh well, too bad? Must not have meant that much to you, then."

"She…it was *everything,*" I snarled.

"Then stop *thinking* and stop feeling sorry for yourself. Man up and fuckin' *do* something about it, then, if she's that important to you."

"Do what?"

He snorted. "The fuck you think? Go find her, tell her you fucked up by letting her go, and beg her for another chance at figuring it out. Put your whole self out there, in her hands, and see what happens. Maybe she'll shoot you down, I don't know. I don't think she will, personally, but I'm not gonna lie and say it's not a possibility. And yeah, if she does, it'll fuckin' suck. You'll be hurt. And we'll all be here for you if that happens. But all you can do is try."

I sat in silence for a very long time, considering his words.

"You are absolutely correct in everything you've said," I said, eventually.

He snorted again. "No shit, Sherlock."

I stood up, shifting from foot to foot. "Sebastian… thank you."

He stood up and wrapped me in a hug. "I'm your big brother, man. It's what I'm here for."

I hugged him back briefly, and then extricated myself. "Still, thank you."

He laughed as he let me go. "Still don't like hugs, huh?" He waved a hand at me. "You're welcome. Now quit all this girly yakking and go find your hot, famous girlfriend and tell her you were a dumbass."

I was on my bike and hauling ass across Alaska within an hour, heading for California.

Harlow

THE ROOM WAS TENSELY SILENT.

Lindsey, Martin, and Emily and I were in a conference room at our production offices attempting to iron out a plan for my career.

The photos of Xavier and I had done wonders for my social relevance, but they came at a cost to my image, to my brand.

There were dozens of articles online and in print full of speculation and rumor and gossip. There were exposés on Xavier and his brothers, on the bar, on me, on my career, on my love life, on my stance regarding nudity and sexuality in movies…you name it, the photos of me and Xavier in Alaska had created a new focus for the info-hungry press.

Martin had received a slew of new scripts for me.

Lindsey was continuing to receive dozens of interview requests, and publicity opportunities for me were mounting up.

But none of these things interested me—I didn't want any of them.

"Low, listen—" Lindsey started, for the tenth time. "You can't just shoot down everything. You're back, right? So *be* back. Martin has a *ton* of scripts, and not all of them are shit. There are some good pieces in there. And some of these opportunities I have are actually very good. If you want to scale back from being as busy as you were before you left, we can work that out. But you have to *do* something, or you may as well just quit."

Martin grimaced as he looked at me. "She does have a point. There are several scripts in here—" he tapped the huge stack of paper, "—that would be great for you. I've vetted everything and this stack represents the best of the best. These are scripts that play to your talents as an actress, they don't have unnecessary sexual content, they don't require nudity, and any of them would push you along a viable path toward a more commercially successful zone—not to mention being more artistically fulfilling."

I groaned. "I don't want to play the simpering,

breathy, weepy love interest, Martin. I've *read* the fucking scripts. Yeah, I could play those roles. Yeah, I'd make money. Yeah, I'd get more roles, bigger and better ones. But that's not what I'm interested in, craft-wise."

Martin flipped through the stack and found a particular script, tossing it at me in irritation. "*Autumn on the Mountain* is a damn good script, Harlow," he snapped. "The character of Judith isn't anything like what you're worried about. She's strong, she's got grit, and she stays true to herself. But she still has a really strong narrative arc. Yeah, she falls in love. Yeah, there's a sex scene, but I spoke with the folks attached to this and they're clear about being willing to work with you on what you will and won't do regarding nudity. But you have to give us a little to work with here."

I pulled the script over and flipped through it. "I hate the name Judith. It's an old lady name."

Martin tossed a pen across the room with a hiss. "Now you're just being difficult."

"What about the Givenchy Couture offer?" Lindsey said, trying to shunt the conversation away from scripts. "It's solid, and they really want you for their brand. The photo shoots are spaced out, and they'll work with your shooting schedule."

"*If* she ever picks something to fucking shoot,"

Martin muttered, more to himself.

I shot up from the table, pacing away toward the window. We were in an office building, way up at the top, and the view from the windows showed most of LA sprawled out beneath us.

"I need to think," I said, eventually.

"You don't have that much time to spend thinking, Low," Martin said from across the room. "Offers will dry up, even damn good ones like *Autumn on the Mountain*. Givenchy will find someone else. Hollywood will move on. The media will stop caring. You need to decide what you want."

"It's not that simple," I murmured.

"No one is saying you have to compromise your values," Lindsey said, "but sometimes, in order to be successful, you have to give a little to get a little. Especially in this industry. And Martin is right—you can't afford to sit around maundering about this forever, not if you want to stay relevant and keep working."

"We're done here," I snapped, knowing I was being unnecessarily nasty, but unable to stop myself. "I'll get back to you with what I decide."

I swept out of the room, but I did snag the *Autumn on the Mountain* script on my way out. Emily caught up with me, her iPad out, stylus moving in a blur, but she was wise enough to hold her tongue until we were in the back of my Land Rover and on the way back home.

Even halfway home, she still hadn't said anything.

Eventually I caught her gaze. "Spit it out," I said.

She frowned. "Spit what out?"

"You're never this quiet." I turned to the window, watching Hollywood fade into Beverly Hills. "I'm sure you have something to say about how I'm living my life, so you might as well just say it."

She shook her head, blonde bob swaying, her gaze not wavering from her iPad. "My job is to be your assistant, not have opinions on your life choices."

I blinked, and turned back to her. "You're more than my assistant, Em. You're my friend."

She went still, stylus freezing. She set the stylus down very carefully, and closed the case of her iPad, finally meeting my eyes. "Your friend?"

"Yeah, of course."

"I'm your employee." She looked away, then, out the window.

"*And* my friend," I insisted. "So if you have something to say, then say it."

She remained silent for a while, staring at her fingernails. When she looked up at me, her expression was wary. "If I speak my mind and you don't like it—"

"I'll probably be a bitch about it, but I won't fire you, if that's what you're worried about. This a friend-to-friend conversation, not a employer-employee conversation."

She sighed, picking up the stylus and flipping around her index finger, a telltale sign that she was nervous. "Okay, then. Martin and Lindsey are just doing their jobs, and you're treating them like shit."

"I'm just—"

"I'm not done," she interrupted, and I went silent, gesturing at her to continue. "You came back from Alaska nearly a month ago, and you've been absolutely impossible to talk to, to work for, and to be around."

"It hasn't been *that* bad," I protested.

Emily just quirked an eyebrow. "Yes, it has. I'm with you all day, every day, and I can say without equivocation that yes, it has been exactly that bad."

I sighed. "I'm sorry, I'm just—"

"You won't talk about Alaska, so I don't know what happened, but I assume a guy is involved, because you've never been like this before, and I've worked for you since you first came to LA."

"It's a complicated situation."

"That sounds like a cop-out—not wanting to talk about it."

I glared at her. "And so what if it is?" I snapped. Then, realizing what I'd said, and how I'd said it, I sighed, rubbing my face with both hands. "God, you're right. That was super bitchy."

Emily smirked. "That was like, a three on a one-to-ten scale of Harlow being a bitch."

I frowned. "For real?"

"For real." She glanced away. "I love you, like a lot, and I love working for you. But I seriously considered quitting the other day."

I felt a hot knot in my throat—something that had been happening a lot lately, which was part of my foul moods. "I'm sorry, Emily. You don't deserve that."

"I know, and I also know this isn't like you, which is why I didn't quit." She smiled at me, then. "So tell me about him, and maybe we can figure out why he's turned you into such a disaster."

I blinked hard, internally cursing myself for still being so damned emotional about this whole stupid thing. "It started with just…hanging out. He's so different, in ways I can't even begin to explain. Sexy. Weird. Funny. So smart it's more than a little intimidating. He's…I want to say innocent, but that's not quite right, and I want to say pure, but that's not right either. God, I don't know."

"Was it good?"

I sighed. "We never really got anywhere, because he's…he's hard to get close to, and there's just…a lot."

Emily eyed me curiously. "You're usually more

articulate than this."

"This is what he does to me," I said, throwing my hands in the air, feeling embarrassed at how emotional I felt. "He…he mixes me up. He's intense, and he's…he's just a lot."

Emily stared at me. "And you haven't even slept with him yet?"

I shook my head. "No. And there's no *yet*. It's over."

"Why?"

I wished I knew how to explain all that Xavier was…but to put his ASD out there without her meeting him first felt…wrong. That wasn't who he was, and it didn't represent him. Not to me. It was *part* of him, but not *all* of him. And it was that part of him I couldn't accurately or concisely explain.

I sniffled. "He's there, and I'm here," I said, with a shrug. "It's just over."

"So? He can't come here? You can't go there?" She shook her head. "'He's there and I'm here' isn't a good enough reason for it to be over, Low."

"You wouldn't understand."

"Because I'm not famous?" Her voice was sharp.

"No." I sighed. "Yes. Sort of."

"Because *he's* not famous?" She snorted. "I've seen the photos, Low, and if he wasn't famous before, he will be now. He is fine as *hell*, Harlow."

I rolled my eyes. "His brothers are all taken, to answer your next question."

She sighed sadly. "Damn." She lifted an eyebrow at me. "They have cousins?"

I laughed. "I don't know. He never mentioned them, if they do."

Emily let the silence stretch out for a while before speaking. "Low, tell me the truth. Why won't it work? You're obviously still hung up on him."

"I know! And I shouldn't be. It's stupid."

"You're not answering the question."

"He can't handle my life, Em! *I* can barely handle my life, and it's *my* fucking life! The paparazzi showed up, not even that many of them, and he—he froze. He panicked. If we were to have a relationship, how would that work? I could never take him to a premiere? Never be seen in public with him, not because I'm embarrassed—because I'm not—but because he can't handle it? What kind of a life is that? For him *or* for me?"

Emily thought for a while, staring at me speculatively. "That sounds like another cop-out, and like a lot of arrogance, if you ask me."

Anger shot through me, but I kept my voice even. "Meaning what?"

"It kind of sounds to me like you're not giving him a fair shot. The first time we got mobbed when

I was with you, I froze too. I'd only PA'd for nameless executives before that, nobody famous. It's scary, and it's overwhelming. They're so aggressive, and the questions they ask are just so inappropriately personal, and the shit they write is ridiculous. I wanted to quit after that first time. But I didn't, because I liked working for you. So I learned how to deal with it, and now it's just part of the gig. You didn't think twice about my reaction to getting mobbed, either—you just expected me to either handle it or quit. You let me make my own choice. You explained when you hired me how it would be and that I should expect it, and that was it. You gave me the choice. I could choose to work for you and accept what came with it, or if I couldn't deal with that aspect, I could quit."

"Exactly! But that's a professional relationship."

"And a personal, romantic relationship is even more reason for him to have a choice, but you're not allowing him that. You're deciding for him that he can't handle it. That's underestimating him, for one thing, and yourself, for another. And it's just you being afraid, for a third." She leaned forward, elbows on her knees. "You have feelings for him, Low, and you're scared, so you're taking away his right to choose a relationship with you and all that it entails in an effort to avoid the fear and possible pain."

"Who are you, Dr. Drew?" I asked, my voice

dripping with snark and acid.

"Your friend, or so you said." Emily leaned back in her seat, crossing her arms over her chest, an eyebrow raised. "But if I'm wrong, tell me."

The knot in my throat, the slam of my heart, the pricking of my tear ducts told me she wasn't wrong. "Dammit."

She smiled at me. "I'm perpetually single, so maybe I'm not the best source of romantic advice, but if you were to ask me what I think you should do—"

"I *am* asking," I put in.

"Give him a chance," Emily said, leaning forward again and taking my hand in both of hers. "Give yourself permission to go for this."

I blinked back tears. "What if he—what if he can't do it? What if he won't even try? What if he doesn't feel for me the way I feel about him?"

"How *do* you feel about him?" Emily asked.

I swallowed past the knot of heat in my throat. "I could fall for him," I whispered. "I *am* falling for him." I hesitated, breathing out shakily. "I already *have* fallen for him, I think."

"Low…" she sighed and started over. "I think you owe it to yourself and to him to ignore all the what-ifs and just…*try*."

I stared out the window as we approached the

gate to my driveway, pushing back the emotion and trying to apply logic to what I felt and what I should do about it.

Enrique, my driver, waited until the gate slid silently apart and then pulled through, the gate sliding closed behind us.

Emily was right. Logic couldn't take me any further than that—she was right, about everything. It didn't make me feel any better, honestly. Worse, if anything.

Because now that I could admit I'd fallen for him, and that I had fucked up by coming back here, by leaving him, by pushing him away—by the way I'd handled the entire situation…now what?

I had no idea. Call him? I'd sent myself that photo from his phone, so I had his number, but call him and say what?

Knowing what I *should* do didn't help me figure out what I *could* do.

"So." I cleared my throat, sitting up straighter. "Business. What's on the schedule?"

Accepting my dismissal of the subject, Emily brought up my schedule. "Ummm…you have a session with Marco tomorrow morning at eight, and then nothing until four in the afternoon, when Francois and his girls are coming over to show you gowns for the premiere, which is in two weeks."

"Okay. That's all fine. Keep my schedule clear through the premiere, otherwise. I'll make some decisions about what to do next after the premiere."

"What to do next about what?"

"Everything."

I just had to get through the premiere. Which gave me two weeks to get back into shape—two weeks to fit into a gown, two weeks to think about scripts and commercial offers...and two weeks to think about Xavier.

Three days later, at six in the morning, the sun wasn't quite up yet, so the world was bathed in gray tinged with soft undertones of pink. The air was cool, and my neighborhood was still and silent. The only sound was the slap of my shoes against the blacktop as I ran. Marco had instructed me, in no uncertain terms, that I had to run every morning, at least a few miles at a hard pace. I hated running, but the dress Francois and I had picked out for the premiere wouldn't zip over my butt, even with his assistants pushing and squeezing my ass cheeks together and pulling the edges of the zipper together, so I had no choice but to trim down. This meant running, intermittent fasting, lots of salmon and lots of salad and lots of HIIT workouts on top of mileage every morning.

Usually when I ran, I had earbuds in and music going, but this morning I'd opted to leave my phone at home, so I could really focus on my stride and let my thoughts wander. As much as I hated the physical aspect of running—the burning lungs and aching legs and jouncing tits and wobbling ass—I loved the mental aspect of it, being able to just dive into my head and let my brain wander.

I was running hard, and despite the cool predawn air, I was sweating profusely. Sweat dripped down my temples, ran off my jaw, trickled in runnels down the valley of my cleavage and into my purple sports bra—which was the only top I was wearing, paired with tight white booty shorts and my favorite running shoes.

I had the circuit through my neighborhood memorized, a nice five-mile route that wound past the homes of other celebrities, up and down several punishing hills, through some nature trails and back to my house, which sat on a cul-de-sac at the bottom of a hill. I was nearly home, coming to the top of the hill and preparing to push myself into a sprint for the last few hundred feet down the hill to my driveway.

I hit the hill, opening my stride and swinging my arms, keeping my eyes on the blacktop just ahead as I barreled pell-mell down the hill, and then turned my eyes to my mailbox, which I always slapped at the end of my run.

There was a sleek black motorcycle parked at the end of my driveway, on the apron just this side of the closed gate.

Xavier sat backward on the bike, his back resting on the handlebars, one foot up on the seat and the other on the footrest, a Kindle in his hand, elbow resting on his propped-up knee. A helmet hung from a handlebar, and his hair was messy and wild, and he was wearing tight black leather riding pants, glossy black boots, and a leather riding jacket, which hung open, showing a plain white T-shirt underneath.

He was so fucking gorgeous I stumbled as I reached the bottom of the hill, my gut tightening, heart twisting, core throbbing.

He saw me.

He placed both feet on the ground, sat forward, and shoved his Kindle into a saddlebag.

I recovered and finished sprinting the last fifty feet, slapping my palm against the mailbox, and stumbled to a stop, lacing my fingers on top of my head and gasping raggedly.

I pivoted away from him, sucking in greedy lungfuls of air, trying to convince myself that the pounding of my pulse and the shakiness in my legs and the tremble in my hands and tightness in my throat was from exertion.

I heard a scuffed step behind me, felt him, smelled him, sensed him.

"Low." His voice was barely a murmur.

"Hi," I said, without turning around.

"Do you need a moment to catch your breath?"

I closed my eyes, filled my lungs, held it, and then turned around as I exhaled. Facing him, looking up at his beautiful face, I lost my breath all over again. Had he gotten better looking? Or had I just forgotten how handsome he was? His eyes were like green fire, his cheekbones razor sharp and prominent, and he'd let his stubble grow in so it was thick enough to be nearly a full beard, which made him look older and more rugged and less boyish.

"You're here," I whispered.

"I drove here," he said, gesturing at the motorcycle. "Or, rather, rode."

"All the way from Alaska?"

"Yes."

"How long did it take you?"

"A little over two days, including stops to catch a few hours of sleep here and there."

"Why didn't you just fly?" I asked.

"I needed the travel time to think."

"About what?"

"What I was going to say to you."

His eyes followed a droplet of sweat as it trickled down my throat, into the valley between collarbones and throat, down my breastbone, and between my breasts.

"What did you figure out?" My heart rate had slowed, but I was still shaky.

I couldn't blame that on the run, though—it was all him.

He shook his head. "Nothing. I ran through half a dozen different speeches, and none of them were right."

I knew the feeling; now that he was in front of me, I couldn't summon a single coherent thought.

Everything was a jumble:

I want him.

Can I straddle him on the motorcycle?

Kiss me, Xavier.

God, he looks fucking sexy in those leather pants.

Kiss me, Xavier.

Tell me you still care.

I'm falling in love and I can't stop myself, so fucking please tell me you're here because you love me back.

He looks so good I could eat him.

I can see the outline of his cock behind those leather pants.

I want to unzip him and suck him off right here,

right now, and fuck what the neighbors will say.

Kiss me, goddammit.

I realized with a start that we'd been standing at my gate, staring at each other, not talking, for over a minute, if not more.

"You want to come in?" I asked.

He swallowed hard. "Do you want me to?"

"Why wouldn't I?"

He just blinked. "Um. Because I showed up without warning? I just...after you left, I couldn't stop thinking about you. And...I—I realized that I feel..." he trailed off, swallowing hard, flicking his gaze away from mine, to the ground at his feet, and then after a deep breath, he met my eyes again. "I feel things for you, and after you left to come back here, I realized I wanted—"

He didn't finish. His hands went to his sides, and his palms tapped against his legs.

My eyes went to his hands, and he abruptly crossed his arms over his chest, tucking his hands under his armpits.

I reached up, untangled his arms, and pushed his hands back to his sides. "Just be you, Xavier."

"It's habit to stop myself, now. Especially when someone is watching."

I realized I hadn't let go of his hands, and both of our gazes went to our hands, our fingers joined.

"Come inside with me," I said. "I think we have a lot to talk about, and I don't want to do that standing outside on my driveway."

"You're not upset I showed up without warning?"

I shook my head. "No, Xavier. I'm…I'm glad you're here."

I used the keypad to open the gate, and Xavier toed up the kickstand of his motorcycle, walking it up the driveway.

"I can't believe you rode that thing all the way here," I said.

"I had to see you."

My heart leapt, hope blossoming inside me. He was here. He had to see me.

I wanted to say so many things to him, but had no idea where to even start.

I used another keypad to open one of the garage doors, and Xavier parked his motorcycle just inside, behind my Land Rover. He followed me through the door and into the kitchen, where Maria was already at work preparing my breakfast.

"*Hola, señora,*" Maria said without looking up from whisking eggs. "Food ready soon."

"Hi, Maria. Thanks." I glanced at Xavier. "Do you want something, Xavier? Maria can whip up just about anything."

He shifted uncomfortably. "I *am* rather hungry.

Eggs would be very greatly appreciated, thank you."

Maria stared at Xavier in surprise—she'd worked for me for several years, and the only people I'd ever had over were Martin, Lindsey, Marco, and my parents. A strange man was an enormous aberration in my life, and she wasn't sure how to react.

"*Sí, sí.* Eggs. You like onion? Queso?"

Xavier hesitated. "However Low is having them is fine."

Maria glanced at me. "Low? Who is low?"

He gestured at me. "Low?"

"Oh, *Señora* Grace. *Sí, sí.*"

I grabbed a couple bottles of water from the fridge, and headed to the outdoor dining area. Xavier followed, gazing around at my home, saying nothing.

Pale pink stucco walls, dark wooden beams, Spanish tile flooring throughout; an open-plan kitchen and living room, with an entire wall of glass doors that opened to create a seamless transition from indoor living space to outdoor. There was a pool lined with more Spanish tile and hand-laid, interlocking slate around it, a four-foot-high rock wall forming the perimeter around the deep end. Beyond the rock wall and the pool was a little oasis—a stand of towering palm trees, flowering cacti, a marble bench, and a small recirculating water fountain, with a ten-foot-high stucco wall surrounding the entire property.

"This place is amazing," he said, after taking it all in.

I smiled, taking a seat. "Thanks. It's actually the smallest house in the entire neighborhood, but it's just me here, so I didn't see the point in buying a huge place I'd only rattle around in."

He frowned. "Small? It must be six thousand square feet, at minimum."

"Seven, including the basement, plus there's a pool house. But by Beverly Hills standards, this place is a dinky little shack."

"I see."

"It's just a house, Xavier."

"I said nothing."

"You only say 'I see' when you don't understand or don't want to sound judge-y."

"The boat, the cars in the garage, this home, the cook…it's a transition for me, to see you in this setting. A reminder that you are far more to the world than just Low."

"Maria isn't just a chef, she's…well, everything, around here. She's like family to me," I said, between long sips of water. "You don't like being reminded that I'm rich and famous."

He glanced at me. "Fame is something I don't really comprehend. But I have wondered how wealthy you truly are." He blinked. "I think that is a rude and inappropriately personal question."

"For anyone else to ask, yeah, it would be. But… you can ask me anything." I twisted the cap back on the bottle. "I'm worth fourteen million, currently. Most of that is from the last two films. I didn't get all that much for the first one."

"Fourteen million dollars." He sighed. "That is an unfathomable amount of money."

"I suppose it is. I don't really spend a lot of time thinking about it, and I didn't get into acting for the money. It's nice to have, and I know I'm spoiled and beyond fortunate. But it's not why I became an actress."

"Why did you?"

"Because I love the craft. I acted in plays all through high school. I fell in love with pretending to be someone else, putting on a mask, channeling this other person who only exists in my mind, and on a piece of paper. I love exploring emotions and characteristics that don't always exist in my own life."

"I watched your films."

I shot him a surprised look. "You did?"

He nodded. "I wanted to know what you did. To try and understand you a little better."

"And what did you think?"

He was silent a moment. "I—it was strange, to be truthful." He shrugged. "It was like…it was you, but not you. It was like watching someone I didn't know occupy your body."

I laughed. "I suppose that's a compliment."

"You are pretending to be someone else, and you are very convincing, which is your job as an actress, so yes, that is a compliment."

"Thank you." I eyed him, seeing something unsaid in his features. "What aren't you saying?"

Maria came out, then, with a tray. She set plates in front of Xavier and me, and then silverware, and then a carafe of coffee and mugs, and a bottle of sparkling water.

"You like anything else, *señora*?" Maria asked.

I shook my head. "No, thank you." I glanced at Xavier, and then made a decision. "In fact, with my—um, with Xavier here, I think you could take the rest of the day off."

Maria's eyes widened. "I only work one hour. I make food for *mañana*. And much housework, also."

"Take the day off, Maria. Paid, of course."

"If you say so, *señora*." She wiped her palms on her apron. "It is my daughter's birthday today. Maybe I bring her out of school and get her ice cream."

"Good idea."

Maria gestured at the kitchen. "Yesterday I make chimichangas, and also, there is a salad."

"We'll be fine, I promise."

She hesitated a moment longer. "I go now?"

I nodded. "Yes, you can go. Thank you, Maria."

"De nada, señora."

When she was gone, we ate in silence.

"Why did you send her home?" Xavier asked.

I set my fork down, hesitating over how much of the truth to tell. All of it, I decided. "So we could be alone."

His eyes searched mine. "Low, I…"

"Why are you here, Xavier? Why did you come all this way?"

He finished his omelet in silence, set his fork down, dabbed his mouth with the napkin, and leaned back in his chair, coffee mug cupped in both hands. "I told you: I had to see you."

"But…*why*?"

"Because I shouldn't have let you leave in the first place." He paused, the silence heavy, thick, tense. "I should have…I should have been stronger. I should have been braver. I was scared."

"Of what?"

"You." He sighed sharply. "Of how you make me feel." Another silence. "Of how I feel about you. Of what I want."

"Tell me," I whispered. "Tell me how you feel. Tell me what you want."

He set his mug down, scooting his chair out and

standing up. He paced away across the slate paver stones, following the perimeter of the pool to the alcove in the corner, where the huge palm trees provided shade from the rising sun, and sat down on the marble bench. I followed him, and we sat side by side on the bench.

My hip nudged his, and my thigh brushed his, and his heat radiated against me; I smelled his leathers, a thin, tangy, sharp scent.

Was I a coward for wanting to hear what he was going to say before I admitted how I felt?

Probably.

The only hint I could give, the only action I was capable of, was to thread my fingers between his, and rest our tangled, joined hands on my bare thigh.

His breath caught. His eyes went to mine. "Low, I…" He exhaled shakily. "I was miserable when you left. I'm here because I want…I want you. I want *us*. I want *this*." He lifted our joined hands. "The things I feel for you are so powerful and chaotic and strange and frightening…it's hard to admit how I feel, because telling you is to…to allow you that power over me."

I blinked back tears—damn this man. *My* power over *him*? God, if he only knew.

"Why are you crying?" he asked, sounding utterly baffled. "Did I say something wrong?"

I shook my head, sniffing. "No, Xavier. This is

just what you do to me."

"I make you cry?"

I laughed, sniffling again. "Yes, dammit."

"I'm confused."

"You make me cry because you make me feel so much…and I don't know how to handle it. I'm not used to being like this. I'm an actress—I'm used to being in control of my feelings. I can cry on command, or laugh, or look sexy, or angry…I can summon all of that at will, because I'm always in control of my feelings. Always in control of myself. But you—you just…you strip away my sense of control. I've been weepy since I've been home, and cranky, and bitchy, and difficult, and miserable. I've been horrible!"

"Why?"

"Why to which part?"

"All of it. Why do I make you feel that? How do I strip away your control? Why have you been weepy, cranky, bitchy, and miserable? This doesn't seem like a good thing to me."

"It's not!" I said, laughing. "It's just…*you*."

"I still do not understand."

"I *want* you, goddammit!" I said, the tears I'd been holding back emerging full force, now. "I want you! I want us. I want this. I want it all just as bad as you do! And I—you may not understand this either, but I don't *want* to want you as badly as I do. But I can't help it."

"You want me? And us?"

"Yes."

"Then why did you leave?"

"Because I'm scared too!" I shouted. "I'm terrified!"

He tensed as I raised my voice. "Please do not shout at me. It negatively affects me, and makes it hard for me to retain my equanimity."

"Sorry—I'm sorry." I sniffled. "I'm sorry. I just—you make me crazy, and I can't handle not being in control. Which is part of why I left."

He looked at me. "I feel equally out of control. There's so much I want to say, but don't know how. So much I want to do, but I'm scared to let myself do it."

"Like what?"

"Show you the things I don't know how to say."

My blood raced, boiled. "What if I told you I wanted you to show me all that?"

"Why would you want that?"

I didn't bother hiding the tears, then. "Because I'm falling for you, Xavier."

"You are?"

I nodded, sniffing, dashing the back of my wrist across my cheeks. "I am."

"There was no falling," he said, holding my gaze with his. "Not for me. I did not *fall* in love with you."

I choked. "You—you didn't?"

He shook his head. "I *drowned* into love with you. I *flew* into love with you. I have been consumed with and consumed by love for you. Love for you swallowed me, became all of me, replaced my blood and bones and organs and thoughts and feelings with you, and you, and you."

I was breathless. "Xavier—"

"I am scared to let myself love you, Harlow. I am afraid of giving in to it. I am afraid I will become obsessed. Addicted. I will smother you. I will need all of you, all the time. I am afraid I will love you with such all-consuming intensity that it will frighten you away. Loving you is—the force of it, the power of it inside me—Low, it is so *much*, so, so much it scares me." He let out a gusting, shuddering breath.

"Xavier, I—"

What to say?

Yeah, that's how I feel?

Same?

Ditto?

Nothing could compare to the way he'd said it.

He wasn't done, though:

"I cry your mercy—pity—love!—ay, love!
Merciful love that tantalises not
One-thoughted, never-wandering, guileless love,
Unmask'd, and being seen—without a blot!

O! let me have thee whole,—all—all—be mine!

That shape, that fairness, that sweet minor zest

Of love, your kiss,—those hands, those eyes divine,

That warm, white, lucent, million-pleasured breast,

Yourself—your soul—in pity give me all,

Withhold no atom's atom or I die,

Or living on, perhaps, your wretched thrall,

Forget, in the mist of idle misery,

Life's purposes,—the palate of my mind

Losing its gust, and my ambition blind!"

I sniffed a disbelieving laugh. "Did you really just quote Keats at me?"

He nodded. "Yes. I did."

I leaned against him, twisting to face him, resting my forehead against his temple. "As if your own words hadn't melted me enough, you had to go quoting Keats at me?" I whispered, laughing through tears. "Damn you, Xavier."

"Damn me? It was a declaration of love, Low. Why should I be damned for that?"

I laughed again, crying, and slid my leg over his, straddling him, facing him, taking his stubbled jaw in my hands. "Because I'm so fucking in love with you I don't know how to feel it or express it or handle it any more than you do."

He blinked up at me, his hands lifting hesitantly, pausing, fingers fluttering like birds, before settling on my waist. "You…you truly feel that way? For *me*?"

I nodded, laugh-crying still, leaning forward to bury my face in his throat. "Yes, Xavier. I fell for you the moment I saw you running down the dock toward me. I fell for you when you helped me and looked at my ankle with such gentility and strength and care. I fell for you when we watched the eagle catch the fish together. I fell even harder when you kissed me for the first time, and I fell for you when you kissed my breasts like they were…like they were the most beautiful and precious gifts you'd ever been given. I fell for you when you went down on me and made me come harder than I've ever come in my life, and I fell for you hardest of all when you told me why you were afraid of letting me touch you, yet still trusted me enough to let me touch you like that anyway."

"We spent a matter of *days* together, Low," he murmured. "How could we have fallen in love so hard, so fast?"

"I don't know. I'm asking myself the same question. How can this be real? Am I deluding myself? Am I just mistaking my sexual attraction to you for love?"

"Hearing your doubts should worry me, I would think," he said. "But it doesn't. It reassures me that I'm not the only one feeling this way."

I leaned back, sitting on his thighs and resting my hands on his shoulders. "If this was only a week after we'd met, and we'd never spent any time apart, I might think it was just infatuation or lust. But we've been apart for nearly a month. I spent that entire month trying to pretend I don't feel how I feel. Trying to make the feelings go away. Trying to tell myself I was better off here alone without you, and trying hardest of all to pretend leaving like I did was best for you. But I can't keep pretending any of that is true. Because none of it is."

His hands glided down my hips, and his fingertips traced the hem of the white stretchy fabric of my shorts, which had rolled up around the inner creases of my thighs, outlining my core in a V. His touch made my heart skip a beat, made my nipples harden inside my sports bra.

"Why do you not want to feel the way you do?" he asked, his eyes meeting mine briefly before skating over my chest and down to where his fingers continued to toy idly with the bunched fabric of my workout shorts. "Why do you not want to be in love with me?"

"I'm afraid of getting hurt. I'm afraid of being vulnerable. As a woman in Hollywood, particularly being as young as I am, I've had to be strong, and in charge and in control at all times. I've put on this strong, in charge facade for the world my whole life. I've never really let anyone in."

"Why? Did someone hurt you?"

I shook my head. "No, I just…I don't know. I watched so many of my friends—famous and not—go through relationship after relationship, falling in love and breaking up, giving their hearts away and getting them broken. All through high school and all through college, I watched my friends go through this cycle of finding a guy, falling for him, and getting their hearts broken, and I just…I never wanted to go through that myself. I was the friend they called for wine and ice cream and rom-coms to get over the breakup. I was the one they cried to. I was the one they complained to about how all men were assholes. And I just…why would I put myself through that? Clearly it never worked. The one guy I ever really actually dated, it wasn't…it was companionship at most. Someone to spend time with. Someone to have the appearance of a relationship with. He wasn't in love with me, nor I with him. I think that's why our relationship, such as it was, worked as well as it did for as long as it did—because it didn't really mean anything."

I sighed. I played with the collar of his leather jacket as I spoke.

"No guy I ever met made me feel anything, so why would I pretend? Why would I put myself through the effort and the inevitable pain of a break-up for some guy I didn't really have actual feelings for? Then I met you, and you threw all that out the window from the first moment I spoke to you."

"How?" he asked.

"Just…everything you are," I answered. "Physically, I'm more attracted to you than I've ever been to any man, ever in my life. That's part of what's so crazy to me—I love sex. I *need* it. I've always had a strong sex drive and I make no apologies for that. But you…you intensify those feelings a hundredfold. Needing you, just the sheer physical *need* for you—that alone is so fucking intense it's scary. And who you are—you just…*fit*, in some way. In my mind, my heart, my body. I don't know how to put it. It's like there was this hole in my life, in my heart, in my soul, in my mind—there was a hole inside me and you showed up and somehow you just fill that hole. Like I was half of a puzzle, and you're the one piece in the whole universe that fits in the jigsaw emptiness inside me."

I pushed the jacket over his shoulders, slowly removing it, folding it, and laying it on the bench beside us, then I let my hands roam over his shoulders and chest and stomach, needing to touch, to feel, to know he was real and here, and that this was happening.

Xavier's laugh was breathless, disbelieving.

"How can any of this be real? You—*you*—Harlow Grace…I'm sitting in your backyard, with you on my lap, touching me and telling me you're in love with me. How can this be real?"

"I'm not Harlow Grace with you, Xavier. Not here, not like this, not in this moment. I'm just…Low. I'm the girl who fell over and hurt herself trying to impress you with my fancy yoga moves. I'm the girl who went fishing with you. Who watched *Spartacus* on my boat with you. Who broke down crying in front of your whole family. I'm the girl who fell asleep in your arms, Xavier." I slid my fingers under the hem of his T-shirt and ran my palms up the warm solidity of his back. "Harlow Grace is…she's someone else. Don't think about her. Think about me. Just…me."

"Can't I think about all of you? Can't I be in love with Harlow Grace the movie star *and* Low, the girl from the boat?" He traced his fingers up the insides of my thighs, over my hips, and up my stomach to follow the underside of my sports bra. "You are yourself, and you are both of those persons—the famous actress, and just the girl. What if I'm attracted to both? What if I'm in love with both?"

"You didn't know I was famous when we met. You didn't know until your family told you."

"After you left, I talked to Bast. I Googled you. I looked through hundreds of pictures of you, and read

He stared past me, over my shoulder, unblinking, unseeing—or perhaps seeing more than I could comprehend. Once again, I allowed him the silence and the space to say what he had to say in his own time.

Eventually, Xavier turned those fiery green eyes to mine, and when he spoke his voice was deep and thick and husky, rough with emotion and need. "You're telling me that if I want to touch you, that I should just touch you. Don't wait for you to ask me, or to show me you want me first."

"That's what I'm saying, Xavier."

"Just take what I want." His eyes flicked to mine. "What if what I want was…rough, or wild? What if I took what I wanted and lost control of how badly I wanted you?"

"You are a gentle person, Xavier. And if you went wild, I would go wild with you." I met his gaze, letting the fire I felt in my blood and bones, in my core and my hands and tongue and lips blaze into my eyes. "Give it all to me. You want rough and crazy? I'll meet you there, Xavier, and take you miles beyond it."

His jaw tensed, flexing, the dark stubble on his jaw shifting in the morning sunlight. His hands slid up my back, roamed over my shoulders. Paused, and then danced up my nape, to the high ponytail that had my hair off my neck and shoulders while I was running. With a slow gentle tug, he pulled the elastic ponytail holder out of my hair, letting my strawberry blonde curls explode around my shoulders.

"I like your hair down," he murmured.

I waited, breathless, for whatever would come next.

He skated his palms back over my shoulders, tracing the band of my sports bra around my back, his fingers running along the lower edge as he'd done minutes earlier.

"So, if I want to see your breasts bare—if I want to nuzzle my face between them and kiss them," he said, his fingertips curling under the elastic band at my diaphragm, "then I could just remove your bra? Right here, right now, and you wouldn't mind?"

I couldn't speak, though a million versions of *go ahead and find out* ran through my mind.

He hesitated another moment, and then slowly lifted the sports bra upward, as if waiting for me to stop him. Instead, I lifted my arms over my head. He tugged the tight purple undergarment up and off, folding it neatly and placing it on top of his jacket.

Naked from the waist up, the air was cool on my skin, and his hungry gaze made my nipples pucker and stand out hard as diamonds, aching, sensitive, and begging for his attention.

He gave them the attention they were begging for—he buried his face between my breasts, his stubble rough and scratchy on my skin, making me gasp and whimper in delight at the contrasting sensations of his soft lips and wet tongue and rough beard. He kissed and kissed, everywhere, over my breastbone and down the upper slope of my breasts, down between them, his beard scratching the insides, and then he kissed his way to my left nipple first, his tongue flicking over the erect nub. I gasped, arching my spine, burying my fingers in his hair.

"God, yes," I breathed.

"You like that?" he asked in a gruff murmur.

"Fuck yes," I growled. "More."

Cupping them, holding them up, he licked and lapped and flicked his tongue against my nipple until I was throbbing all over, and then he transferred his mouth to my other breast, teasing his way from the underside and around the circumference of it and across the slope before finally taking my aching, begging nipple into his mouth again.

"Jesus, Xavier—"

I was panting, breathless, and my core was throbbing. I seriously felt like I was approaching the edge of orgasm just from his mouth on my breasts.

Abruptly, he pulled away, brows furrowed, eyes narrowed, jaw flexing. His hands latched onto my hips and he pushed me off his lap.

"Xavier, what are you—" I began, confused by

the sudden absence of his touch and heat and mouth.

He stood me up, facing him, his hands resting on my hips. Keeping his eyes on mine, he hooked his fingers in the stretchy white fabric of my running shorts, which was all I had on, nothing beneath them except bare skin. I exhaled a tremulous breath; my thighs clenched together, core aching. His eyes raked over my body, pausing at my tits before traveling down to the V between my thighs.

"If I want to taste you again—if I want to bury my face between the warm silk of your thighs and taste the sweetness of your pussy—" his voice dropped to a whisper at the last word, his cheeks flushing as he said it, "then all I would have to do is this…"

He drew the shorts down a few inches, baring the upper swell of my pudendum, his eyes on mine, waiting for the demurral, the reproach—and when I didn't offer one he tugged them off all the way, picking them up as I stepped out, folding them and placing them on the pile with my bra.

Naked, then, I stood aching and trembling, flesh pebbling from the cool air and from desire, nipples damp from his mouth and throbbing for more, my pussy seeping the essence of my need, clenching around nothing.

He didn't move, just sat staring at me, his eyes roaming my body as if no matter how long and hard he looked, he simply could never get enough, could never believe I was real, that I was for him.

"Touch me, taste me, kiss me, make me come," I whispered. "Take me inside and give me a dozen orgasms in a row." I swallowed hard, licking my lips, shaking all over. "Please. *Anything*."

He reached for me, his hands cupping around my buttocks and pulling me closer, so I was standing between his knees. "Anything?"

"Anything," I repeated. I ran my hands through his hair, gazing down between my breasts at his handsome face. "Everything."

"Show me your bedroom."

I took his hand and led him inside, through the gleaming marble and stainless steel of my kitchen, past the heavy dark beams and stark white walls and white leather of my living room, up the stairs and to my suite of rooms, which took up the whole upper floor. My bed faced a wall of windows, with a view of LA spread out beyond, the hillside falling away. Dawn bathed the room in shades of gold and orange and grapefruit-pink light.

I led him to my bed, and I sat down on the edge, holding his hands. He stood over me, a lean, masculine god in black leather and white cotton, his hair gloriously messy, his eyes sharp and fiery and fiercely green. His zipper bulged, his erection straining behind it.

He leaned forward, bending over me, taking my face in his hands and tilting my mouth up to his, and he kissed me breathless, kissed me stupid, kissed me dizzy.

"I want to make love to you," he murmured, his lips moving against mine, his voice a rough whisper.

"God, please…" I murmured.

He lay me down on the bed, bent over me, kissing my throat and my tits. "Allow me to clarify." My feet were still flat on the floor, my ass at the edge of the bed, and he dropped to his knees in front of me. "I'm going to go down on you until you scream, and *then* I'm going to make love to you."

Fuck.

Could he get any more perfect?

His tongue hit my clit and I realized that yes, in fact, he could.

Xavier

SHE WAS GASPING RAGGEDLY, AND I FELT HER LEGS shaking against my face as I slowly nuzzled my way up between her thighs.

At first, as I spoke boldly and touched her and did what my desires told me, I felt like an imposter—I was always waiting for her to tell me no, to stop me, to change her mind. But she never did. The opposite happened, in fact—the more explicitly I told her what I wanted and what I intended, the more boldly I touched her, the more she seemed to enjoy it. The more she seemed to want me, the more she seemed to want what I was doing, what I was saying.

So now, I parted her thighs with my hands,

spreading her legs wide, exposing her core. I smelled her essence, and inhaled deeply. I was tempted to close my eyes in enjoyment of her scent and to focus on the feelings, but I didn't. I wanted to see her. I took my time exploring her—I used my thumbs to spread apart the petals of her womanhood, examining the lovely pink flower within. I slid my index finger inside her, slowly and gently, feeling the wet slick heat clenching around the digit, and I explored the inside of her, watching her, studying her reactions. When I turned my palm face-up and curled my finger in a come-here motion, I brushed against something inside her and she jerked, gasping a shriek.

I flicked my tongue against her clitoris, and she jerked again, but in a different way, and her whimper was different then, too. Different kinds of pleasure?

I did both things at once, touched her inside where it made her flinch and circled my tongue around her clit as I'd discovered she liked best last time; now she arched up off the bed, her heels sliding up my spine. I cupped her ass with my free hand, holding her up, and she clung to me with her thighs, and I massaged that spot inside her and licked her clit, and she went wild. Screaming wordlessly, writhing, panting, moaning.

I kept my eyes open, watching every movement of her body. Her tits shook and swayed and trembled as she ground her core against me, and her stomach flexed and her face twisted into a rictus of ecstasy so potent it looked almost like pain.

I knew the moment she reached orgasm: her voice broke on a whimper, and her spine arched, and her inner walls clamped down hard around my finger, and the taste of her essence burst in my mouth, sweet and tangy and musky and thick and pungent. I pushed her through the orgasm, licking and massaging until she settled back onto the bed limply, panting raggedly.

"I know I said to make me come a dozen times," she gasped, "but…fuck, I need a minute."

I lifted her in both hands and settled her higher on the bed, gently depositing her head on the pile of throw pillows, and then moved to sit on the edge of the bed, watching the way sweat dappled her skin, watching the way her gasps for breath made her breasts twitch and sway.

When she'd caught her breath, she opened her eyes and turned her head to look at me. "Jesus, Xavier. You make me come so fucking hard it's crazy."

"I love watching you orgasm," I said, running a hand along her thigh from knee to hip, wanting to touch her again, to make her come again, to watch her come apart from the way I touched her.

She rolled toward me, moving to her hands and knees, crawling across the bed like a primal beast, like a tigress. Her shoulder blades shifted and her breasts swayed and her hips undulated sinuously from side to side, the explosion of red-gold spirals of her hair illuminated and made more red and more gold by the sun.

"My turn," she purred.

I swallowed hard. "Your turn?"

"To watch you come apart."

"I want to make love."

She grinned hungrily. "We will. I'm not letting you leave until we've made love so many times we pass out." She slid off the bed, kneeling on the floor in front of me. "But first, there's something I want to do."

"What's that?"

"Something I've fantasized about since the first time I saw you."

She peeled my shirt off, tossing it carelessly away. Then she trailed her fingertips down my chest, stuttering them over my abs, pausing at the button of my riding leathers. Biting her lip, she undid the button and lowered the zipper. My cock sprang out, still restrained by my underwear. She hooked her fingers in the belt loops at my back and tugged—I lifted up and let her yank the leather pants down my legs and off. Now inside out she threw them aside. Her eyes were greedy, full of blatant lust as she removed my underwear. She did this slowly, however, deliberately tugging the elastic away from my erection, and then tugging them down past my buttocks. Off, then, and the underwear were tossed in a third direction, and now I was sitting naked on her bed, as she had been minutes before.

My erection jutted upward, laying flat against my stomach, straining, aching.

Low remained on her knees on the floor, sitting on her heels, shimmying closer and closer until she was kneeling between my wide-spread thighs. Her eyes met mine, and her hands danced up my calves, over my knees, and slid up my thighs. I had stopped breathing.

I needed her touch like I needed to breathe.

"Low—" I breathed. "If you touch me, I won't last but a moment."

She smiled, biting her lower lip. "I know." She traced my abs, and then ran a finger down my belly next to the column of my raging erection.

"I don't want to—"

"Just sit and watch. Enjoy what I'm going to do." She palmed my cheek, rubbing my cheekbone with a thumb, her smile sweet. "Trust me, okay?"

I exhaled carefully. "Of course I trust you."

"Then let me make you feel good."

"Okay."

"Good," she breathed, and wrapped her hand around my cock. "And Xavier?"

I couldn't breathe, and barely managed to grate out a reply. "What?"

"Don't hold back. Not a single thing."

I smiled in acquiescence. I couldn't have held back, even if I'd wanted to.

Her fingers slid down, ringed around my cock, stroking my flesh with a slow, loving caress. On the upstroke, her thumb rolled against the tip. Her eyes flicked between my face and what her hands were doing. I clenched my fists at my sides—despite what she'd said, I was holding back…not out of embarrassment, but because I didn't want this to end.

Her touch was fire, all-consuming, but this time, instead of overwhelming me, I let the sensations own me. I delved into them, accepted them, and lost myself in them.

A few slow caresses, then, first one hand and then the other, and then both, and I was aching and throbbing, breathing hard. Still holding back. Wanting more. Wanting her to touch me forever, wanting the feeling of her hand around my cock to never stop, never end.

She paused, then, with one hand around the base. Her eyes flicked to mine, and then down to my cock again, and the corner of her lower lip caught between her teeth in a smirk that was hungry and lustful and wild and eager all at once. With a toss of her head, she shook her hair so it draped down over her shoulder, obscuring her right breast in red-gold spirals. My lungs seized, and I wondered if she was about to do what I thought she was.

She pulled my cock away from my torso, angling it outward. Leaning forward, she bent over me, and her hair trailed down my thigh, tickling, and the crown of her head brushed my stomach, and then I felt wet tight heat around my cock, sliding slick and smooth and so wet and so hot, and my whole universe shrank down to that sensation, to this moment. Her mouth, on my cock.

More, and more. Sliding down, rising up.

As she moved her mouth upward, her lips around the tip, she took me in her hands and caressed me in slow smooth long strokes, and then her mouth plunged down again and her hands moved with it, a collage and clash of sensations, her hands now moving faster than her mouth, stroking and pumping, and her tongue circled and flicked and licked as she rose up. I heard a wet sucking noise and the ache in my balls was an agonizing throb, and my shaft pulsed, and I felt her mouth pulling off of me with a loud suckling popping sound, and I only barely restrained myself from coming right then.

My cock was wet with her saliva, and she straightened and gazed at it, watching her hands spreading her own slick spit all over me, and then, before I could catch my breath or formulate a thought, she bent over me again. This time, she tilted her head to one side and gazed up at me as her mouth stretched around my organ.

I groaned, the sight of her lips wrapped around me and the lust in her eyes did something to me, made me crazy, wild, with need. She smiled at the noise I made, her eyes crinkling and brightening, and then she wrapped both hands around me again and stroked me as her stretched lips slid slowly downward.

I gasped, gagging on a groan, arching my back and flexing my hips, need overtaking me. She moaned in surprise as I flexed my hips, and her eyes widened, the movement of my hips thrust my cock deeper into her mouth.

"I'm sorry, I'm sorry—" I gasped. "I didn't mean to—"

She backed away until I fell out of her mouth, but only to lick her tongue up the side of my cock. "Don't apologize. Not for anything." She grinned up at me, then. "Give me everything, Xavier."

She guided me into her mouth again, and this time her hands just held my cock away from her body, and her mouth did all the stroking, plunging down and up, down and up, tongue flicking and licking and circling.

"Oh...oh god," I groaned. "I'm...I have to...oh god, Low...Low..."

She moaned, and the vibration buzzed through me like an earthquake.

I watched every moment of it, groaning, gasping as her mouth plunged down around me.

And then I was gone. Unable to stop myself, the orgasm struck with the swiftness of a lightning strike.

I felt myself unleash with a hot pulsing rush, and I heard Low moan in surprise, and then I heard her gulp, and then her lips popped as I slid out of her, and she was caressing me in smooth fast strokes with both hands over my wet slick cock. I pulsed again, and cum dripped out of me, and she glanced at me as she lapped it up, and then plunged her mouth around me in a fast sucking greedy movement, and I pulsed and came and groaned.

When she finally stopped, cum was dripping down the side of my cock and glistening at the corner of her mouth, and she lifted up, smiling up at me, climbing to her feet and onto the bed.

Her tongue flicked out as she lay on her back, licking away the droplet of my seed, and I followed her onto the bed. I ached, still. I'd just come harder than I'd thought possible, but the sight of her stretched out on the bed, breasts heavy, nipples puckered and hard, her pussy glistening and wet with need…I felt myself filling and throbbing with renewed fervor for all of her.

She wiped her mouth with her wrist, and then I was levered over her, kissing her, tasting myself on her tongue and lips, tasting her on mine.

This time, the kiss didn't end.

We writhed together in the bed, lips tangling and shifting, tongues darting. She was on top, then, somehow, tits smashed soft and thick against my chest; she ground her pussy against my thigh; she was beneath me again, and I had her neck cupped in one hand, clasping her into the kiss, into the embrace, and her hips flexed, and I knew she was as wild with need as I was.

Kissing, writhing, breathing, touching, hands all over, lips everywhere, bodies sweaty and moving and sliding.

I ached.

Throbbed.

After an all too brief eternity of kissing ourselves breathless and wild, I broke away, gasping, levered above her.

"I need you," I murmured. "Low, I fucking need you. I need to make love to you."

SIXTEEN

Harlow

He was everywhere, he was everything. Lean and hard, wolfish and hungry and wild with desire, kissing me as I've never been kissed; passion bled through his pores, and need blazed in his eyes.

Love gnashed in his kisses.

"I need you," he whispered, his voice rough, ragged with desperation. "Low, I fucking need you. I need to make love to you."

I felt him, his cock throbbing hard against my belly. How long had it been since he'd come? Minutes? God, this man. So potent, so hard. The taste of his cum still lingered in my mouth, and I tasted my own essence on his lips.

My core ached. I wept with my own need.

"Then make love to me," I whispered back.

He hesitated. "Do we need a condom? I don't have one. I wasn't expecting this. Hoping, and wanting, but not expecting."

"No," I said, gazing up at him. "But I'm on the shot, and I'm clean."

He knelt between my thighs, his hard muscular body shifting as he stared down at me. "Low, are you—"

"I'm sure." I grasped his cock, nudging the thick, fat crown between the lips of my pussy, notching him just inside me. "I want you—I *need* you. I need you like this, with nothing between us. And you're—you're the only one I'll have ever been bare like this with. *Ever*. I swear on my soul."

He wasn't breathing—he was simply staring down at me, his eyes wild with need.

"I love you," Xavier said, and thrust into me.

It was a slow, careful thrust, gentle and exquisite. Filling me, ever so slowly, until he was buried inside me, our hips meeting.

"Oh god…" he whispered, shaking all over. "Oh *fuck*, Low. *Harlow*, god, you feel…"

"Tell me," I breathed.

"Like heaven." He planted his face between my breasts; pulling out and then plunging back in, harder.

"Like... *home.*"

I wept. I couldn't not. He was exactly right—this was heaven, this was home.

Utter perfection.

He filled me until I ached, stretched me until I burned, but it felt just right. Just enough. When he next thrust fully into me, I was split apart until I couldn't breathe or think or feel anything except *him,* his cock inside me and his body above me and his breath on mine and his lips on my tits and his thighs against the inside of mine.

I wrapped my legs around his back and clung to him, wrapped my arms around his neck and clung to him.

I breathed on his cheek, panting, whimpering shrill gasps against his ear. I writhed against him, aching and tingling and pulsing all over. Desperate and wild, crazed with him, enveloped by him. Weeping unashamedly with the manic crushing onslaught of love coursing between us.

He kissed my tears and didn't have to ask why I was crying—the desperation and the love in my eyes when he pulled away to stare down at me told him all he needed to know.

"I love you," I whispered, taking each of his thrusts and meeting them with my own.

His body was so hard, so strong, and his thrusts

sped up, grew in need, grew in potency, and he filled me and left me empty, filled me and left me empty—his voice growled in my ear, primal and wild and unleashed, and my heart swelled at this Xavier, this side of him, the need and the desperation and the love and the power.

"Say that again," he grunted, pausing with his cock buried deep, one fist in the pillow by my face, the other caressing my breasts lovingly, possessively. "Tell me again."

I locked my heels tighter around his back, thrusting against him, grinding and rolling my hips against his, fucking him from underneath him. Locks of dark hair clung in damp curls against his forehead and draped over his eyes, and I brushed them away with my fingers, clutched the back of his neck and kissed his cheekbones and his jaw and the corner of his mouth as I undulated against him.

"I love you, Xavier."

"Harlow—" he grated, teeth clenched, pushing into me. "Fuck!"

"Yes!" I breathed, his cock sliding against my clit and sending shivers of climax-inducing ecstasy through me. "All of you, Xavier—show me—show me, god…oh god! You feel so good, Xavier! Give me more, give it to me harder, give it to me faster!"

He snarled wordlessly, crushing his lips against

mine in a brief slashing kiss.

And then I knew he'd gone beyond all control, and I cried out as he slammed into me. He was all over me, inside me, around me, above me—he was everywhere, he was everything. His body was hard against mine, his face against the side of my throat, his arms wrapped around my body, lifting me up and crushing me against him, clutching me in a furious death grip I wanted to live in and die in and never leave, and then he let go.

He fucked me with perfect love.

Each thrust was slow and hard, grinding with shuddering power into me. I gasped his name as he reached orgasm:

"Xavier! Yes, god yes, yes, more—Xavier! Oh god, Xavier…"

And I was there, so close, riding the edge, and I felt him explode inside me, filling me with his hot wet seed and thrusting against me desperately and whispering my name in my ear as he moved, and I needed to come, needed to—

I clung to him with arms and legs and rolled, and he went with me onto his back, and I rose above him, hair wild and breasts heaving, feeling like a goddess in that moment, a creature of raw wild primal sex, and his eyes blazed love and worship. He was throbbing and thick inside me, his cum wet and hot and slick and intoxicating, and he was so deep…

I planted one hand on his stomach and leaned back and rolled my pussy against him, riding his cock, grinding him where I needed him…but it still wasn't enough.

He knew, though. He knew what I needed.

He wrapped his hands around my flexing thighs and pressed a thumb to my clit, pressing in circles, and I cried out as the orgasm rose up inside me at his touch, and I abandoned myself to taking this moment in all its glory, taking what I wanted and what I needed.

I clutched my breasts in both hands, leaning way back, spine arched, hair flying, hips rolling, and his touch sent me there, took me there, and his cock thrust into me and—

I came.

I didn't just come, though.

Or explode, or shatter.

No, this was something else.

Our eyes met and the climax smashed through me and shook me and wrenched me and tore screams of his name out of me—and this was love. Sex as it had never been, fucking as it never been—love in its rawest and most primal and perfect form.

Love shared.

Love created.

I fell forward onto him, sobbing through an orgasm that never ended or else became two and three in succession, so fast it was all one, each more powerful than the last.

Xavier knew the precise moment I started coming.

His eyes locked onto mine, and there cannot be any moment so raw and intimate and vulnerable as when you lock eyes in the midst of an orgasm and know you love him and he loves you, and you can't look away even though he's seeing into you, and you feel exposed, beyond naked, soul bared, heart open and tender and there for the taking.

He took it, then—he took my heart.

And I took his.

That intimacy was in his eyes, and I knew he was mine for all time, and I his.

"Low…" he whispered, sounding as broken as I felt.

I finally stopped coming and clung to him, shuddering, sobbing. "I know, Xavier. I know. Me too."

"Everything, Low. That was…"

"It was everything," I finished. "I know. Me too."

Xavier lay beside me, asleep.

What time was it? I decided I didn't care.

I texted Emily: *make sure absolutely NO ONE bothers me at home until I text you again. No one. For any reason, including death or the end of the world.*

You got it, boss, she texted back; a brief pause, and then another text popped up from her: ***He's there?***

I snapped a photo of his face, sleeping, peaceful, heart-stoppingly beautiful, and sent it to her: *Between rounds.*

He's even more gorgeous than I thought. Jesus, Low. You're SURE he doesn't have any single cousins? ;-)

LOL I'll ask.

A pause, the dots jumping, and then she hit back. ***You love him?***

And then some, Emily. I smiled to myself as I tapped at the keyboard. *Thank you.*

What else are assistants for? Another brief pause. ***Bring him as your date to the premiere.***

I hesitated over the idea, but deep down I knew if he wouldn't go, neither would I, consequences be damned. *I'll ask. I'll need a tux fitted last minute, if he'll go.*

Easy enough. I'll get someone on call right now. The message popped up, and the dots appeared again right away. ***Make sure you eat something...Besides him, I mean.***

I'll try, but no promises.

"Who are you texting?" I heard Xavier ask from beside me, his voice sleepy.

"Emily, my assistant."

"About what? Or is that personal?"

I laughed and showed him the phone. "Nothing's personal between us anymore, Xavier."

He read, and then handed it back. "I think I remember my dad mentioning an estranged brother when I was a kid, but I know nothing about any cousins."

I laughed, turning the phone off and putting it in the drawer. "She's just jealous because I get you."

He smiled vaguely, and then glanced at me. "She wants you to take me to a premiere?"

I lifted his arm up, settled into the warm strong cradle of his arm. "Of my latest film, *December's Last Light.*"

"Do you want me to go with you?" he asked, his hand traveling up my back and down to my butt in slow, roaming caresses.

"Yes." I looked up at him. "But it's going to be a big event, Xavier. Press will be there in force. Lots of cameras, and lots of questions. If we go, we'll be out there. You and me, as a couple. People will write about you, and us, and make things up about me cheating on you or fake breakups and shit like that."

He was silent for a long, long time. "This is a big part of your life, and they're important to your career, these premieres."

"Yes, but you don't have to—"

"I'll go," he cut in. "I want to go with you."

"You will? You do?"

He smiled down at me. "Yes. I want to share your life."

I gazed up at him, my heart melting. "I'll be proud and honored to walk that red carpet on your arm, Xavier."

He blinked hard. "You will? Proud and honored?"

"One hundred percent truth, Xavier. Yes. Proud and honored. There's no one I'd walk the red carpet with but you."

He rolled over on top of me; his arm still cradled under my neck, and kissed me. "Come on," he said, abruptly rolling off me and hopping out of bed.

"Where are we going?" I asked, laughing as he hauled me out of the bed after him to the stairs, both of us still naked.

"I'm going to feed you," he said, starting down the stairs with my hand in his, "and then I'm going to fuck you."

"Why, Xavier! How crude of you!" I said, giggling.

He paused halfway down the stairs, turning to glance up at me in consternation. "I'm sorry. I thought it would be funny, and perhaps sexy."

I laughed even harder, leaning down over him from two steps up and palming his hard, taut ass. "It was. I was just playing along." I reached between us, fondling his burgeoning erection. "Where exactly were you planning to fuck me, Mr. Badd?"

"Ah…I was thinking the couch. Or the kitchen counter. Or the floor." He found my slit with his fingers. "Or right here on the stairs."

I gasped as he circled my clit with a light, delicate touch that sent me into a paroxysm of pleasure. "Why pick one?" I breathed. "There are a lot of surfaces in this house to christen."

"Christen? As one christens a child in a church?"

"Yeah." I frowned down at him. "You've never heard that expression?"

"No."

"It means the first time a particular place is used for sex. We just christened my bed, because I've never had sex in that bed until today. We're about to christen my stairs, because I've never been fucked on these stairs. After you feed me, we'll christen my kitchen island, because I've never been fucked there, either. And then my couch, and everywhere else you can think of to fuck me, because you're the only man I've had in my home."

"Harlow, you do know when I say I'm going to

fuck you, that I really mean—"

I lifted up and bit his lip. "Make sweet, passionate, beautiful, affectionate, attentive, gentle love to me. Yes, Xavier. I know." I sat down on the stairs and lay back, pulling him down with me, and slid him inside. "Can I tell you a secret?

"Anything," he whispered, and moaned as he filled me.

"I know you love me. And I love making love with you. But I'll also love it if you just…*fuck* me."

"Then fuck you I shall. *And* make love to you." He paused. "At the same time," he clarified.

"Perfect," I said, giggling breathlessly.

And so he did.

On the stairs.

And the kitchen counter, after we'd eaten. And the couch. And outside, in the pool, half in the water, splashing as we came together.

I lost count of the number of times he told me loved me, and repaid him with a countless number of utterances of my own.

"I love you" became a chorus. A song. A poem.

It became an invocation, evoking our future.

SEVENTEEN

Xavier

THE TUX WAS FITTED TO MY BODY, CUT TO MY PRECISE measurements and made of some sleek, stretchy, breathable material. It moved with me, stretching, not constricting. The tie was tight, but I could breathe, after insisting the top button be left undone behind the tie.

Low was in the limo beside me, breathtaking in a custom gown that looked like it had been crafted from spider silk and starlight, molded to her curves and allowing tantalizing glimpses of her skin without revealing anything.

The limo ahead of us disgorged its occupants—Low's co-star, Dawson Kellor, and his wife Grey. Once they finished waving to the gathered crowd of photographers, they moved up the carpet and away from the staging area outside the front of the theater, and our car pulled forward and it was our turn.

Low squeezed my hand. "Are you ready, Xavier?"

I swallowed my fear, lifted my chin, and recited pi to the thirtieth digit before answering. "Yes."

She laughed. "Liar. You're never ready for this part. I know I'm not." She let out a shaky breath as the valet opened her door, and gave my hand another squeeze. "Smile, breathe, and just be you."

She slid out gracefully, adjusting the train of her gown as she stepped aside so I could exit behind her, and then there was a blinding barrage of flashes and voices.

"Smile, baby," Low murmured, tucking her hand into the crook of my arm.

I smiled, focusing on her, on how lovely and perfect she was, on how lucky I was, and my smile was as genuine as it could be. The flashes never seemed to stop, but these voices weren't desperate or clamoring, and once I remembered to breathe, my nerves subsided some. There were a million questions, mostly about me, and Low didn't answer any of them.

We moved to stand in front of a black and white checkered background stamped with sponsors and posed for more photos, Low subtly guiding me where she wanted me. An older man wielding a cell phone like a handheld recorder leaned into her space.

"Harlow! Who's the guy, honey?"

She seemed to know him, and smiled. "Hi, Benny, how's the wife?"

Benny, the reporter, grinned. "Bah, she's as contrary as ever."

"You love her that way, and don't pretend otherwise," Low said, laughing.

He guffawed. "Got me there, Harlow, but don't tell her that." He eyed me, and then shoved the phone at her again. "Now come on, hon, give me something. Who's the guy?"

She tucked both hands around my arm and leaned into me. "This is Xavier Badd."

"He's your boyfriend?"

She gazed up at me as she answered. "He's my everything."

Benny turned the phone to me. "Xavier, how do you feel about landing the woman every man in America dreams about?"

"I have died and gone to heaven," I said, unable to stop myself from lapsing into formal eloquence. "And I will thank you not to wake me, should this prove to be but a dream."

Ben laughed. "Hot damn!" he laughed, pocketing the phone. "What a sound-bite, kid!"

I glanced at Low for translation, and she just laughed, pulling me toward the theater entrance. "That's a good thing," she assured me.

The rest of the night was a whirlwind. I met a hundred different people as we milled outside the theater, memorizing names and faces, and we watched Harlow be brilliant on the screen and I applauded louder than anyone, and then we were whisked away to a party on a rooftop somewhere.

I found myself with my socks and shoes off, pant legs rolled up, feet in a pool with Low beside me and Dawson Kellor on the other side and his wife beside Low, talking among the four of us into the smallest hours of the night. Even though I was nervous enough to lapse into Spock-speech, and though I forgot myself enough to lecture the director about everything I'd read on film theory, no one seemed to care, and everyone was amazing, and it was the most fun I'd ever had.

And then, with dawn approaching, Low nudged me. "Time to go home," she said, sleepily.

"Okay. Is there a car to take us?"

She smiled mischievously, blinking sleepily and rubbing her eyes. "Not quite," she said, gesturing at a sudden welter of noise from across the rooftop.

A helicopter was landing on a designated pad on a higher portion of the roof.

I glanced at her. "A helicopter?"

She just yawned. "Now that the premiere is over, I'm done in LA for awhile. We're going home."

"We don't need a helicopter to get your house from here," I said, still confused. "It's only a few miles."

"No. Home to Ketchikan."

I blinked. "Oh." I smiled. "Home to Ketchikan, then."

"We'll have to crash in your room until my yacht gets there, though."

I laughed. "You have a yacht and a multimillion-dollar home in Beverly Hills, and you're going to crash with me in a three-bedroom apartment I share with my brother and his wife."

"As long as you're there, I don't care where we are."

"Oh. I see," I said, not understanding at all, but—like Bast had advised—I didn't question it.

"I do have plans, though." Low smiled up at me.

"Plans? For what?"

She shrugged. "Buying a place in Ketchikan and building you a proper lab so you can play evil genius to your heart's content."

"I'm not an evil genius," I protested.

"So you can play Tony Stark, then. Genius billionaire playboy philanthropist." She bumped me with her shoulder. "The point is, I'm gonna build you a big, fancy lab with all the most expensive equipment we can find. I need something to spend my money on."

I blinked at the prospect. "You don't need to do that, Low."

"Obviously. But I want to."

"Because you love me, and it would be a way to show me that," I said, explaining to myself out loud.

She yawned again. "Exactly. And you can show me you love me by letting me sleep on your lap on the way."

"There are other ways I could show you I love you," I said.

Low giggled. "Later, big boy. When we get home."

"That's not what I meant."

"Yes it is."

I laughed. "Okay, maybe it was. But I also meant—"

She touched my lips, quieting me. "I know." She gestured at the helicopter, idling with its rotors slowing. "For now, just take me home."

The End

Author's Note

All of our books are special to us, and if you know anything about Jack and I, you know we like to pull from real life and personal experience when we create characters and situations. The touch of real life makes everything feel more real, we think.

That being said, Xavier Badd is truly special to us. We have children on the spectrum, and so writing Xavier's story was a particularly emotional experience for us. We didn't intend to publish this book in the middle of World Autism Month, but we find it a lovely bit of serendipity.

To learn more, go to www.autismspeaks.org/what-autism. It is a fantastic and informative website, and it answers pretty much every question you might have on this topic.

Jasinda Wilder

April 2018

You didn't really think I was done writing about
Badd boys, did you?

Keep reading for a sneak peek of

BADD KITTY

EPILOGUE

Roman

THE TRAILER WAS HOT, STUFFY, AND SMELLY.

Of course, that's to be expected when you're sharing a double-wide in the ass-end of Oklahoma with three other men.

I was bored.

And cranky.

And horny.

And I needed a drink, but my brothers and I had agreed to keep the trailer dry, for Dad's sake. Not like it'd do any good—the ornery old bastard was bound and determined to drink himself to death no matter what my brothers and I did.

Remington was out breaking horses with our

neighbors, the Callahans, and he wouldn't be back for hours yet, and Ramsey was out on a bender, and had been for a week, so I didn't expect him back for another day or two.

Which left me here alone, with Dad, babysitting his grouchy, surly ass.

Speak of the devil—he blinked awake from his nap, and glared at me. "Rome. Get off your lazy ass and get me a beer, dammit."

I flipped channels until I found a daytime replay of a celebrity gossip show, which I left it on, because there were often highlights of hot celebrity chicks.

"You're on the wagon, you old drunk." I heaved my carcass off the protesting, sagging, creaking, ancient couch and snagged a diet Coke from the fridge, tossing it to him. "No more booze for you."

"Fuck that shit," he snarled. "I been a drunk for thirty years. Ain't quittin' now."

"Doc Mullins says you'll die if you don't quit."

"Doc Mullins can kiss my ass." He popped the top of the soda and slugged back half of it. "And who gives a good goddamn, anyway?" he groused.

"Uh, well, Rem, Ram, and me, for one."

"That's three, dipshit."

"Yeah, but we're identical triplets, so it counts as one."

"'Cause you can only muster half a shit between

the three of you?"

"We came back, didn't we?"

He lit a cigarette and puffed angrily. "Yeah, and who asked you to? Not me, that's for fuckin' sure."

"You had a heart attack, Dad. How're we supposed to be effective smoke jumpers when we know you could keel over dead any minute? You're all the family we got."

He had nothing to say to that, and we watched highlights of a fancy dancy Hollywood movie premiere from the night before. The main actor, Dawson Kellor, I'd seen in a few flicks—and his wife was hot as fuck. The next to pose for photos was Harlow Grace, and standing with her was a tall, lean, dark-haired guy with green eyes; something about him struck a chord in my head somewhere, and I paused the image on the TV.

"He look familiar to you, Dad?" I asked.

Dad peered. "Maybe a little. Why? You know him?"

I shrugged. "Naw, but that's why I asked you."

"Well un-pause the fuckin' TV, and maybe they'll say his name."

So we watched them pose and then the narrator rambled on about Harlow's recent hiatus from acting:

"Recent photos of Harlow surfaced recently, showing her locked in what appeared to be a passionate kiss with

this same guy you're seeing her with now. She vanished more than two months ago after a lewd video was leaked online, only to be discovered in a dive bar in Ketchikan, Alaska, making out with this guy…one Xavier Badd. Who, apparently, is the youngest of eight brothers—"

A female voice cut in. *"Eight brothers who are mighty damn fine, I might add."*

"His last name is Badd? What are the chances of that?" I paused the TV again, glancing at Dad. "Ketchikan. Ain't that where you grew up, Dad?"

He was staring at the TV, frowning furiously at the close up of the dark-haired kid, who looked freakishly familiar.

"The fucker had *eight* kids?" Dad murmured. "Thought for sure I'd have beaten him there, at least."

"Who?"

"Your uncle."

I gaped at him. "Uncle? What uncle?"

Dad heaved himself out of the chair and shuffled into the kitchen, digging around in the cabinets.

"What are you looking for?" I asked. "I threw away all your booze."

"Even the stuff I had hid in the cereal?"

I laughed. "Yeah, even that."

He growled like the bear he resembled—six-four, heavy and huge and hunched, with shaggy hair that had once been grizzly bear brown, but had now gone gray. "Damn you."

"What fucking uncle, Dad?" I demanded.

He gestured at the TV. "Him. The bastard."

"That's just a kid, you idiot. Can't be more than twenty, twenty-one."

Dad hurled the empty Coke can at my head. "I know that, you dumb sonafabitch. His dad—my twin brother."

I shoved up out of my chair and faced my dad; we were of a height, and I had the build he'd had when he was young—bear-strong, bull-necked, heavy in the shoulders and chest.

"The fuck are you talking about, old man?" I snapped. "You don't have a brother."

"Fuck you know about it, boy?" he snarled back, straightening to his full height and reminding me why he'd been so feared in his time. "I *had* a brother, just never told you about him. He's dead now."

"You're not making any damn sense."

He glared at me, eyes bloodshot and sagging. "Get my trunk from my room."

"Why?"

"You wanna know, or don't you?" He gestured at the TV. "That kid is your cousin. An' apparently you got eight of 'em."

I groused under my breath as I fetched his antique seaman's trunk from his closet and set it by his chair. He flipped the lid open and rummaged around in it, hunting through overstuffed manila file folders and stacks of paper bound with twine, and bags of trinkets and sheaves of old photos, until he found a tattered leather photo album covered in dust. This he opened, flipping through the pages until he found what he was looking for and tossed it onto my lap.

"Look there," he said, tapping at a particular photo. "See what you see."

One of a handful of old black-and-white photos featured two young men, big and burly and strong, thick-shouldered, with shaggy hair and beards and flannel shirts, their arms around each other's shoulders, standing in front of what looked like a log cabin. They were identical twins, and looked to be in their early twenties. Happy, grinning, in the prime of life.

It was clearly Dad, and an identical twin I hadn't known he had.

I stared at him. "You had an identical twin fucking brother, and you never told us about him?"

"Weren't none of your business."

I glanced at the other photos, all of him and his twin, and a stunningly beautiful woman with black hair, seen sitting on the lap of…one of the twins—I certainly couldn't tell which.

"Who's the hot lady?" I asked.

Dad didn't answer, toying with a loose flap

of Formica on the edge of the counter. "Your aunt Lena."

"Meaning, the wife of the uncle I didn't know I had? The one who's dead?"

"She's gone now, too."

"She was gorgeous."

There was a butter knife crusted with old peanut butter on the counter; and in a swift, angry movement, he hurled it across the room where it smashed handle first in the fake wood paneling by my head, and then fell to the thin, threadbare carpet with a dull thump.

"The fuck, Dad!"

He didn't answer, instead stomping across the trailer, kicking the screen door open, and pacing out into the tall grass beyond the trailer.

I gave him a minute, and then followed him into the blazing Oklahoma air. "What the hell is going on, Dad?"

He bent and snagged a blade of grass, breaking it apart in his thick fingers. "You think it's coincidence I had multiples?" he asked, his voice surprisingly quiet. "Liam and me were twins, as alike as you three are. We were as tight as the three of you are, too. Did everything together."

"So what happened? Why is this the first I'm hearing of him?"

"What do you think could happened that could split up twins?" He gestured back at the trailer. "Lena happened," he spat, and paced farther away.

"You fought over a woman?"

"Not just any woman. *The* woman. Lena Dunfield. Most beautiful woman either of us ever saw."

"You loved her, and she loved him."

"Bingo."

"So you never spoke to him again because of it?"

He spat. "Ain't tellin' that story twice. Get your brothers back here and I'll tell it all at once."

"I have cousins," I said, after a long silence, trying the thought on for size.

"Eight of 'em, it seems."

"I've always wanted to visit Alaska," I remarked, watching him for his reaction.

He laughed bitterly. "Be my guest. Just leave me out of it."

I had eight cousins, living in Ketchikan, Alaska. One of whom was apparently shacked up with the hottest actress in Hollywood.

This could prove to be interesting.

I pulled out my cell phone and called my brothers and told them to get their asses back home. And while I waited for Rem and Ram, I did some Googling on my phone.

Apparently my long-lost cousins had a bar in Ketchikan called Badd's Bar and Grille…

When the boys got back, demanding to know what the panic was, I shot them a wolfish grin. "Have I got some news for you."

BADD KITTY

Book 9 of the Badd Brothers series…
Coming soon!

Jasinda Wilder

Visit me at my website: **www.jasindawilder.com**
Email me: **jasindawilder@gmail.com**

If you enjoyed this book, you can help others enjoy it as well by recommending it to friends and family, or by mentioning it in reading and discussion groups and online forums. You can also review it on the site from which you purchased it. But, whether you recommend it to anyone else or not, thank you *so much* for taking the time to read my book! Your support means the world to me!

My other titles:

The Preacher's Son:
Unbound
Unleashed
Unbroken

Biker Billionaire:
Wild Ride

Big Girls Do It:

Better (#1), Wetter (#2), Wilder (#3), On Top (#4)

Married (#5)

On Christmas (#5.5)

Pregnant (#6)

Boxed Set

Rock Stars Do It:

Harder

Dirty

Forever

Boxed Set

From the world of *Big Girls* and *Rock Stars*:

Big Love Abroad

Delilah's Diary:

A Sexy Journey

La Vita Sexy

A Sexy Surrender

The Falling Series:

Falling Into You

Falling Into Us

Falling Under

Falling Away

Falling for Colton

The Ever Trilogy:

Forever & Always

After Forever

Saving Forever

The world of *Alpha:*

Alpha

Beta

Omega

Harris: Alpha One Security Book 1

Thresh: Alpha One Security Book 2

Duke: Alpha One Security Book 3

Puck: Alpha One Security Book 4

The world of Stripped:

Stripped

Trashed

The world of *Wounded:*

Wounded

Captured

The Houri Legends:

Jack and Djinn

Djinn and Tonic

The Madame X Series:

Madame X

Exposed

Exiled

The One Series

The Long Way Home

Where the Heart Is

There's No Place Like Home

Badd Brothers:

*Badd Motherf*cker*

Badd Ass

Badd to the Bone

Good Girl Gone Badd

Badd Luck

Badd Mojo

Big Badd Wolf

Badd Boy

The Black Room
(With Jade London):

Door One
Door Two
Door Three
Door Four
Door Five
Door Six
Door Seven
Door Eight
Deleted Door

Standalone titles:

Yours

Non-Fiction titles:

You Can Do It
You Can Do It: Strength
You Can Do It: Fasting

Jack Wilder Titles:

The Missionary

To be informed of new releases and special offers,
sign up for
Jasinda's email newsletter.

CPSIA information can be obtained
at www.ICGtesting.com
Printed in the USA
FSHW01n1551240418
47405FS